# THE
# RUNESTONE
# INCIDENT

# THE
# RUNESTONE
# INCIDENT

## THE INCIDENT SERIES #2

### A NOVEL BY

# NEVE MASLAKOVIC

47N⬤RTH

Published by 47North
P.O. Box 400818
Las Vegas, NV 89140

ISBN-13: 9781477849507
ISBN-10: 1477849505
Library of Congress Control Number: 2013945539

*for my mother*

# PART ONE:
# THE STONE

# 1

It started with a knock on my office door—and ended with us carrying a dead body back from the fourteenth century.

Scratch that. The story actually starts much earlier, a year before I began working at St. Sunniva University, before the school even had a functional time travel lab. I was still working at the local gym when a new member walked in. He was tall, blond, dressed in white from head to toe, and had a tennis racket swung jauntily over one shoulder.

I was expecting the standard pick-up line, but when he slid his crisp new membership pass toward me, flashing a toothy grin, he said, "Ever heard of the Kensington Runestone?"

Good looking *and* an interesting conversationalist.

I took the card. "Yes, it's supposed to be a fake, right? Rigged to look like it was carved by Vikings who came here years before Columbus."

*Here* was the middle of Minnesota's glacial lakes and hills country. More precisely, Kensington, a couple of towns over from Thornberg.

"Oh, it's not a hoax," he said confidently. "My grandfather watched it come out of the ground. His name was Magnus Olsen—I'm Quinn Olsen, by the way." He extended a hand and shook mine with a firm grip.

"Olsen?" I said, looking down at his membership card.

"Yeah, why?"

"I'm an Olsen, too. Julia."

"Very pleased to meet you, Julia Olsen. Hmm, I hope we're not related. That could be a problem." There was that charming grin again.

I pushed the gym card back toward him. "Plenty of Olsens in town. Mine are from Norway."

"Good, because mine are from Denmark. I guess it just means we both have an ancestor who was the son of an Ole."

It almost seemed like we were fated to be together, I remember thinking.

I was a lot younger then.

That night, over lingonberry pancakes and wine at Ingrid's, which is what passes for a fancy restaurant in Thornberg, Quinn told me his grandfather's story. *Farfar*, he called him—father's father. "Here, you want to see a photo of Farfar with the stone, Jules? Is it all right if I call you Jules?"

He had the photo in his wallet. At the time, I thought it was sweet. Perhaps it was. I should have realized back then that it was an obsession for him. He passed the photo to me over the lit candle in the middle of the table. The black-and-white square showed a middle-aged man in a suit standing stiffly, as if at attention, next to a rectangular gray stone propped up on a couple of wooden boxes. On the back of the photo someone had written in careful cursive, *Magnus Olsen and the Kensington Runestone, 1928.*

"What are those squiggles on the stone?" I asked.

"Runes. You know, the alphabet used for old English and Norse before we developed our *A* to *Z*s."

"And your grandfather found it under a tree?"

"One of his neighbors did. He helped. He was just eight at the time."

"He looks so serious," I said, handing the photo back. "I wonder when people decided it was okay to smile in photos."

"Maybe when their teeth stopped looking so yellow. More butter?"

"Thanks."

"But that's not the only reason he looks so serious. No one believed him or the farmer who found the stone. Magnus was accused of being a liar and even lost a job over it. After that, he became a bit of a nomad, earning money by trying his hand at various odd jobs and schemes. I'm happy to report that he did eventually settle down, after he met Farmor. One day— yes, I don't mind saying it—one day I intend to prove that he told the truth. That the stone *was* carved in 1362 by Vikings. Most people have never heard of the runestone. I intend to change that."

Quinn moved in five months later, and, a couple of years down the road, we were married on a San Diego beach at sunrise.

∞

Fast-forward six years or so to a Friday morning.

I was now working as assistant to the dean of sciences at St. Sunniva University. My small office was two buildings over from the balloon-roofed Time Travel Engineering (TTE) building, where our historical researchers stepped into a maze of mirrors and lasers to hop into the past and return with invaluable photos and notes. The plants on the lone windowsill of my office had just gotten their weekly watering from Oscar, the security guard from the TTE building. I appreciated the interest he took in my plants, and I'm sure they did, too, given my notorious black thumb. The door had just closed behind him when it opened again with a peppy knock.

I thought Oscar might have forgotten his watering can and automatically glanced around for it, but it wasn't his wiry figure standing in the doorway.

It was Quinn. We hadn't seen each other in what was for him a calendar year and a bit less for me, given the time skip that had occurred on the way back from my one and only run into the past, a stumble into ancient Pompeii. He was sporting a tan, an expensive haircut, and a large yellow umbrella with frogs on it. The umbrella was still dripping from the September rain tapping out a beat on my window. He threw a look around my office and said, "So, Jules, where do you keep it? The Time Machine?" as if he expected to see it nestled in a corner nook.

I set aside the incoming student orientation booklet I'd been working on while chatting with Oscar. I knew why Quinn had come back to town, and I was not happy to see him.

"It's out of the question, Quinn. You can't just waltz into the TTE lab and expect to go on a run into the fourteenth century." I had already told him this back in June when he had called from Phoenix. Since the rest of the summer had passed without another word from him, I had assumed that Quinn had moved on to his next grand scheme, whatever that was. The last I'd heard he was flipping houses. But now here he was, on my office doorstep.

Or more precisely, in the chair across the desk from me. He shook the frog umbrella, sending raindrops cascading onto my rug, and hooked it on the chair back. He flashed a familiar grin at me. "But you're in charge of the Time Machine, aren't you, Jules?"

"Hardly. I only oversee the roster. You know that. Dean Braga reviews all time travel proposals and approves or rejects them at her discretion. And don't call it the Time Machine," I added. "Its name is STEWie."

STEWie was short for *SpaceTimE Warper*, and I was pretty sure I had mentioned this to him more than once in the months before he had taken off for Arizona with one of our campus security officers. Speaking of which—

"How's Officer Jones?" I asked.

"I wouldn't know. She's moved on."

"Sorry. Did you bring the divorce papers—signed, I hope? You did get them in the mail, didn't you? My lawyer hasn't been able to reach you on the phone."

"I don't have them with me. Never mind that. Let's talk about the runestone, Jules."

I noticed he didn't actually say whether he had signed the papers or not.

"Not *that* again. The runestone is just a hoax."

"I disagree."

"A prank that got out of hand, an example of pioneer-era humor, a bit of fun by Scandinavians proud of their heritage—"

"I believe Farfar's story."

"If you're so sure your grandfather was right, what do you need me—and STEWie—for?"

"To prove it . . . and film it. It's going to make a fantastic pilot for a reality TV series. Look, it'll be simple enough." He rubbed his hands together in anticipation. "We jump to 1362 to shoot the Vikings carving the stone—wait, let's make a stop first in 1898 to film Farfar dig it up—or is it better to do it the other way around, 1362 first and then 1898, the way history intended? Either way is fine with me. Do you want to turn to a fresh page and start a list of the things we'll need?" He nodded at the notepad on my desk, where I had jotted down a few notes about the grad student orientation booklet. "And," he added, "shouldn't you be offering me a cookie or something?"

He knew from experience that I tackled all problems by (a) offering food and (b) making a list of what needed to be done.

"You want a list?" I said, sliding the cookie jar toward him. He lifted up the lid and cheerfully took out a couple of the fudge mints as I ticked off the points on my fingers. "Here it is. To go on a STEWie run, you need to (a) be a professor, postdoc, or grad student in one of the departments here at St. Sunniva; (b) submit a research proposal for approval by Dean Braga and the TTE department, a process which typically takes a month or more; (c) secure a roster spot, which takes a few more months; and— probably most importantly—(d) have funding. STEWie runs are expensive.

"And more to the point," I added, "Dean Braga would never sign off on your plan because STEWie cannot be used for personal matters. You have to be a historian looking to answer a research question. Or, failing that, an archeologist, anthropologist, paleontologist, linguist, geologist, or evolutionary biologist."

"*You* went on a run. And you're none of those things." He popped a third fudge mint into his mouth.

"I'm just a science dean's assistant, yes. But Pompeii was a special case." He hadn't meant it as a put-down, I knew. He honestly had trouble understanding how someone could stand, much less enjoy, a nine-to-five desk job (or, in my case, more like seven-thirty to seven).

"How's the luxury-home-flipping business?" I asked.

"I have a couple of properties in play."

I got to my feet. "Then I suggest you use your time to renovate them instead of wasting it trying to prove that the Kensington Runestone is real and that your grandfather told the truth. There is nothing you can say that would make me want to help you in the present, much less the past."

"I have proof that you brought the Pompeii girl back."

# 2

I didn't ask how he knew. It was obvious. He must have let himself into the house to snoop around after everyone had left for the day. I'd never gotten around to changing the locks. He had probably waited behind the droopy willow in the front yard until Sabina—or the Pompeii girl, as he had called her—got on the school bus and I drove off to work in my aged Honda with Abigail Tanner, the third member of our household, in the passenger seat. Today, Abigail had forgone her usual mode of transportation, her bike, because of the rain.

I had gotten up to close the office door. That we had brought thirteen-year-old Sabina back from my one and only STEWie run was not common knowledge and I wanted to keep it that way. Five of us had ended up in Pompeii—with me had been Abigail, who was a graduate student in TTE and now Sabina's legal guardian; Chief Nate Kirkland of campus security; a Shakespearean scholar by the name of Dr. Helen Presnik; and a second TTE graduate student, Kamal Ahmad. We had been marooned in the past by Dean Braga's predecessor, who had planned to take control of the TTE lab by framing a senior professor for the crime. We had battled locals, disease, and Vesuvius's fury—thereby confirming first-hand the correct date of the volcanic eruption in 79 AD—and had returned from the wild ride back through History with two extra people.

The first was one of our own St. Sunniva professors, who had relocated to the past for reasons of his own.

The second was dark-haired, bright-eyed Sabina, daughter of the merchant Secundus, granddaughter of the backyard herbalist and inveterate schemer Faustilla. We had rescued her from certain death in the eruption. That was how it went with time travel and its rules. You couldn't change the course of History, not one of its twists or turns or side alleys, so if there had been the slightest chance that Sabina would have survived the eruption, we wouldn't have been able to bring her back. Her footsteps would have been irreversibly intermixed with those of others along History's road, and History protected itself. The very fact that we were able to pull her into STEWie's basket with us meant that her life in 79 AD was over.

My ineptitude with plants and other things that needed nurturing aside, I had been prepared to act as the girl's guardian, but Abigail had quietly stepped up instead. She had grown up as a foster child and had no family—and, also of some importance, had a working knowledge of classical Latin. The two of them, Abigail and Sabina, were living in the mother-in-law suite in the back of my bungalow, where Sabina had the small bedroom and Abigail the sofa bed in the equally small living room. Sabina had been living with us for the past four months, facing head-on the peculiarities of twenty-first-century life, from Twitter to toothpaste to canned tomato soup.

"How much do you know?" I asked Quinn, sitting back down and eyeing him from across the desk. He had helped himself to a couple more of the fudge mints while I'd been lost in thought. I pulled the cookie jar away from him.

"How much do I know? That you all broke a bunch of rules bringing her back."

"Protocol. We broke protocol." There *were* rules of time travel, like I said, four of them in fact, with one being the afore-mentioned *History protects itself.* I resisted the urge to list it and the other three for Quinn.

"Protocol, whatever. I couldn't help but notice that that part of the story never made it into the news. That's her, right?" He turned the frame sitting on my desk in his direction and examined the group photo in it. It was the seven of us who had returned from Pompeii at a Fourth of July picnic by Sunniva Lake. Quinn's bangs slid over his forehead as he bent over the photo, his hair looking blonder than ever against his Arizona tan. His peach-colored short-sleeve shirt and perfectly seamed beige khakis seemed out of place in a rainy Minnesota September. I wanted to slap his hand away.

"Hey, Jules, what happened to your glasses?" He looked up from the photo. "Did you get Lasik or something?"

I couldn't believe it. We had been married for six years—still were, technically, until the divorce proceedings went through—and he had forgotten that the glasses I used to wear were plain glass. I had worn them in an effort to be taken more seriously in my official capacity as the science dean's assistant, having been confused for a student one time too many. Picture a small nose and round face under wavy brown hair that refused to stay pinned up. The brown of my hair was matched by the brown of my eyes, which was a bit of a mystery—I looked nothing like my parents, and the family pictures I had of my grandparents, who were long gone, all showed light-haired, prim-looking Norwegians.

Deciding that it was a wonder that Quinn had even remem-bered which building I worked in—the science dean's offices were on the ground floor of the Hypatia of Alexandria House, a two-story brick building as old as the school itself—I explained about the glasses, hoping to change the subject away from Sabina.

"Huh. I thought you needed them for reading. You look better this way anyway. The glasses made you seem too bookish. I'm planning on plastering the Pompeii girl's—what's her name again?"

"Sabina," I said reluctantly.

"I'm planning on plastering Sabina's story all over the Internet if you don't help me prove that the runestone is real, Jules."

So much for changing the subject.

Who knew what evidence he possessed? If he'd been inside the house, he had no doubt seen the Pompeii photos that Sabina had taped up in her room. Also the lists Abigail and I had added all around the house to help her deal with modern oddities like which trash went into the garbage can and which into the recycling bin, and when to eat with your fingers (pizza, French fries, and chicken wings) and when with silverware (pretty much everything else).

"Wait," I said, realizing something. "Is that why you've held off on signing the divorce papers? To blackmail me into doing this?"

He leaned back in the visitor's chair, his arms clasped behind his head. If there had been room in my cramped office, he probably would have put his feet up on my desk. "Well, when you disappeared, we all thought you were dead, and there didn't seem to be any point to signing the papers. Then when you showed up alive and well after five months, telling tales about the past, it occurred to me that the Time Machine would be just the thing to confirm Farfar's story."

"I can't get you a STEWie run."

"It would be quick, isn't that true?"

"What would?"

"Going into the fourteenth century. Time zips by in the past but drags in the present, no? It's a turtle here but a hare there when you compare clocks."

"Something like that," I said. So he did know something about the rules of time travel, because that was another one of them. Each hour spent in the past corresponded to only 133 ticks of the second hand on the lab clock. No one quite knew why.

"So we could get this pilot filmed and be back the same day, couldn't we, Jules?"

"The answer's no, Quinn," I said firmly.

He leaned forward and took my hand. "Julia. The sooner we settle matters, the sooner I can sign the divorce papers. And do my best to keep Sabina's story from going public, of course. Hey, do you want a spot on my new reality show? It could be arranged."

At this point I might have been asking myself what I ever saw in the man, but I knew. He was a charmer, with his easygoing ways and handsome grin. His grand plans—like flipping houses in Arizona—and now this...well, it was just his way of doing things. He had hated his job as an accountant for the town's electrical plant, the sameness of it day in and day out, but had given it a try for our sake, and I understood that. He had ultimately failed and, drawn by online photos of Phoenix bungalows and cactus gardens basking in perpetual sunshine, had left town with Officer Jones. I couldn't bring myself to hate him, not even now. He was a disappointment to me—no more, no less.

"No, Quinn," I said, letting go of his hand. "I can't get you on a STEWie run. Not for a story passed down in your family, and certainly not for a reality show."

He went on as if I hadn't said anything. "I'm thinking of calling it *History's Dirty Secrets*. I even have a tip on where I can get backing for the show. Wouldn't it be something if I can prove that Farfar was right and that the Vikings really did come to the US? Once we film that, it'll set the ball rolling, and we can move on to the JFK assassination, the Roswell Incident, and other mysteries... I'm full of ideas."

I tried a different approach. "Look, I don't know that what you have in mind is even possible. Big questions and important people are often the hardest to tackle. It's just how time travel works."

He grinned at me and got to his feet, cheerfully unhooking the frog umbrella from the chair back, not looking discouraged in the least by my refusal. Listening had never been one of his stronger characteristics. "Take the weekend to think about it, Jules. I'll be in touch. I'm staying at Lena's Lodge—unless you'd be willing to let me sleep on the couch?"

"I don't think so."

# 3

I was dialing the phone before the door had closed behind Quinn. Helen answered after the second ring. The no-nonsense historical linguist had been on many a STEWie run, including the Pompeii one. She was well known for having proven that Shakespeare *did* write his plays, by returning from a run to Bishopsgate in 1590s London with some well-shot footage. She was a senior professor with research interests that included, in addition to Shakespeare, classical Latin and Greek. She was also a good friend.

I told her everything.

"I hope I did the right thing in sending Quinn away, Helen," I said, switching the phone to my left hand so that I could reach into the cookie jar for the last of the fudge mints. "I'm not sure what to do. I can't get him a STEWie run like he wants, but we can't let him expose Sabina either. It's hard enough to be the new kid in school. Imagine how mercilessly she'll get teased if the other kids find out that she's from the first century. And if the media gets a hold of the story..."

Though every historian at St. Sunniva University would have given an arm and a leg to sit Sabina down and hear what life had been like for an ordinary person in the ancient Roman Empire, something that rarely made it into the accounts that had survived into the present before STEWie, we had agreed that privacy trumped academics. Sabina had not asked to be brought here, and we were not going to make a celebrity out of her. If she decided to share her story with the world when she was older— well, that would be her choice.

"You did the right thing, Julia." Helen's voice, trained by years of classroom lecturing, carried strong through the line. "And if he does break the news—well, the truth was bound to come out one day. When it does, Sabina will be fine. There might be some awkwardness for us here at St. Sunniva about how the whole thing was handled, but we'll deal with it. Why does Quinn care about finding the runestone anyway? Historical finds rarely make anyone rich."

Helen knew Quinn somewhat, having met him at a few of the school functions we'd attended as a couple.

"He seems to think the runestone would make a great pilot for a time travel reality TV show with him as the star," I explained.

"It might, I suppose, though I would have thought the JFK assassination or something of that sort would be more marketable. It's the first idea that people always bring up."

"He's saving that for a future episode. His grandfather played a role in digging up the stone, so he thinks that makes it perfect for the pilot."

"I see."

I slid the lid into its place over the empty cookie jar. "If Quinn asked for money so he could finance the reality show, I might have given him some. But not this, not an off-the-books STEWie run."

"I wouldn't worry about it, Julia. Still, I suppose we should prepare Sabina just in case. We can talk more about it this evening."

I was hosting a get-together of our Pompeii family to celebrate Sabina's first week of high school. "If you don't mind, I'd rather you didn't bring it up, Helen. I don't want to ruin Sabina's party. Plus, I don't want…uh, the others to know that Quinn is in town."

"How are things between you and Chief Kirkland, anyway? Has he asked you out yet?"

Nate and I had formed a friendship on the Pompeii run, but that was the extent of it. I obviously still had some Quinn-related issues, and Nate had personal stuff he needed to work through as well. At least we'd come back from Pompeii with him calling me Julia instead of *Ms. Olsen*. It was progress. He had been gone most of the summer, which was quiet time at the school, on a team-building retreat. I hadn't seen him since the Fourth of July picnic.

"There's nothing going on between us," I said into the phone. "Besides, he just got back."

"The course of true love never did run smooth," said Helen, who was given to quoting the Bard at odd moments. "Do you need me to bring anything tonight other than the balloons?"

"Let me check." I moused the computer to life, closed the orientation booklet I had been working on, and opened the party to-do list. I'd already crossed off most of the items on it. "We're looking good, if the weather clears up. I'm picking up the cake on the way home, and Nate is bringing the burgers."

Cooking and I did not mix, even on outdoor grills, so Nate's offer of being the designated chef was a welcome one.

"See you tonight, Julia—oh, wait, I have an idea. I should have thought of it immediately when you mentioned the runestone. Why don't you send Quinn to talk to Dagmar?"

"Who is she?"

"Dr. Dagmar Holm is a postdoc here in the department, a runic linguist. She might be able to explain to Quinn why the runestone story is just a myth—a popular one, but a myth nonetheless. Maybe he'll accept an objective opinion better than a refusal from you."

"I'll see if I can catch him."

"I'll let Dagmar know."

I hung up the phone and stuck my head out the window. The rain had tapered off. Quinn was in the courtyard, leaning on the frog umbrella as he chatted with a female graduate student. I thought I saw the dean's straight back and black umbrella in the throng of students milling in and out of the courtyard on their way to class, so I waited until she had disappeared into the building before calling out Quinn's name.

He turned in my direction, said something no doubt charming to the graduate student, and took a few steps over to the still-dripping white birch outside my office window. "Did you change your mind, Jules?"

"No. But there's someone I want you to talk to. Her name is Dr. Dagmar Holm and she works in the English Department." I pointed to the square cement building, somewhat of a campus eyesore, which squatted by the bend in the lake. Though everyone called it the English Department, its official name was the Department of Classical, Medieval, and Modern Languages. "She'll be expecting you."

"Julia, is there a problem?"

I waved Quinn along and turned from the window. The dean had poked her head in on the way to her office next door. Formerly of the Earth Sciences Department, Dr. Isobel Braga was a geologist by training and my new boss. She was *not* one of the few people who knew the whole Pompeii story.

"Just a personal matter," I explained. I grabbed the stack of referral letters that needed her signature from my desk and accompanied her to her office. "How was the meeting?"

Dean Braga had been showing potential donors around the *History Alive* exhibit at the campus museum. The exhibit represented the fruits of the STEWie project. One of its star attractions was a somewhat blurry photo, enlarged and taken from behind a bush, showing the muscular, tanned, and bearded builders of Stonehenge in prehistoric Britain. In another corner of the exhibition hall, heartbreaking footage of the sinking Titanic taken from a time-traveling buoy looped in ten-minute intervals.

Dean Braga deposited her black umbrella with perhaps slightly more force than necessary in the coat rack just inside the door. "It didn't go terribly well. I think I just wasted an hour."

"They weren't impressed with the exhibit?"

She shook her head. "It's not that. They've heard that MIT is constructing a bigger STEWie."

That happened to be true.

"But bigger is not necessarily—"

"—better, yes. I tried to get the point across that the reason we've had trouble getting near primary historical figures is because of History's constraints, not any fault on our part, and that MIT will face the same problems." She dropped into the leather chair behind her desk and shook her head.

"They always ask why we don't try again the next day and the day after and the day after that, as if each STEWie run isn't such a large drain on energy and resources. I explained that research is never easy and that results rarely just fall into one's lap—that confirming who shot JFK, which seemed to be their main interest," she said, echoing what Helen had said moments earlier, "will take longer than the months of planning that the Department of American History has already put into the project. Hiding a fleet of cameras around Dealey Plaza is no easy task. And we have to make sure that the people placing them and retrieving go under the radar, too."

"Did you explain that maneuvering in a time period not your own is 'like navigating a maze?'" I asked, quoting Dr. Rojas of the TTE lab, who was on a well-deserved sabbatical, having gone through the stress of being wrongfully accused of murder. "That our researchers cannot always go where they want to, not to mention that there are ghost zones to worry about?"

"I'm not sure I got the point across. This salesman side of being a dean is going to take some getting used to. Their other idea—really not an original one to suggest to a geologist— was to go back in time to film the dinosaurs. The energy expenditure to go that far back, not to mention the danger to our researchers, the unknown factors they would encounter... I mean, the air itself was different." She shook her head wearily, slid on her reading glasses, and held her hand out for the referral letters. She commenced reading the top one. After her predecessor, Lewis Sunder, had been arrested for sending five of us into a ghost zone and trying to frame Dr. Rojas, I'd joked that the new dean, whoever it turned out to be, could not be worse.

Dean Braga came close. Lewis Sunder had preferred to leave the day-to-day running of the dean's office in my hands, dedicating himself to fundraising and to addressing the big issues, like whether theoretical researchers needed bigger offices than experimentalists, who also had lab space. Dean Braga attended to the details of STEWie roster assignments, funding requests, and conference travel forms with the same zeal she would have given a particularly interesting rock specimen in her career as a geologist. Saying she micromanaged did not do justice to the fervor with which she followed the path of every penny in the eight science departments under her care and checked every signature on every piece of paper. I hoped it was a temporary stage and would pass once she settled into her new role.

"You said you were dealing with a personal matter, Julia?" she asked, checking the figures in the letter against her notes.

I had considered telling Isobel about Sabina after she took up the post of dean, but was concerned that she'd think it her duty to tell the world. And she'd no doubt be furious with us for breaking time travel protocols.

"That was my ex," I explained. "My soon-to-be-ex husband, actually. There were some matters we needed to settle."

She took a pen and applied her signature to the first of the letters. "Let's try to keep personal matters outside of work hours, shall we? Now, about the first pass at the spring class schedule..."

∞

By mid-afternoon, I had rearranged some chemistry lab sections in the spring semester class catalog as requested by Dean Braga, helped a foreign student dealing with a visa problem, and listened to a phone message from a sophomore who had *completely* forgotten to turn in her final essay ("On the Early History of Weather Prediction"), but the professor who had taught the summer class had already gone on a sabbatical and was not answering her calls, so she had e-mailed the essay to me instead, and could I please forward it to him so that she'd get a passing grade—all of this even though the deadline had long since passed and the fall semester had already started. I jotted down a note to deal with it later in the day. Quinn's words— *"I'm planning on plastering Sabina's story all over the Internet if you don't help me prove the runestone is real"*—kept running through my mind as I filled out budget forms. Finally, I decided I'd had enough. Dean Braga wanted personal matters kept out of the office and so did I. The best way to accomplish that was to make sure that Dr. Holm had been able to convince Quinn that his plan was unrealistic.

Besides, I wanted the matter settled before Sabina's party tonight.

I looked up Dr. Holm's contact information in the internal campus database, hesitated, then sent her a text message introducing myself and asking if she'd be available for a short chat.

She texted back, *Am in Coffey Library, in the stacks, come by.*

I found Dr. Holm between a pair of floor-to-ceiling bookcases, sitting cross-legged on the carpeted floor of the library. Hardcover books lay open all around her, and one was nestled in her lap. She was, I guessed, in her late twenties, with fine auburn hair held back by a sky-blue hairband. I've been told often enough that I look young for my age, but Dr. Holm took it to a whole new level. The tip of her tiny nose turned to one side ever so slightly, which, coupled with the small ears that held the blue headband in place, made her look like an erudite pixie as she bent over the textbook. Above black leggings and flats, she had on an oversized white T-shirt with photos of a Viking ship on the front and back.

"Sorry to disturb you," I said in the measured tone everyone automatically adopts in libraries. "I'm Julia Olsen, assistant to Dean Braga over in the science departments."

She looked up, blinking to adjust from reading printed materials in the low library light, and nimbly sprang to her feet and shook my hand. She was petite, as befitted a pixie, and had a suitably high-pitched voice. "Pleased to meet you. You're the one who went on that accidental run into far time, aren't you? Let me put these books away and maybe we can grab a smoothie or something? I went for a jog this morning, and I'm famished."

I wasn't into jogging. In my opinion, people who jog always look like they're suffering—it's not often that you see a smiling jogger—but I could see how it would make a person hungry.

"Nice T-shirt," I said as we headed out of the library to the student café next door. The photos printed onto the front and back of the custom-made T-shirt had been taken from shore. One showed a long and agile wooden vessel with a dragon figurehead on the prow, a single mast, and tightly packed, bareheaded figures expertly manning the oars. The other showed a work-horse vessel, its open cargo hold overflowing with cattle, sheep, and other goods as it sailed away to unknown lands.

"Thanks. The one the front is a longship, used for raiding. The one on the back is a *knarr*, a cargo ship of the kind used to settle Iceland and Greenland. The photos were taken by Dr. May on her runs to eleventh-century Europe. The longships were up to thirty-five meters in length. They were sturdy enough for long sea voyages, yet shallow enough to navigate up rivers as well." The academic language made for a strange partnership with her girlish voice. "Most people think the Vikings wore horned helmets, but as you can see, they didn't."

After she got her smoothie and I got a caffeinated pop, we wound our way through tables where students sat engrossed in their various electronic devices nursing coffees and energy drinks, only a few of them carrying on conversations.

"Dr. Holm, I don't want to take up too much of your time…" I said once we sat down, having chosen an inside table since the outside ones were still wet from the rain. Realizing that I didn't even know for sure that she and Quinn had spoken, I suddenly felt foolish.

"You're Quinn Olsen's wife, right?"

"I am," I admitted. "Look, I don't know what he told you—"

"That there's a family legend concerning his grandfather and the Kensington Runestone." She took a long sip through a straw that was the same pink color as her strawberry smoothie, then went on. "I told him the runestone *is* real, of course— it's a two-hundred-pound slab of graywacke inscribed with rows of runes and you can drive half an hour to Alexandria to see it."

This, of course, was not the Alexandria in Egypt, but the biggest town in the county and its seat.

"The real question is, who carved it?" She paused for another sip of the smoothie. "Norse explorers who sailed to North America more than a century before Columbus and reached as far inland as the Great Lakes, like the text on the runestone claims? Or a nineteenth-century Swedish immigrant with a talent for hoaxes?"

"You sound as if you think there's a chance the runestone is authentic," I said, pulling the paper wrapping off my straw. This was no good. She was supposed to discourage Quinn, not add fuel to his latest wild scheme. "That it was carved by Vikings."

She shook her head. "It wouldn't have been the Vikings. The Viking Age—of raiders, Thor-worshipers, and masters of sea and river travel—ended in the eleventh century. The medieval Norse were traders who had converted to Christianity." She paused for more smoothie, then said in a measured tone, "The stone is almost certainly a hoax."

"Almost certainly? You didn't tell Quinn that, did you? He's perfectly capable of taking that as an encouragement."

"Well, to be honest, he didn't seem discouraged in the least by what I had to say." She paused for another long sip, then said, "I'm somewhat familiar with the details of the runestone finding. I don't remember any mention of a Magnus Olsen, though I thought it would be rude to mention that."

"He was just a neighborhood kid, eight years old." As I related the tale, it suddenly occurred to me how much alike Quinn and his grandfather were. Perhaps the runestone hadn't been as influential on Magnus Olsen's life as family lore had it. Maybe it was in the genes, this dislike of being tied down to a steady job that paid the bills. Whatever it was, Quinn certainly had it. Before the flipping-houses-in-Phoenix thing, Quinn had invested our savings in a restaurant that failed immediately, started several blogs that never went anywhere and didn't bring in any money, and even suggested we move to Hawaii to open a snorkeling business, something neither of us knew a thing about. Though I didn't obsess over it—the end of our relationship had been a long time coming—I had always wondered if I'd said or done something to finally make him leave. Now I realized that it didn't matter. In the end, it didn't have much to do with me, after all; it had everything to do with his quest to make his mark on the world.

Dr. Holm had downed her drink before the edges in the ice cubes in mine had the chance to round. She took a loud slurp of what was left in the bottom of her cup and said, "It's sweet that your…that Mr. Olsen wants to clear his grandfather's name." I didn't think so, especially given that he had resorted to blackmail. And Quinn was probably just as motivated by the thought of getting his face on TV as anything else. He certainly seemed to have exercised his charms on Dr. Holm, I noted.

She added, "I'll pass on what I told him. I tried...I wrote up a STEWie proposal to investigate the runestone last year. Dr. Payne said no. In his opinion, runic linguists should stick to European sites and go no farther west than Greenland, which the Vikings reached in 982."

I realized why her name was unfamiliar. I had never seen it on the STEWie roster. She hadn't been on a run yet. The Dr. Payne she had mentioned was a senior professor of American history. Several of his research proposals, all written densely and with elevated prose, had crossed my desk on their way to the science dean's office. They were usually approved, unless there was some technical reason prohibiting the run. I had seen the thin-haired, stooped professor in period costume—coat, waistcoat, and knee-length breeches—around the Time Travel Engineering building. Rumor had it that those Toliver Payne mentored—his postdocs and grad students—had a hard time getting the professor to sign off on projects that had not originated in his own brain.

Dr. Holm confirmed as much. "In the two years I've been a postdoc here at St. Sunniva University, I've written forty-nine proposals for projects I thought would make good research topics. I've managed to obtain funding for only three—*three!*—and none for a STEWie run. Since Dr. Payne had mentioned Greenland, I got the idea to study the Kingittorsuaq Runestone, which was found north of the two Viking settlements there, and establish a full translation and date of carving for it." As before, her words, those of an authoritative researcher, sounded odd when coupled with her high-pitched voice. Not that a personal characteristic of that sort should have much bearing on the prospect of a professorial position down the road—at least, not in an ideal world. What makes someone a good teacher is his or her ability to connect with students and get the best out of them, not his or her method of delivery.

"Unfortunately," she sighed, "Greenland turned out to be a kind of a no-man's land academically speaking—no one can decide if it belongs in American history, Dr. Payne's domain, or European history, Dr. May's domain. Dr. Payne told me to submit to Dr. May, and Dr. May told me to submit to Dr. Payne."

I was familiar with her complaint. Getting funding in academia was no easy matter, and securing a STEWie roster spot was an order of magnitude harder. Tenured professors enjoyed priority and were the most frequent visitors to the cavernous lab with its maze of mirrors and lasers. Postdoctoral researchers like Dr. Holm occupied the gray area between graduate student and junior professor. Postdocs were relatively cheap, highly trained, and worked long hours without any guarantee of a professorship down the road. It often took three or four postings—usually at different research centers around the country and abroad, each lasting only a year or two and requiring uprooting and relocation each time—before a tenure-track faculty position was offered, if the person was lucky. I decided to try and give Dr. Holm what little help I could, which amounted to no more than putting her STEWie proposals in front of Dean Braga when she was in a good mood and not at the end of the day, when she was rushing to get things done. I owed Dr. Holm that much at least for trying to talk Quinn out of his plan.

As if echoing my thoughts, she commented with a self-conscious laugh, "I'd bribe Dean Braga or treat her to dinner or something if I thought that would get me a run. She always looks so severe, though, that I barely dare to say hello to her. Uh—I don't suppose you have any influence over who gets chosen for runs, do you?"

"Not much, no. Sorry."

She tugged at the hairband. "What was it like?"

"Which?"

"Going to Pompeii. Other than the danger presented by the volcano, obviously, and being marooned against your will."

"It was... *extraordinary*. I'm sure you'll get your chance," I said.

"I know, good things come to those who wait and all that." She got to her feet. "Did you want to see it, your runestone? There is an excellent life-size reproduction in the map section of the library."

∞

A couple of minutes later, our drink cups dispensed with, Dr. Holm led me to the lower level of the library and a large glass cabinet. This was where historical maps and manuscripts obtained on STEWie runs and through more conventional means were made available to students and other library visitors in a sort of disorganized, overflowing fashion. She rummaged around a bit and finally pulled out a rolled-up poster from the back of a low shelf. I followed her to a free table, and when she unrolled the poster, I helped her pin down its corners with four library books that had been discarded by previous patrons.

Perched on the table next to the poster, her tone and the T-shirt with the Viking ships making her seem like a perky museum guide, she said, "Farmer Olof Ohman was the one who found the stone. He was clearing a new field on his homestead with the help of his two sons. One of them noticed the stone clasped in the roots of a tree they had just uprooted. This is what they said they found."

The poster displayed the front of the stone:

There was also a view of one side, where a shorter bit of text had been carved:

"Can you read it?" I asked Dr. Holm, looking up at her from my chair.

"The runes? Oh, yes, though there are differing opinions about the translation. I'll give you the gist of it, though." Running a finger over the poster, she quoted:

*Eight Gotlanders and twenty-two Northmen*
*on a journey from Vinland to the west.*
*We had a camp one day's journey north from this stone.*
*We were out fishing one day.*
*After we came home,*
*We found ten men red from blood and dead.*
*Ave Maria save us from evil.*

I followed her hand as it moved over the text and spotted the abbreviation that stood for Ave Maria, as that part was chiseled in clearly recognizable letters: *AVM.*

"Gotlanders?" I asked, vowing to study up on my Scandinavian history. I had picked up bits and pieces from the historical snippets that accompanied each STEWie run proposal, but I hadn't come across Gotland before.

"It's the largest island in the Baltic Sea. Part of Sweden today. And Northmen probably refers to Norwegians. Hypothetically speaking, we can imagine they might have been explorers looking to establish a new trade route, perhaps for fur, which was a luxury item at the time." She added, "Here on the side, it says: *Have ten men by the sea to look after our ships, fourteen days' journey from this island. Year 1362.*"

"It's quite a tale," I said, "if it's true. On a journey from Vinland... I've heard that term before—it's used in the Norse sagas, right? But where was it?"

"No one is quite sure." She tugged at her hairband again. "All we know is that there was a settlement at Lancey Meadows—"

"I'm sorry, where?"

She spelled it out for me. "L'Anse aux Meadows. The settlement was built just around the turn of the millennium—early eleventh century—on Newfoundland."

"Sorry," I said again, "my geography of the, er, northern part of the Americas is rusty."

"Newfoundland is the large island in the North Atlantic Ocean off the coast of mainland Canada. Twenty years after his father, Erik the Red, founded the Greenland colonies, Leif Erikson sailed to Newfoundland—or at least we think he did. It hasn't been confirmed yet with a run. The settlement, with its Viking artifacts, is at the northernmost tip of the island. *It is the only confirmed Norse site in North America.*" She followed the statement with a moment's pause to underline its significance.

The implication suddenly hit me.

"Wait," I said. "If there was a Viking village in Canada, doesn't that conclusively prove that—"

"—the Vikings reached the Americas five hundred years before Columbus? It does indeed. Before L'Anse aux Meadows no one had believed it."

Thanks to a recent run by the Dr. May she had mentioned, we now had a snapshot of Columbus. The picture showed a man on the tall side with a hooked nose, his red beard and hair shot through with white. It surprised me that I hadn't heard that a Viking archeological site had been found. My Norwegian ancestry meant there was a high possibility that I had Viking blood in my veins, though I didn't actually know of any ancestors who had gone pirating, pillaging, and exploring. My parents were not big on ancestry and that kind of thing— except for a few family photos, the knickknacks in our house were mostly mementos of the stories my parents had written for the town newspaper over the years. But you couldn't grow up in Minnesota, where it was impossible to swing a cat without hitting someone of Scandinavian descent, without absorbing some Viking lore.

"When was the settlement documented?" I asked, expecting to hear that it had been filmed on a STEWie run while I was in Pompeii. "Lancey...what did you call it again?" It occurred to me that I should have brought my notepad, if only to list all the new names I was learning.

"L'Anse aux Meadows. The name is an anglicized version of the French for Jellyfish Cove. The settlement—what was left of it—was found in 1960 by the Norwegian explorer and archeologist pair Helge and Anne Stine Ingstad. I thought it was worth a shot for a STEWie run. No luck so far, though," she said. I thought she meant no luck in confirming that it was the Vinland of the runestone and the Norse sagas, but she elaborated by lowering her voice to quote Dr. Payne. "'There is no need for you to go, Dr. Holm, where there are no runes.'"

I took another look at the poster, this time with different eyes. "So if the Vikings reached L'Anse aux Meadows at just about the turn of the millennium—"

"—could a small group have made it inland all the way to Kensington some three hundred fifty years later?" She continued with the caution of an academic. "There are linguistic problems with the runes on the stone that point to a forgery. I explained that to Quinn—to Mr. Olsen. I hope you're not disappointed."

"Not in the least. Thank you, Dr. Holm."

As she rolled up the poster and turned back to the cabinet, I stopped her. "Why *did* you want to go to L'Anse aux Meadows if there are no runes there?"

I recognized the hesitation. She didn't want to share an idea that she hadn't published yet. "Well—think of all we would learn about the Old Norse language if we planted microphones throughout the settlement. It's true that most of the conversation would concern ordinary things like *What's for dinner?* and *I hope the rain will taper off by tomorrow.* But that's exactly what we need to supplement the meager texts that have survived. It's unlikely that L'Anse aux Meadows itself was Vinland, the place of wild grapes, but if we should happen to overhear the villagers mention where it might be..." She didn't finish the thought.

The rolled-up poster in her hand, with its black-and-white reproduction of the runestone, was like a window into the past. I raised an eyebrow at it. "What killed them?"

"Who?"

"The ones who stayed behind at the camp on the runestone. Unfriendly locals?"

"Hypothetically speaking, that's been the assumption ever since the stone was found. If we knew where to look, perhaps we could find the skeletons of ten men and their effects within a day's journey on foot or boat from Kensington. Now that would be something...Just think of it—they probably thought they had reached Asia from the west, just as Columbus would assume years later."

For someone who didn't believe in the authenticity of the stone, she sure seemed to know a lot about it. As if she could sense what I was thinking, she added, "Still hypothetically speaking, of course. Some of the runes are unusual, like this part here, *opthagelsefarth.*" She unrolled the poster a bit again. "Did the carver mean to suggest a journey of acquisition or a journey of exploration? And the camp where the fisherman left their companions is described as being near two landmarks. In my opinion, the word refers to—"

"Wasting your time, Dr. Holm?" a voice rasped. "Don't you have a department meeting to attend? Or were you not planning to grace us with your presence?"

It was Dr. Payne, a bound book in one hand, his thinning hair combed over an ever-expanding bald spot. The raspiness of his voice was from years of chain smoking in the courtyard of the American History building.

"I'll be at the meeting, Dr. Payne, I was just showing Julia here the runestone poster she's from the science departments. Even though the stone's not authentic, it's still a valuable nineteenth-century artifact..."

"I expressed an interest," I explained calmly. "There is a minor connection on my husband's side of the family."

The professor sent a look of contempt in the direction of the poster in Dr. Holm's hand. "All this talk of who discovered America—Columbus or the Vikings—is utter nonsense. Ancestral Indians got here fifteen thousand years ago, or more, by crossing the Bering Strait from Siberia. Columbus didn't discover America. Indians discovered Europeans on their shores, much to their detriment. A hoax like the Kensington Runestone...well, let's just say that it only makes a historian's lot harder."

He sniffed derisively and went on his way.

# 4

Sabina came home on the school bus and cheerfully dropped her backpack onto the deck, where Abigail and I were setting things up for her party. Truth be told, I was happy the pair had moved in with me. While I didn't exactly miss Quinn, the house had seemed empty when I was the only one living there. Sabina greeted me as Aunt Julia, which was nice, even though it made me feel older than my thirty-five years.

Sabina and Abigail went to dig up a Frisbee in the garage. Helen had phoned to say she was running late, but Nate and Kamal arrived a few minutes after the appointed time in our security chief's Jeep. They had Wanda, Nate's spaniel, in tow. She ran off into the yard and Kamal sank into one of the deck chairs immediately, already sweating. Nate nodded at me and said, "Where do you want these, Julia?"

He was carrying a large plate heavy with vegetables, with a stack of metal skewers waiting for them. There were also some plump, pink disks.

I eyed them. "What on earth are those?"

"Salmon burgers."

"Salmon? I thought you were bringing normal burgers."

"These are normal. You've never had a salmon burger?"

My palate was more of the "grilled meat and potato chips" type, except, oddly, for finger foods—since they were the life's blood of the fundraisers and other school events I frequently organized, I was well versed in fancy cheeses, fondues, shrimp cocktails, and other delicacies that could be eaten standing up. Well-versed in ordering them, that is, not making or enjoying them.

"I suppose I can give the salmon burgers a shot. In here." I slid the deck door open and he followed me into the kitchen. "How was the team-building retreat?"

"Good. And your summer?"

He was not a particularly chatty person, as if he was the one with the Norwegian ancestry instead of me. His own ancestry was wonderfully mixed, which had resulted in a uniquely appealing set of features, I had to admit—from his jet black hair and eyes to his height. He was so tall and lanky that his campus security uniform probably needed to be specially made. I had always meant to ask him about that.

"Sabina started school this week, right?" he added. "How's she liking it?"

"She hasn't said much about it," I explained. "I think she's reserving judgment."

"Well, it is high school, and she is the new kid."

I sighed. "I know. That rarely goes well for anybody."

Having left the food by the sink, we went back out onto the deck, where Nate turned his attention to lighting the charcoal. Sabina and Abigail had returned with the Frisbee and Sabina twisted it in her hands as, with a mixture of relief and pride, she launched into an account of her first week at school. "This *puella*—girl—she called me 'pizza lover,'" Sabina mimicked, her accent (which seemed to be diminishing day by day) only adding to the tale.

I wasn't happy that someone had teased her, but at least it sounded like the back story we had come up with, that she was an immigrant from Italy living with Cousin Abigail and Aunt Julia, had been accepted without question. Besides, it was sort of true. "Just try to ignore remarks like that," I said, moving the deck chairs into the shade. The rain had cleared up, leaving behind a strong afternoon sun. Summer had continued seamlessly into September, and the heat had yielded a fresh crop of boxelder bugs. The black bugs, with their familiar red markings, coated the sunny side of the house, harmless nuisances that they were.

Sabina ignored the chairs and hopped up onto the deck railing. "I wasn't offended. I like pizza, this is true, no?"

"I can go to school with you if you'd like. I'll punch anybody who needs it," Kamal announced, edging his deck chair deeper into the shade. The senior graduate student, who was not athletic in the least and would probably sprain a finger if he *did* punch anybody, added, "Happy to do it."

"Not to worry, Kamal. I can handle. And I made friend. Kim. She nice." Sabina fingered the amulet hanging from a thin chain around her neck, a crescent moon made of orange-brown amber. The amulet was a lunula—a symbol of Diana, the goddess of the moon, the hunt, and childbirth. It was Sabina's one link to home and a source of great strength for her. I hoped she wouldn't get teased about the odd piece of jewelry at school.

An overweight scruffy dog waddled up the deck steps and curled into a ball by her feet, which she was energetically swinging from her perch on the railing. Celer had also returned with us from Pompeii. The leisure-loving dog's name, pronounced with a hard *k*, meant *Speedy* in what was clearly intended as a joke. Celer's opposite in personality and looks was Wanda, who was currently chasing a squirrel up the oak tree that shaded the deck, her tongue hanging to one side. While Celer was grayish and of indeterminate ancestry, Wanda's silken white-and-chestnut coat could have won her a dog contest. Nate had inherited her from a previous case, back when he had worked in law enforcement in the Boundary Waters Canoe Area Wilderness, by the Canadian border.

"Wanda, behave yourself," he called out, then went back into the house to prepare the food.

Sabina, watching Wanda, commented, "Most hard word... sk—skoo..."

"*Sqwo-ral*," Kamal said helpfully. His parents were diplomats, and he spoke four languages fluently, including his native Arabic.

"Skoo-ral." Sabina added, "I forgot to say. We get in school—what is it... *lah-kers*, yes."

"Shoot, sorry, I forgot to explain about those," Abigail said. The two had bonded during the few days we had spent in the past, and their bond had only grown stronger in the four months since our return. "Did you get a combination for it?"

"Yes, three numbers. I memorize."

Abigail's short hair changed color so frequently that Sabina and I joked that it was like living with a different person each week. The current, somewhat odd shade of green made her look rather like a hungry insect as she untwisted the top of a salsa jar. Sabina hopped off the railing and, following Abigail's example, tentatively scooped up some salsa with a corn chip. She looked at it for a moment, then popped the whole thing in her mouth.

"Good," she said after some crunching.

"I know, right? Julia and I bought something new for you to try for dessert, too—*cheesecake*. It's yummy. Not for you, Celer, sorry," Abigail added as the dog stirred at the familiar word. "It's made from chocolate, which, as you found out, is bad for dogs."

Chocolate, corn, pizza—these were all newfound tastes for Sabina (and Celer); the Roman world of their time had been a place of grapes, figs, and olive oil. I felt a twinge of sadness as I watched the girl dig into the chips and salsa, wondering if she missed Pompeii fare like the flavorful goat stew we'd eaten with hearty bread, or the pungent but popular Roman sauce *garum*. Her father had manufactured it in large sunken jars in the garden behind his shop, just next to the pear tree, by fermenting fish for months at a time. Well, it wasn't likely we'd be able to duplicate that one, but the others we could try at future get-togethers. I headed back inside, sliding the screen door behind me quickly so that no boxelder bugs could get into the house.

Nate was by the kitchen sink with his sleeves rolled up as he popped vegetable chunks onto metal skewers. I offered to help him prepare the food and received a friendly chuckle in return. "For everybody's safety, perhaps you'd better not. Some things are best left to the chef."

"Hey, I'm only dangerous to the food, not to my guests."

"You want to do the wine?"

"I was about to."

As I reached for a bottle of red wine on the countertop, the front door opened and Helen hurried in, maneuvering a thick bunch of balloons in with her.

"Sorry I'm late, Julia. My lecture ran longer than I expected, then I had to stop to pick up these. I wasn't sure which would be the most suitable for Sabina's first week of school in the twenty-first century, so I got them all. Hello, Chief Kirkland. How was your retreat?"

"Good. And your summer, Professor?" Nate asked from the sink.

"Most productive. I managed to recover a copy of Shakespeare's lost *Cardenio*."

"Well done."

"Is Dr. Mooney with you, Helen?" I asked. I hoped she would remember to not let it slip that Quinn was back in town. "I thought he was coming."

"Xavier texted to say he got held up at the conference and missed his plane. He was showing them his new and improved Slingshot." She tossed her silver hair, which she kept long for STEWie runs to Shakespeare's time, behind her shoulder with her free hand as if she was irritated at Xavier for changing his plans without consulting her. Xavier Mooney was a senior professor of Time Travel Engineering. He and Helen had been married once, and our shared Pompeii ordeal had rekindled their somewhat stormy relationship. The Slingshot was the laptop-size device that the professor had used to bring us back from Pompeii; he had been perfecting it ever since. "He won't be back until tomorrow," Helen added.

"Can't he just use the new and improved Slingshot to get back?" Nate suggested half-jokingly.

"I guess it's not quite ready for that sort of thing."

After helping Helen tie the balloons to a kitchen chair (there were ten of them, with a variety of messages, from *Congratulations!* to *Good Luck!*), I returned my attention to the wine bottle and opened it with a sharp twist of the corkscrew. I poured the wine halfway up a large pitcher, then went to the sink to top it off with cold tap water, a procedure that probably would have puzzled anyone who hadn't gone to Pompeii with us. If serving watered-down wine to a thirteen-year-old girl was odd, well, so were many things at our house.

"How are the coals looking out there?" Nate asked as I poured the rosy mixture into two glasses, passing one to Helen and leaving the other on the counter for him.

"They always look the same to me, pink-gray. I don't know how you decide when they're ready."

"Years of grilling experience, Julia."

As Helen held the deck door open for me, I noticed a twinkle in her eye and mouthed *Stop it* at her. I set the pitcher down next to the lemonade already sitting on ice on the deck. Lukewarm had been the Roman way of serving the watered-down wine, but I didn't think Sabina would mind on such a hot afternoon. She and Abigail were on the sunny part of the lawn, tossing the Frisbee around, Wanda nipping at their feet as she ran back and forth following the path of the Frisbee. Kamal was slumped in a lawn chair with a glass of lemonade in his hand and Celer in his lap. "I'm exhausted. It's a lot of work putting together a thesis defense. Celer, get off. You've gained too much weight."

It was true. The dog hadn't been exactly lean and energetic when he'd arrived in the twenty-first century in Kamal's arms, and he'd only gotten chubbier since. Used to eating scraps in the Pompeii shop run by Sabina's father, he had turned his nose up at the notion of pre-bagged dog food and simply shared ours—a lot of it.

Luckily, Sabina hadn't followed suit. Though she was no doubt eating more food than she had grown up on, her habit of moving around most of the day countered the extra calories. She helped with chores, tended to the yard, and spent afternoons exploring the campus; with her height, she could have easily been mistaken for a college freshman instead of a high school student. Hers was a familiar face at the TTE lab, where she often hung out by Dr. Mooney's workbench watching him tinker with STEWie parts.

Right now, her jeans and T-shirt made her look like a typical American teenager as she sent the Frisbee flying above Wanda's head. She wasn't. Having worked at both a laundry business and her father's garum shop, she was used to hard physical labor. Just a few days earlier, I had caught her stockpiling empty shoe boxes and pop bottles. Sabina had explained that she thought that they might come in handy for something or other. Why give them to the truck that came down the street every week and drove away with the neighborhood's discarded possessions? I felt a rising tide of anger toward Quinn. How dare he let himself in to snoop around, interfering with the fragile peace Sabina had made with her situation?

"Does Chief Kirkland need any help in there?" Kamal asked as his stomach gave a low growl. He nudged Celer off his lap and the dog gave the senior graduate student a look of profound hurt before settling down in the shade against the deck railing.

I set aside my concerns about Quinn and said, "He seems to have things under control. Here, have some corn chips."

Kamal hailed from the more well-known Alexandria, and his Mediterranean coloring was similar to dark-eyed, dark-haired Sabina's. His hair was on the long side at the moment and stubble covered the bottom half of his face. No need to shave for STEWie runs to the Neander Valley of so long ago that the notations in STEWie's roster were not in AD *or* BC. He'd been spending time in 30 ka, as in thirty kilo-annum, as in thirty thousand years ago. I imagined that his thesis defense next week would find Kamal with his chin baby smooth, his black hair trimmed to a fine degree, and his somewhat stocky frame clad in a suit. The T-shirt he was currently wearing announced $\sqrt{-1}\ 2^3\ \sum \pi \ldots and\ it\ was\ delicious$, which had puzzled me until I'd heard him explain to Sabina that the symbols on the shirt, which spelled out *i 8 sum Pi*, had a second meaning. Sabina was an avid reader of math textbooks, and knew all about pie and $\pi$.

Letting Wanda have her way with the Frisbee, Abigail and Sabina returned to the deck. Abigail's short green hair stood up perfectly still in the light breeze, as if the styling mousse had imparted a statue-like quality to her head. She poured the diluted wine into glasses for herself and Sabina—Kamal didn't drink alcohol. Slumping into a chair, she took a long sip.

"Ahh, I needed that," she said. "Wait, that came out wrong. I didn't mean the wine—although I'm not complaining about that part—it was hot trying to keep up with Wanda." She downed some more of the watery wine and turned to Kamal with a snicker, though not a mean one. She was very fond of him in a platonic, sisterly fashion. "There's the man of the hour."

"What's this?" I asked.

Kamal puffed out his chest. "The run to Neander Valley I just got back from was *quite* fruitful, so to speak."

"It's big news all over campus. He got footage, didn't you hear, Julia?" Abigail snickered again. "Of an early human and a Neanderthal *making out*—"

"Just thirty seconds worth," Kamal interjected. "From a distance."

"—and maybe even interbreeding. Though we'd probably have to wait nine months to find *that* out. Which way?" she asked as Kamal took another serene sip of his lemonade.

"Which way what?"

"Cro-Magnon woman or man?"

"Oh. Cro-Magnon man, Neanderthal woman, though we saw other examples. It was a ten-day run. Which is why I'm hungry." He reached for more chips.

Kamal's ten-day run would have passed in just about as many hours in the lab.

"Was it a lovers' tryst in a cave or something?" Abigail asked in a somewhat dreamy voice. Sabina interrupted before Kamal could answer. "What is *Ne-ander* and this *mate*-ing?"

Abigail gave her a somewhat muddled explanation of the matter, drawing on her knowledge of academic Latin enriched by colloquialisms Sabina had taught her. Both of them ended up in a paroxysm of giggles.

After their laughter subsided, I asked, "Kamal, you're not thinking of showing any…uh, inappropriate footage at your defense, are you?"

Kamal shook his head over the lemonade. "Don't worry, Julia. It will all be very tasteful. The slides will be the whipped cream on the pie of my defense."

"I'll bet," said Abigail.

I wasn't so sure my definition of tasteful coincided with Kamal's, so I decided that I'd better drop by his office on Monday morning to do a quick check before his defense that afternoon. Besides the three professors who would form the chairing committee, there would be students and other guests present, especially if the rumors about Kamal's latest results got around, which I strongly suspected they would. Nothing stayed secret for long on St. Sunniva's campus. In fact, I was surprised the news had taken this long to reach me—I must have been distracted by the whole thing with Quinn.

"I wish I could come to your defense," Abigail said regretfully, "but I have a run with Dr. B on Monday. For some more data on Antoine and Marie-Anne."

I felt a small and completely unexpected stab of envy at how casually they talked about time traveling. Dr. Holm and Quinn were both desperate to use STEWie—and, truth be told, I wouldn't have minded having a second chance myself, perhaps to see the Beatles perform in concert after all, like we had originally planned before being sidelined to Pompeii. As for Dr. B, she was Dr. Baumgartner, a junior TTE professor and Abigail's advisor. Antoine and Marie-Anne were Monsieur and Madame Lavoisier, an eighteenth-century chemist and his assistant wife, the latter of whom was the topic of Abigail's thesis.

"Jacob Jacobson, will he be at defense?" Sabina asked. She had a bit of a crush on the ginger-haired, social media–addicted second-year grad student who shared an office with Abigail and Kamal.

"I suppose so," Kamal said in the tone of one who couldn't care less.

Nate came out carrying the food, with Helen on his heels. She quickly closed the screen door behind her at our call of *Boxelder bugs!* Helen greeted everybody and Nate, after stirring the charcoal, began arranging the burgers on the grill.

Just as I had, Abigail eyed them with suspicion. "What are we having?"

"Salmon burgers, Miss Tanner," Helen said, taking a seat in one of the deck chairs.

"You'll like them," Kamal said.

"Fish, yes?" Sabina said as Nate made room for her to help at the grill.

"Give them a try," I said as Abigail pulled a face. "I have some hotdogs in the fridge if the burgers don't work out."

The first time the mention of hotdogs had come up, we had hurried to reassure Sabina that they didn't contain dog meat, of course, but somewhat disconcertingly, she hadn't seemed particularly bothered by the idea.

After he and Sabina had set the cover back on the grill, Nate turned to ask Abigail and Kamal how their research was coming along, which brought up the topic of the Neanderthal and Cro-Magnon social relations again. Helen, as befitted one well-versed in history, was most interested and asked Mr. Ahmad, as she called Kamal, for a full account. Nate seemed to be paying close attention, too.

My cell phone, which I had set down on the table with the drinks, rang, interrupting Kamal, who was providing details about the Neanderthal family structure. "Sorry, I thought I turned it off," I said and glanced at the caller ID. Quinn. Great. I swatted away a boxelder bug, said, "I better take this," and went back into the house to take the call.

"Still at the office, Jules?"

"No, I left a bit early today," I started to say, then realized I didn't owe him an explanation. There was no reason for me to be defensive about my long work hours anymore. "What do you want, Quinn? The answer is still no. I can't get you on a STEWie run."

"Guess what, Jules—I signed the divorce papers. I'll put them in the mail tomorrow."

"Oh. Er…thanks. What about Sa—…the runestone? You're not still expecting me to take you into the past, are you?"

"Certainly I am. You'll figure out a way to do it." He added, "How was Sabina's first week at school? Can't be easy getting used to a new place."

The question sounded genuine. He wasn't heartless, just an opportunist. No, that wasn't right either. A better description was that he was self-centered, cheerfully and optimistically so, like many a freshman newly arrived at St. Sunniva University. To Quinn, the world existed for him…and him alone. It just hadn't realized it yet.

"Sabina's first week went okay, as far as school can," I answered as I tried to figure out whether I had any leverage on *him*. I came up empty. "She was surprised to find that we've outlawed corporal punishment, and that boys and girls go to school in equal numbers."

"Modern society got some things right, didn't it?" His good mood was evident even through the phone. I didn't like it.

"Listen," he continued. "I gotta run, sorry. I'm meeting someone at Ingrid's."

I wondered if the *someone* was the female grad student he had been chatting up in the courtyard outside my office. I almost said, *Enjoy the lingonberry pancakes*, which was his favorite dish there. Mine too, as it happened.

"You have my number, Jules," he went on. "Let me know when you set things up. I'll check in after the weekend. If you haven't gotten things sorted, I'll start making calls to news stations."

He hung up.

I left the phone on the kitchen counter and turned to go, only to see that Nate had come back inside, noiselessly sliding the screen door open and shut behind him. I wondered how much he'd overheard.

He headed for the sink to drop off the empty food platter.

I cleared my throat. "Quinn is back."

"Is he?" Nate said without turning around as he rinsed the plate.

I realized he might have misunderstood me. "No...not in that way. He—we—have some paperwork to take care of, that's all. It's nothing important."

Nate gave me a frank look over one shoulder. "Good, then."

He held the screen door open for me as I carried the buns and condiments out onto the deck. Abigail and Sabina had gone back to playing Frisbee with Wanda the spaniel. Kamal and Helen were keeping an eye on Nate's salmon burgers cooking on the grill. Celer was curled up in the shade, asleep.

Sliding the screen door closed behind me, I wondered how much longer my Pompeii family would be safe.

# 5

After the others had left, Abigail and Sabina helped me clear up and then retired to their side of the house. I turned on the dishwasher, then sat down with a cup of coffee to check my cell phone for further communiqués from Quinn—there weren't any—and to see if I could think of any solutions that didn't involve running Quinn over a moonless autumn night. I could hear the muffled sound of Abigail and Sabina's laughter through the walls now and then. I suspected that Jacob Jacobson's tweets were being read and discussed next door. We had decided not to expose Sabina to TV just yet, but the Internet was unavoidable, especially since she had needed to use the computer for the online English as a Second Language crash course she had been taking over the summer. She was the only person in the world whose mother tongue was Latin. The thought made me sad for a moment. Like I said, her knowledge of first-century Latin and the customs of the time would have made her an invaluable research subject to historians and linguists, starting with Helen; but Helen herself had drawn a sharp line in the sand. Sabina was not to be treated as a research subject. If scholars wanted to thicken their classical Latin dictionaries, they could apply for a STEWie run like everyone else. Sabina was just a kid who had lost her family. I gritted my teeth at Quinn's meddling.

Another peal of laughter drifted through the walls.

Jacob was a harmless crush on Sabina's part—if anything, it made me feel better about her chances of acclimatizing to twenty-first-century life. After a leap of more than two thousand years, there were inevitably a few bumps, like frequent visits to the dentist, which thirteen years of decay, deposits, and no brushing had necessitated. Sabina didn't enjoy that aspect of modern life one bit. A different sort of surprise to her was the fact that we weren't going to marry her off. Back in Pompeii, Sabina's grandmother and father had arranged for her an early marriage (by our standards) to a young pottery shop apprentice. Of course, they were all long gone now—whether in the Vesuvius eruption or later, of natural causes. We had never found out and probably never would.

I got up from the kitchen table and did a loop around my small living room, mentally dividing the furniture into items that had already been in the house when Quinn and I had moved in, after my parents had left for Florida (where they were in charge of a retirement community), and items that Quinn and I had picked out together. In this second group were the big-screen TV and the ladder shelf with books and DVDs on it. Also the wall color behind the shelf, a muted orange we'd argued over because he had wanted a more manly steel blue, which I'd felt would give the house the feel of a hospital. It was one of our many arguments— other times we'd grappled about my long work hours, whose turn it was to do the dishes, Quinn's desire to move to one coast or the other, and many more domestic grievances.

Sounds of some kind of noisy activity drifted through from next door. I knew what it was. Abigail and Sabina had decided that Celer was overdue for a bath (a new element in his life) and that tonight would be the night. Celer fought baths with the only avenue available to him; that is to say, he made himself as heavy as he could and refused to budge from behind the door to the bathroom. It took two people to get him into the tub, and one to hold him down while the other washed. The bathroom floor and walls took a beating with each dreaded bath. I heard the water turn on and sounds of encouragement. I would have gone over to help, but two people and one dog was the limit for the small bathroom of the mother-and-law-suite.

So the divorce papers were on the way, or would be the next day. I tried to gauge how I felt about that, not to mention Quinn's date at Ingrid's Restaurant, and decided I felt perfectly fine about both things, aside from the fact that he was using the divorce papers and Sabina in a carrot-and-stick approach to get what he wanted. I wondered who he was having dinner with. Someone we had both known socially, or a new acquaintance, like the grad student he had been talking up in the courtyard of the Hypatia House? Whoever it was, it was none of my business.

I took out my laptop and flicked it to life. Perhaps needing to symbolically say goodbye to my married life, I changed the passwords to my social media accounts, which Quinn knew, wondering why I hadn't done it sooner. It didn't take long, as most of my time at the computer was spent on work, not personal matters. I was about to head off to bed when I remembered that somewhere on my computer was a photo of Quinn's grandfather, the one with the Kensington Runestone. I hadn't looked at it in years.

Some digging around through old files produced one that was simply saved as *Farfar's Photo*, as if it had been the only one ever taken of the man, which was highly unlikely. I had never met Quinn's grandfather—Magnus had died when Quinn was still a toddler, no doubt a charming and trouble-making three-year-old. I searched the mustachioed face for similarities to Quinn, but found it difficult because of how expressionless Magnus's face was—his grandson had never *not* had a grin in photos, even our wedding ones.

Like Quinn had told me, and I had in turn told Dr. Holm, Magnus had tried his hand at various things in search of that elusive fortune before marrying and fathering a child late in life, at age fifty. He never did amass a fortune, but he established a comfortable life with Ellen Olsen, who was now also gone. They had owned a magic shop in Rochester, which Quinn remembered fondly as stocking everything from whoopee cushions to gear for more serious magicians. It didn't bode well for Magnus Olsen's veracity that he had become a connoisseur of the art of illusion and trickery.

Which suited me just fine. I moved the mouse to delete the photo, but something prevented me from clicking. Instead, I washed up and headed to bed.

It did make for a good tale, admittedly. A party of explorers from the unknown land of wild grapes, Vinland. I imagined the Norsemen as rugged, self-sufficient types, with mud on their boots and suntanned, wind-bitten features, driven to face the dangers of exploring what was (to them) a new land. What had sent them on their journey? Economic hardship, a Europe in the grips of the Black Death…or the desire to chisel their names into history, a personality trait that Magnus and Quinn shared, although Quinn was hardly the danger-seeking type? Whatever it was, something had gone badly wrong. Those who had lived to tell the tale had done so with stone and chisel. Six hundred years would pass before an immigrant farmer would find their memorial clasped in the root of a tree.

Or not. I fluffed up my pillow and turned toward the window, where the just risen half-moon was peeking out from under the bedroom shades. I realized that I wanted the stone to be a hoax because Quinn believed in it. But it wasn't only that. The bottom line was that if the stone *was* real—well, it would be that much harder to send Quinn on his way.

# 6

Saturday morning I got up with the realization that for Sabina's sake I could not just sit back and wait for Quinn to lose interest in time travel and leave town. There *was* a simple way out of this, and that was to find proof in the present that the runestone was a fake. Because here was the thing: When Quinn called back on Monday, I wanted to be better armed. If the Vikings-in-Minnesota story was a myth, then there had to be proof of that in the present. And I wanted to be able to shove that proof under his nose.

And if the runestone was real...well, there should be proof of that, too.

I had two days to find it. Something that no one had managed to do in more than a hundred years.

I figured the best way to start would be by following one of one of time travel's unwritten rules, *Do your library research first.* Wikipedia only got you so far.

After eating a quick breakfast and showering, I grabbed a light jacket and my shoulder bag and left the house, careful to close the front door quietly so as not to wake Abigail and Sabina. I decided to walk to campus—it was just a twenty-minute stroll to the Coffey Library, on the opposite side of the lake from my office. I hadn't been to the library much since graduating with my business degree. And here I was about to ascend its steps for the second time in as many days.

It was a weekend, but like all student spaces on campus, the library hummed with activity, albeit of the quiet kind. Headphoned students sat holed up in corners, studying. The librarian at the front desk, Scott, greeted me cheerfully and asked if I needed any help. I shook my head and asked how the funding drive for the new library wing was progressing. The expansion, still in the planning stage, was meant to house our steadily increasing store of ancient texts, most of them painstakingly obtained on STEWie runs with the aid of handheld scanners and currently stuffed into the glass cabinet in the basement. The tug of war between the campus museum and the Coffey Library on the matter—the museum had the space, but the library offered hands-on accessibility to visitors—had been resolved by Chancellor Jane Evans, who made the simple suggestion that the manuscripts should be made available in both places. Scott explained that the fundraiser was progressing as they usually did—slowly—and pointed me to the library computers.

I ran into Dr. Payne by the computers. He nodded at me and asked what I was doing there, as if the library was reserved for academics only.

I explained.

"You're wasting your time, Julia. I hope Dr. Holm hasn't been encouraging this." He chuckled mirthlessly. "Even *if* we went back in time to watch the farmer stumble upon the stone, what would it prove? That he probably planted it there himself."

"I'm just killing a free Saturday morning," I said mildly.

"You should have better things to do."

That was probably true.

"Since I'm here already," I said with a shrug, "I might as well grab a book or two on the subject. If you'll excuse me—"

He went on as if I hadn't said anything. "The runes on the stone are completely…ah, shall we say, *unexpected*. And the inscription is long, ridiculously so. The bottom line is that no artifacts or historical accounts lend credence to the story of medieval Norse reaching what is now the state of Minnesota."

"Then my visit here will be short."

"Feel free to consult me if you need an opinion on any of the materials. Some of the so-called authors on the runestone issue are hacks." He swiped a hand over his comb-over and let out a sharp laugh, as though what he had said was hilarious. "Some? Most!"

With that, he turned on his heel and burrowed deeper into the library. I sat down at a computer terminal to do a quick search and soon was headed into the stacks armed with several call numbers.

The books concerning the runestone seemed to be spread evenly between two shelves, one devoted to general-interest history books, and one whose subject matter, according to the shelf label, was *Impostors, Forgeries & Fraud*. A cursory glance at the covers revealed a wide range of opinions. One called the stone "the most important artifact in US history," while another dubbed it a "transparent hoax." I picked up a couple of the most objective-seeming books from each shelf, carried them to a free table by the window, and settled in for a morning of reading. As everyone connected to the STEWie program knew very well, much of History was made up of threads set in motion by a single person, and Olof Ohman had been one such person, whether the stone was real or not.

There were only a few pictures of the major players because the stone had been found at the turn of the century. The first showed the young Ohman family not long after they had settled on the farm. After emigrating from Sweden, Olof had purchased a forty-acre parcel in 1890 for $300, later expanding his farm with additional parcels. The farm was described as being three miles to the northeast of Kensington's rail station on the Soo Line, which was the Minneapolis, St. Paul & Sault Ste. Marie railway. Olof had a heavy beard, and all of the Ohmans were looking unsmilingly at the camera. Then there was a jump of a few decades to a photo that was eerily similar to the one of Quinn's grandfather next to the stone. A middle-aged Olof Ohman was standing stiffly in a suit by the stone at some sort of ceremony, flanked by a pair of soldiers in full garb, his hand resting lightly on the stone as it stood up propped on wooden boxes. Again, he looked dead serious, as Magnus had in his photo, not at all like a man with a bent for practical jokes. There was one last photo, of Olof and Karin Ohman in their old age standing side by side on their land, a year before the good farmer would pass away, both white-haired, bespectacled, and seemingly shrunken by life. It was no wonder—they had raised nine children.

I came across a sworn affidavit that Olof had given to the county register or someone of similar official standing regarding his unusual find. It began with his swearing in and continued,

*I am fifty-four years of age, and was born in Helsingeland, Sweden, from where I emigrated to America in the year 1881, and settled upon my farm in Section Fourteen, Township of Solem, in 1891. In the month of August, 1898, while accompanied by my son, Edward, I was engaged in grubbing upon a timbered elevation, surrounded by marshes . . . Upon moving an asp, measuring about 10 inches in diameter at its base, I discovered a flat stone inscribed with characters, to me unintelligible. The stone laid just beneath the surface . . . with one corner almost protruding. The two largest roots of the tree clasped the stone in such a manner that the stone must have been there at least as long as the tree . . .*

I turned the page and found a letter written in the farmer's own hand in his native Swedish, dated December 9, 1909. The four pages of tightly scribbled text included a small sketch, which showed the stone-harboring tree—the tree's thick roots had grown horizontally over the width of the stone, making a right angle before continuing deeper into the ground.

Below the letter a translation had been supplied:

> *I saw that the stone was thin, Olaf Ohman, who was fifty five at the time, had written. I simply put the grubbing hoe under it and turned the under side up...My boy Edward was about 10 years old. He was the first to see that there was something inscribed on the stone. The boys believed that they had found an Indian almanac...*

I read some more and found out a few additional details, such as the name of the other son, Olof Jr., then age eleven. Magnus Olsen wasn't mentioned anywhere in the book, but perhaps no one had remembered—or thought to mention—the presence of a neighborhood kid. There was a Sam Olson, a neighbor, but presumably there were quite a few families with the last name of Olsen or Olson on the plat maps and town records of the time. I wondered in passing how historians kept track of all the similar names. Magnus Olsen, Olof Ohman, Olof Jr. A lot of them seemed to begin with *O*.

The detail about the roots having a square kink to them, aside from seeming like a math joke, struck me as authentic. But perhaps that was the hallmark of the true hoaxer, and he had supplied the detail to hide his sleight of hand, like a magician would. I wondered how Olof's wife, Karin, had felt about the runestone, but there were no quotes from her.

I pounced on the farmer's words from the letter in Swedish: *The boys believed that they had found an Indian almanac. I myself also saw that there was something written. But to read it was a mystery to me.* How could someone born in Sweden, who had spent the first twenty-five years of his life there, *not* have recognized runic writing?

Unfortunately for my theory of the farmer's guilt, he wasn't the only one. After being dug up, the stone was moved to the local bank, where the public viewed it, with its strange symbols and ancient look. An enterprising townsperson, thinking the inscription was, of all things, Greek, sent a copy to a Minneapolis newspaper. The editors forwarded it to University of Minnesota, where the Greek scholars recognized that the text was, well, Greek to them and got it to the right place, a university expert in Scandinavian languages, who gave the stone a thumbs down. After hearing the news, Olof Ohman promptly stored the stone in his grain shed.

That was how things went before STEWie.

I leafed through a few more pages. A half-hearted effort had been made to excavate the spot and to look for the skeletons of the ten dead men, but neither they nor any additional artifacts had been found. Two witnesses, both acquaintances of the family, cancelled each other out, with one person swearing that he'd helped Olof carve the runes and the other that he had seen the stone unearthed with his own eyes. From that point onward, the opinions varied, with professional linguists and historians firmly on the *no* side and amateur enthusiasts and the occasional geologist leaning toward *yes*.

I didn't like assuming anyone was a liar or that Dr. Payne was right, but the most likely scenario was that Olof Ohman had carved the stone in his barn soon after settling on his new farm, then buried it under the tree only to "discover" it several years later, giving the roots plenty of time to curl down over the rune-stone. It didn't embroil the two Ohman sons or Magnus in the hoax...unless the boys had been in on the whole thing, eager to participate in the prank, a rare bit of fun in the hard-scrabble immigrant life.

I left the library thinking that the matter should have a simple answer. Either the stone was real, or it wasn't. Though I highly doubted he had bothered to do much research, I was beginning to see why Quinn had thought a STEWie run might be just the thing.

# 7

The following morning, I awoke to the chirping of birds and the thought that I only had a day left. It was high time for me to see the runestone in person. Not on a STEWie run, but in the museum over in Alexandria.

The thing was, I wanted someone else's opinion on whether the whole thing was a hoax...and who better than an expert in crime?

I called up Nate to see if he felt like taking a Sunday drive. It was only after I hung up the phone that I realized what I had done. One, he must have thought I had just invited him on an unofficial date. Two, had I? I could just as easily have called our retired chief of security, Dan Anderson, and asked him to come. Dan didn't get out much these days and would have probably enjoyed the company. Three, this was hardly the time to be thinking about romance, with my almost-ex husband back in town with blackmail on his mind...so did that mean I should dress down in a ratty T-shirt and sweatpants to prevent any misunderstandings about the nature of my invitation? Or four, did it mean I should dress up, because that would make Nate less suspicious that something else was going on?

I rather thought Nate wouldn't notice either way and decided to stay with my jeans and button-down shirt.

He showed up an hour later in slacks and a windbreaker, his hair wet and freshly combed. Wanda burst out of the Jeep and ran inside to greet Celer, who submitted to the other dog's sniffing without bothering to get up. Nate suggested we take his Jeep and not my aged Honda, and we left, leaving Abigail and Sabina to decide whether they wanted to take the dogs on a walk to the nearby apple orchard or drive them. It was certainly a nice day for it—the apple-picking season was in full swing, and Friday's humid rain had been replaced by sunshine and a crispness in the air that hinted that winter was not far off. I promised the girls that we'd try making an apple pie in the afternoon.

Nate drove the half hour to Alexandria on Highway 94 through gently hilly farmland while I looked out the window, watching the scattered farmhouses with their red barns and dome-topped corn silos, the pointy Lutheran church spires peeking above treetops, and the small lakes surrounded by tall grasses, wondering what the area had been like when Olof Ohman had arrived from Scandinavia in search of a better life. Here and there cows and buffalo grazed placidly, not bothering to look up at the highway traffic zipping by. Fields laden with yellow corn rippled gently in the wind. The billboards disfiguring the scenery on both sides of the highway would not have been there in Olof Ohman's time, of course, nor would the road itself, for that matter. A wagon and horses would have been used for transport. And in the fourteenth century, the date given on the runestone, travelers would have relied on the waterways.

The runestone matter had grown more urgent. Quinn hadn't been bluffing about having evidence. Abigail had noticed that a photo was missing from Sabina's room. It was one we had taken of the girl sweeping the street in front of her father's shop on the morning of our last day there. Celer was also in it, lounging in a shaft of summer sunshine. As I had pointed out to Abigail, we had no way of explaining their presence in a photo of a bustling Pompeian street, complete with a single-domed, pre-eruption Vesuvius in the background.

"Sure there is. Creative editing," Abigail had suggested. "Photoshop."

"Yes, but I doubt that the fake background we've given her as an Italian immigrant would stand up to more than a casual inquiry if Quinn posts the photo online. Not to mention that Sabina doesn't speak Italian like we claimed but a very early version of it." I added with perhaps more optimism than the situation warranted, "I'm hoping that Quinn will return the photo with the signed divorce papers."

"I wouldn't hold my breath," Abigail had said.

She and I had agreed that it was best not to say anything to Sabina, not until it was absolutely necessary. Luckily she hadn't noticed the missing photo yet.

As for Nate—I knew that if I told him what was going on, he'd turn the car around to find Quinn and arrest him for blackmail and theft, letting the chips fall as they may. Instead, I went with a half-truth. I wasn't proud of it, but I had to put Sabina's welfare first. All I wanted was for this to go away quietly.

So when Nate asked me why I was interested in the runestone, I told him I was just brushing up on local history, in case any related STEWie requests popped up. If he assumed that it was just a pretext for spending the day with him, well, so be it.

Nate nodded at my answer and, speeding up to pass a U-Haul truck, asked, "What *are* runes, anyway? Foreign languages are not exactly my strong point."

He had mentioned that before. As a child of grandparents who had come from four different backgrounds, he'd had plenty of opportunity to pick up languages other than English, but apparently none of them had stuck.

I had garnered a bit of information from reading the books on the runestone. "It's the early alphabet of the Germanic languages—what Old English was first written down in. The Scandinavian version is the *futhark*, named for the first six letters, F, U, TH, A, R, and K. Runes were developed for writing on wood, so they have few curves. They look a little like stick figures," I said, thinking of the poster Dr. Holm had shown me in the Coffey Library. I rattled off a few more facts and added, "By the way, thanks for coming out with me."

"Happy to do it. So is this thing real, this stone?"

"That's what I need your opinion on."

"I'm not a historian."

"I've already got an opinion from a historian. Dr. Payne—his specialty is American history—said that the stone is a hoax, and a poorly executed one at that. Dr. Holm, whose specialty is runic linguistics, sounds like she thinks there might be something to it and would be happy to tackle the problem with a STEWie run or two, if only she could secure a green light from Dr. Payne and funding. I'm guessing you've come across hoaxers before?" I asked before remembering what had made him leave the BWCAW. A photographer he had been smitten with had been setting wildfires throughout the Boundary Waters wilderness. Why she had done it never became clear, but before Nate and everyone else had caught on, one of the fires got out of hand, killing a park ranger. The pyromaniac was now in prison. Wanda had been her dog. But I wasn't sure that counted as a hoax exactly.

Apparently neither did he, because all he said was, "Only of the identity theft kind. It doesn't apply in this case."

"Yeah, I don't think the runestone was carved for financial gain. The good farmer got all of ten dollars for his find from the Minnesota Historical Society after the stone changed hands." As an aside, I added, "If it had been me, I think I would have charged people who wanted to see where the stone was dug up. Nothing wrong with making a bit of extra spending money."

"It makes him seem like an honest man, this farmer of yours."

"I guess."

Nate had once told me that in his experience most crimes came down to one of five motives: greed, desire, fear, jealousy, or desperation. We discussed them each in turn and ruled out fear and desperation as motives for Olof Ohman, and also, per our discussion, greed. That left the Scandinavian immigrant community's jealousy of the Italian immigrant community over the whole Columbus issue...or, a shade more nobly, Olof's desire to see his Viking ancestors get their dues.

Nate gave a small shrug. "If it was a hoax, then your farmer—"

"Olof Ohman."

"—Olof Ohman may have done it just to get his name into newspapers. Generally speaking, to run a successful scam— whatever the motive, money or fame—you have to give people what they want, something big for their eyes to feast on. Like a letter saying you've won a million dollars and they'd be happy to send you the money after you pay the small transfer fee of $250. If you were already enthusiastic about the idea of Vikings in Minnesota— and I'm not talking about the football team—then I suppose farmer Olof Ohman's 'find' would have been just the thing."

"Yes, that makes sense. The runestone would be the missing link between the Vikings of old and the Scandinavian-Americans who live in the Kensington area. It's what people want."

He brought up another possibility as he slowed down to turn onto the exit for Alexandria. "Could it have been a joke that got out of hand?"

"You mean Olof Ohman might have made it up because he wanted something to do during the long Minnesota winters?

Could be. It's just that he looks dead serious in all of his photos. But then they all did."

"It can't have been an easy life, not for an immigrant farmer trying to eke out a living. Then again, I would think his family and neighbors would have noticed if he had lugged a stone into his barn and started spending a lot of time in there."

"Why would they?" I said a bit more snappily than I intended.

He glanced over at me. "I just meant that it was a tight-knit community. Nowadays people spend years living across the street from someone without ever meeting them. It wasn't like that back then."

He was right, of course. Even the neighbor I knew best, Martha, probably wouldn't have noticed if I'd taken to carving stones in the privacy of my garage. But that was how it went today—we didn't rely on our neighbors for help with daily problems or even a cup of something hot in the evening. Our support networks were geographically broader—my parents lived in Florida, my cousins were in Austin, and my best friend from college had moved to Seattle.

Nate slowed down to a stop at a red light. "Hey, how come you haven't seen this stone before? Didn't you grow up in this area?"

"I was sick the day of the school trip. My parents wrote about this kind of stuff, but they never thought to take me along. They ran the local newspaper—not the campus one, the Thornberg one—back in the days when everyone read it and you could make a decent living selling ad space." Quinn had always meant to take me to see his grandfather's stone, but we had never gotten around to it. And by the end of our relationship, I was tired of hearing about it.

Since Nate had asked me a personal question, I decided it would only be fair play if I asked one in return. "What about you, how did you end up with such a motley collection of grandparents?"

He flashed a grin at me. "You mean, one-fourth Dakota, one-fourth Scottish, one-fourth Sri Lankan, and one-fourth Quebecois? Simple. My grandmother Mary met my grandfather Duncan at a picnic—that's the Dakota and Scottish connection. Two months later they married and in due course had seven children, one of them being my father, Nate Senior. On the other side, my grandmother Renée met my grandfather Nimal at school, thereby cementing the Quebecois and Sri Lankan side of the family. They had one child, a daughter named Gigi. Gigi and Nate Senior met in college, and I'm the result."

"That's quite a family story. Mine's pretty simple."

"Everyone is of Norwegian ancestry?"

"Pretty much. Lots of blue eyes and blonde hair in the family, except for me. I'm the black sheep—or rather, the brown one," I added, giving myself a mental kick for comparing my hair and eye color to a sheep's.

"And Quinn?" he said as the light changed and he sped up.

"What about him?" I asked.

"Every other person in Thornberg seems to be from Scandinavia. Is his family from Norway as well?"

"Oh, that. No, they're Danish. They never quite warmed up to me, since I was from a Norwegian family and all."

"People are funny sometimes, aren't they?"

"I'd say as a rule they are, yes."

"Julia?"

"Yes?"

His attention was focused on the road. "I seem to remember promising to make shrimp curry for you again one of these days."

The first time the shrimp curry had come up had been at a garum shop, as we waited for Professor Mooney to swap some goods with Sabina's father for a tunic for Nate and a dress for me. The shrimp curry, which Nate had made at a celebratory picnic after we got home, had indeed been delicious, as promised.

"So how about next Friday, at my place?" he went on.

Maybe I should have worn a ratty T-shirt after all. I wasn't sure I was ready for this, for dinner with Nate. After all, dinners led to other things. I rolled down the window a bit. The inside of the car suddenly seemed too hot.

"Julia?"

"Friday night it is," I said. I hoped the whole thing with Quinn would be over by then. I wanted him to stay firmly in my past. And once he was gone for good, maybe things with Nate would be clearer. It was quite possible that I was reading too much into it anyway, and he was just being polite. Perhaps all of Helen's goading had gone to my brain.

∞

Restaurants and shops lined Alexandria's wide main street, Broadway; a lot of them incorporated the word *Viking* into their name or had some sort of Scandinavian motif. The Runestone Museum was at the north end of the street. We parked, grabbed a quick bite of lunch at a diner, then walked down past the museum for a closer look at Big Ole, a thirty-foot-tall Viking statue. Big Ole sported a red cape, a winged helmet, and, in one muscular fist, a spear. His shield proudly proclaimed:

*ALEXANDRIA*
*BIRTHPLACE OF*
*AMERICA*

"How do they figure?" Nate asked, looking up at Big Ole.

"The runestone. If it's real, it's the earliest record of Europeans stepping foot on future US soil."

"But still...it wasn't really the start of anything, America or otherwise. And there were already people living here. My people—a quarter of them, at least."

"It's good for tourism."

"Besides, wasn't the runestone found near Kensington?"

"Alexandria is the county seat."

"Vikings, all the way here." He shook his head.

"Actually, according to Dr. Holm, they wouldn't have been Vikings by that time. Christianized Norse, she said."

We waited to let a car pass, then crossed the street to the museum. Before going in, we stopped to look through the fence into the area behind the main building. There was a barn, a smokehouse for curing meat, a washhouse, and several other pioneer-era structures, whether replicas or original I wasn't sure. We headed inside and stopped to pay the admission fee in the gift shop. The gift shop, which turned out to be a precursor of the museum itself, seemed to have a bit of everything—Big Ole bobbleheads shared shelf space with teepee Christmas ornaments. There were plastic Viking helmets, as well as runestone T-shirts, runestone mugs, and runestone license plate frames. As we waited for a customer to finish paying at the cash register, I rifled through the T-shirt rack to find one for Sabina and turned to see that Nate had donned one of the plastic helmets. It was gold, with horns like elephant tusks sticking out on either side, like he had a big *U* on his head. It looked ridiculous on him.

"Well, what do you think?"

"They didn't really wear them, you know," I said, suppressing laughter. "Dr. Holm told me that."

"Really? I'm crushed. I think I'll buy it as a souvenir anyway."

"Should we tell them?" I nodded toward the cash register, where a museum staffer was ringing up a purchase.

"I expect they'll find out soon enough."

We bought the helmet along with the T-shirt for Sabina and headed into the main display area. The small museum was nearly empty, and most of the guests were families with small children in tow.

Propped up on a stand inside a protective glass case, the runestone held the spot of honor. Around it, wall panels explained the meaning of the runes and the history of the stone. Off to the side were more display rooms with exhibits on pioneer and Native American life.

My first impression was that the runestone seemed small, smaller than I had expected from the poster in the Coffey Library and the picture of Quinn's grandfather with it. About the size and shape of a tombstone, it was dark gray, except for the lower left corner, where there was a triangle of lighter gray. A nearby panel noted that the stone weighed just over two hundred pounds.

My second impression, possibly influenced by all the kitsch we had just seen in the gift shop, was one that immediately made me relax: *It's fake.*

Because these were not runes carved in a hurry; they couldn't have been. Steady hands had worked neatly and painstakingly—stick-like symbols followed one another in careful row after row, nine rows in all, covering well over half of the face of the stone. As if the carver had decided to give up and switch surfaces upon reaching the light-gray and rougher bottom third of the stone, the text continued on one side. The three additional rows of runes were there, and, near one edge, someone had chiseled an *H*. I was pleased to see that the modern letter didn't look any different from the runes themselves—that is to say, neither the runes nor the *H* seemed very old at all.

"Which part is the date?" Nate asked, consulting some of the support materials on the walls.

"Here." I pointed. "The symbol that looks like half a T, that's the number one. The one that looks like an F is the number two, and so on. The six has that funny loop."

We circled to the other side of the glass cabinet, where a detail on the back of the stone caught our attention. Parallel scratches ran down the uncarved side, as if the stone had been dragged across something sharp.

Nate explained that it must have been the other way around. "I've seen those before. Glacial markings. They're from when the stone was part of the bedrock and a glacier passed on top of it, dragging rocks with it. Those tracks were made before the stone itself was dislodged and moved by the glacier."

At an angle across the back of the stone were two wavy lines, newer and sharper looking, thin and white, with one continuing down the side of the stone. The roots of the aspen, tracing out a path as the tree grew over the stone? I didn't like it. It matched Olof Ohman's account.

"Looks like the tree roots left a mark. How old was the tree when it was cut down?" Nate asked.

I remembered that from my reading. "A decade or two seemed to be the consensus."

"Doesn't that put Olof Ohman in the clear? He had bought the land, what, only a few years previously?"

"I suppose."

"Really, Julia, I'm beginning to think you have a personal stake in this stone being proven fake. I would have thought, having Scandinavian roots and all, you'd want it to be real."

"It just seems to me that it's quite possible that the stone spent time underground before Olof Ohman found it, carved it, and reburied it."

"Yes, but that's not the simplest explanation, is it?"

I sighed. "No, I suppose not. Occam's razor."

"What's that?"

"A creed everyone in the science departments lives by—*Don't complicate matters. The simple solution is probably the right one.* Occam was a medieval English philosopher," I added. "The razor part of it has to do with 'shaving away' unneeded assumptions."

Nate nodded thoughtfully.

"Well?" I demanded.

"Well what?"

"What do you think?"

"Of what?"

"Of the stone. Is it real?"

"Like your Occam and his razor say, the stone is probably what it says it is."

It wasn't what I'd hoped to hear. "Let's go see the place where it was found," I suggested, hoping we'd see something there that would definitely damn the stone.

∞

A fifteen-minute drive took us over the highway and to the old Ohman homestead, which was now part of Kensington Runestone Park. The county park, wooded and serene, lay in the middle of gently rolling countryside dotted with lakes and cabins. Nate pulled the Jeep to a stop in a small parking lot. We seemed to be the only visitors.

We peeked into the windows of the old Ohman house, which was white with a brown roof, but didn't go inside because both doors were padlocked. Nearby stood the old Kensington train depot building, which had been moved into the park from its original location. Next, we dodged some bees and ducked into the dairy barn. Big and red, it housed an indoor picnic area. Copies of plat maps lined the walls and there was a replica of the runestone just outside. After exploring the areas around the house, we left the car and walked up the road to the small hill where the runestone had been found.

Though not exceptionally high even by Minnesota standards, Runestone Hill had a 360-degree view of the surrounding countryside. Beyond it lay a large marshy lake, and, on the opposite side, there was a small teardrop-shaped pond. At the top stood a monument, with a bench and four flags—for the United States, Sweden, Norway, and Minnesota. Nate bent down to look at the monument and I suddenly realized how quiet it was, other than the chirping birds and the occasional car in the distance. Highway 94 wasn't visible from where we were, but I knew it was there, cutting across the land in a southeast to northwest line from the Twin Cities to Fargo, North Dakota. Only a few of the cars streaming in both directions would make a stop here. This area, scenic as it was, was home to only a few; for most, it was just a place to drive through. A term popped into my head that I had heard chemistry and engineering professors use on occasion to describe a bit of research or an experiment—*steady state*. Other than the change brought upon by the seasons, this was not a place of flux and motion. A new lakeside cabin might be built or a different billboard erected on the side of the highway, but that was about it. This was a place set in its serene ways.

Which was all well and good but perfectly useless in helping me decide what to do about Quinn.

Nate and I took a few photos of the hilltop monument and left, no wiser for our visit.

∞

Nate's phone beeped with a text message on the way back—it was Officer Van Underberg reporting that eleven student bikes had been stolen that afternoon. Since the girls weren't expecting me yet, and I wanted to figure out who had carved the modern *H* on the runestone, Nate dropped me off at the library before continuing on to the campus security office, which was lucky as we spotted the missing bikes arranged in an artistic metal-and-rubber sculpture in the library courtyard. Apart from the cut locks, it didn't look like any of them had been damaged, only lovingly and gravity-defyingly woven into a pyramid. Just an early-in-the-semester student prank.

Nate waved off my offer of help and started untangling the bikes as I continued up the wide steps of the library. Scott, looking a bit surprised to see me again so soon, waved cheerfully as I walked past his desk. I needed to get over the feeling that I didn't belong here.

I carried my books to an armchair by one of the tall library windows, passing a table with four sleep-deprived students slumped in chairs. I wondered if they had been responsible for stacking the bikes, but they all had scripts in front of them, like they were practicing lines for a play. I left them to it, and, making myself comfortable in the armchair, started where I had left off, which was with the stone being stored up in Olof Ohman's shed.

The runestone might have stayed there but for a young graduate student from the University of Wisconsin by the name of Hjalmar Holand. I guessed that he, like many a grad student, needed a research topic, and the runestone captured his excitement and energy. Olof Ohman gave the young scholar the stone, and Holand became its biggest fan, taking it to Europe, writing books about it, and weaving a somewhat unlikely story that its carvers were soldier-missionaries sent by the King of Norway and Sweden who had ventured beyond their intended destination of Greenland. In an era in which artifacts weren't treated as carefully as they were nowadays, he was the one who had carved the *H* on the side of the stone—the equivalent of someone carving their initials into a favorite tree.

The play-reading students in the corner raised their voices for a moment and received a stern look from Scott, which resulted in giggles and a torrent of whispers. I wondered how the detangling of the bicycle practical joke was proceeding outside.

I was amused to read about a much more elaborate prank that had been pulled by a group of grad students from one of our nearby academic competitors, the University of Minnesota, which involved a runestone. In 1985, the students had headed to the hill Nate and I had just returned from, armed with a hammer, a chisel, and a copy of the runic alphabet. Runestone Hill turned out to be "too public" for their purposes, so they headed to a nearby one instead. During this stage of the proceedings, one of them managed to get caught in a barbed wire fence and needed to get a tetanus shot later. After selecting a boulder, they started chiseling it. Finding the process more difficult than they'd imagined, they wrapped things up after carving *AVM*, one runic word, and the supposed date (1363), after which they tried to turn the boulder over so that the inscription faced downward. They weren't able budge it. When the stone was found sixteen years later, I read, there was some excitement, but two of the former grad students, now university professors, confessed. All of which went to show two things—it was both easy and hard to pull off a good hoax.

Pulling out my yellow legal pad, I drew a vertical line down the middle of the page and, in what I hoped was a scholarly fashion, penned *Pros* on top of one column and *Cons* on the other. It was time to see if the evidence weighed more heavily on one side. I did the pros first to get them out of the way and ended up with six items:

1. *Olof Ohman, unlikely hoaxer.* The immigrant farmer, father of nine, never had any run-ins with the law and never tried to make money off the stone.
2. *The Norse.* They built a settlement in L'Anse aux Meadows at the turn of the millennium, so surely it was plausible, perhaps even likely, that their descendants had ventured farther inland over the next four hundred years.
3. *The length of the inscription.* Two-hundred-some runes. As far as hoaxes went, it was an unnecessarily elaborate one, requiring days of carving. Something shorter—say, *Ole and his buddies from Vinland were here*—would have been easier to carve in the privacy of a barn and might have been more convincing to historians and linguists. Why go to the effort of crafting what was essentially a tale complete with protagonists, action, and an enemy?
4. *The stone itself.* Geologically sound, with tree roots traced into it.
5. *History.* If there was one thing that had come out of the STEWie program, it was the realization that History was rarely neat and tidy. A stone that didn't make much sense at first glance might actually do so.

6. Finally, and somewhat personally, there was Magnus Olsen's account, which corroborated Olof Ohman's. Was it really fair to blame Magnus for the way his grandson turned out?

I did the cons next, taking my time with them:

1. *Olof Ohman, likely hoaxer.* The elephant in the room: What were the chances that an immigrant of Scandinavian descent would find an artifact of Scandinavian origin?
2. *Where were the other artifacts?* Finding the skeletons of ten men of European ancestry or their campsite would have helped matters greatly.
3. *The inscription.* The stone's very appearance, with its neatly carved rows, felt modern. The length of it must have required several days of carving, surely unlikely under the purported circumstances. The men's comrades had just died a sudden, violent death. Why linger in the vicinity?
4. *The stone itself.* Unusual, so out of place, mysteriously under a tree.
5. *Minnesota, in the middle of the country.* Venturing inland from Vinland, other than rhyming quite nicely, would have required a light boat, portages, and a lot of luck and drive. It would have been no small undertaking, even for a crew of hardy Norsemen.

And, finally:

6. Magnus Olsen was related to Quinn, and Quinn had been known to stretch the truth on more than one occasion when it suited him.

I stared at the list for a moment. Well, it was maddeningly even. How did historians cope before STEWie? It was no wonder Dean Braga was besieged with requests for roster spots. Depending on how you looked at it, the stone and its runes either exhibited unique characteristics or tell-tale signs of fraud. I tried reading the arguments from the linguists, but all I could gather was that some of the runes were too modern. I decided that the thing to do would be to talk to Dr. Holm a second time. She herself had mentioned that there were issues with the runes. I was pinning my hopes on that.

Consulting her would have to wait until work hours on Monday, however. I'd done what I could for now. Besides, there was apple pie to be made. I folded my list of pros and cons into my bag and went outside to wait for Abigail and Sabina. They were on their way back from the orchard with Celer, Wanda, and a basket of apples, and were swinging by to pick me up. Boy, did I have a story to tell them, and it didn't involve the runestone.

Nate had invited me to dinner.

# 8

Monday brought a pile of paperwork. I found time to send a text message to Dr. Holm asking if she could meet with me at her earliest convenience, then rolled up my sleeves and got to work. Just before noon, when the stack of information packets for prospective students had reached an impressive height on my desk, I checked my phone—no reply from Dr. Holm yet—then grabbed a sandwich I'd brought from home and a can of pop from the vending machine and headed out to the lake. After dodging a couple of bicycles, I settled myself on my usual bench and dug into the sandwich and tried to enjoy the view. Ducks bobbed on the surface of Sunniva Lake, sending ripples through the buildings, trees, and fluffy clouds reflected in the water. Students milled to and from classes on bikes, skateboards, and occasionally on foot. I kept an eye out for Quinn, expecting him to appear any minute, Sabina's photo in one hand and a video camera in the other at the ready for the STEWie run he imagined I was going to take him on.

As the noon hour struck on the clock tower by the Coffey Library, the throng of students thickened and I spotted a familiar face. Not Quinn, but Sabina's crush, Jacob Jacobson, on his way to the Time Travel Engineering building, where he had a desk in the grad student office. The hood of his sweatshirt hid his ginger hair as he propelled himself on his skateboard, weighed down by a heavy backpack. His attention was wholly engrossed by the cell phone in his hand as he weaved around the slower walkers. I hoped he wouldn't run into anyone.

Seeing Jacob reminded me that I had meant to check on Kamal's presentation for his thesis defense. Deciding that the rest of the information packets could wait—the mail didn't go out until four o'clock anyway—I headed after Jacob. If Quinn dropped by, he wouldn't find me at my desk, which was undoubtedly for the best.

I exchanged a few words with Oscar, who was at his post just inside the door to the TTE building, then headed to the graduate student office. Kamal was feverishly pacing around his desk. Clean-shaven, with freshly trimmed hair, he had on a slightly wrinkled gray suit and a tie dotted with mathematical symbols. He looked pale, like he was about to throw up. This was normal. All graduate students looked that way just before their dissertation defense. Kamal's was set for three o'clock, so he had a good two and a half hours to get through.

"Where is everyone else?" I asked, looking around at the empty desks. "I thought I saw Jacob heading over."

"He dropped off his backpack and then went to help Abigail prepare for her run with Dr. B. Well, not exactly *help*—more like Abigail's helping *him* learn the ropes. Now that Jacob's been here for a year, he *really* needs to pick a research topic and start going on STEWie runs. The department doesn't like grad students hanging around without engaging in active research." After this very mature sounding statement, Kamal added, "And everyone else went to lunch. I didn't want to risk food stains on my suit. Besides, I'm not really hungry."

"You should eat something. We don't want you fainting during your defense."

"I might if someone asks me a question I don't know how to answer."

"It'll be fine." I spotted a box of granola bars on Abigail's desk and pushed one in his direction. "Here, eat this while I look over your presentation."

He turned his laptop toward me. "Don't tell me if you find a spelling mistake, Julia. Wait, no, tell me—I still have time to fix things."

He took the granola bar, dropped into a chair, and started munching, contorting unnaturally to avoid getting crumbs on his suit.

I quickly looked over his slides—the ones featuring Neanderthal and early human coupling, while not exactly tasteful, weren't any worse than others I'd seen in biology or medical sciences presentations. Most of the photos had been taken from afar, with a long-focus lens. Kamal had also included a few photos that showed just the prehistoric landscape, unspoiled by electrical wires or roads. The meat of the presentation was the computational method he had used to find safe landing zones, culminating with a 3-D map of the zones in Neander Valley and nearby locations, with time as one of the coordinates. There were also red dots on the map—ghost zones, like the one in Pompeii where he and I had almost perished. Ghost zones were wells in time you did not want to fall into.

I looked up from the last slide, the one titled *Acknowledgements*. Kamal had moved onto his second granola bar. He was lost in thought, and I had to ask my question twice. "Dr. Payne is on your committee?"

"Yeah." He swallowed quickly. "I needed someone from outside the department. Why, have you heard anything I should know about? He's not extra tough on students, is he?"

"I wouldn't worry about it. Dr. Mooney and Dr. Little have followed your work closely and signed off on it. There's no reason to expect anything but a positive outcome."

"Whenever anyone tells me that, I worry even more."

I left him to his worrying and, on my way out, caught sight of Xavier Mooney in his office down the hall. He was on his knees on the carpeted floor. I went in to investigate.

The professor didn't hear my approach. He had printed out a dozen sheets of paper and placed them on the carpet in a long line. His graying hair, which he had kept shoulder-length after Pompeii, hung to one side as he bent over the sheets to tape them together. He was humming as he worked. I was happy that the professor seemed to be in a better mood—he had been a bit down since our return from far-time, which was understandable. Being grounded in the present and watching the two junior TTE professors, Erika Baumgartner and Steven Little, do the time jumping had been hard on Dr. Mooney. He was one of the original creators of STEWie, the other being his lab partner Gabriel Rojas, who was on his well-earned sabbatical. The symptoms of the immune disease that had sent Dr. Mooney into self-imposed retirement in ancient Pompeii had all but disappeared with a change in diet. Still, even a slightly subdued immune system made him at risk for bringing back an eradicated disease like smallpox—or worse, something we didn't know how to treat.

A bookshelf behind him held the professor's collection of musical instruments, most of which he'd collected on STEWie runs before his illness. The didgeridoo that used to lean against the wall had been lost in the eruption of Vesuvius (it was the one little bit of home that the professor had brought with him), and the spot of honor was now taken by a pair of mismatched Cuban conga drums.

When the professor shifted his position to better apply the tape, he caught sight of me. "How do you like it, Julia? It's a timeline of social inventions."

I squatted on the floor next to him and looked over his creation. Each of the printouts had a horizontal line down the middle and short chunks of text above and below the line at irregular intervals. A mark at 1888 caught my attention and I saw that it was a tick for under-arm deodorant, the commercial kind. From there my eyes automatically flicked to the end of the fourteenth century, the date on the runestone still fresh in my mind.

"King Richard the Second invented the handkerchief?" I said, looking over at Xavier. "I didn't know that."

"Not many people do. Which is why the timeline is going up on the wall in STEWie's lab. I figured people could use a quick reminder before each run—no handkerchiefs on runs to pre-fifteenth-century Europe unless you want to get odd looks. Here, can you help me with the tape?"

"How was the physics conference?" I asked as I took charge of the tape. Last year there had been rumors that Dr. Mooney and Dr. Rojas, as the co-inventors of STEWie, were on the shortlist to win the Nobel Prize in physics. The notion had been put on hold since everyone had suspected Dr. Rojas of murdering his colleague. That had turned out to be very much false—Dr. Mooney was clearly alive and well—but the scandal had placed their Nobel chances on hold. The Nobel committee tended to err on the side of inaction.

"Everyone was most interested in the Slingshot. I gave a presentation on the steps I've taken to address the stability problem. There are still some kinks to be worked out, of course. A bit more tape?"

The Slingshot had a tendency to send time travelers into ghost zones. As the first human testers, we had been sent to a sequence of them after escaping Pompeii: a beach in advance of a tsunami, the Great Fire of London, a blizzard, the shores of a Tunguska lake just before the great meteorite impact, and a World War II air raid. We had been extremely lucky to make it back alive. Now that the professor could no longer go on time travel runs, he had focused all his energies on fine-tuning the device.

I helped him roll up the chart and we met in the middle.

"I just came by to check on Kamal's slides," I explained.

"Ah yes, how's he holding up?"

"He's nervous. Given his topic, I expect he'll draw a larger crowd than usual. Come to think of it, perhaps I'd better double up on the refreshments." I had meant to do it earlier, but worrying about Quinn had pushed the thought out of my mind.

After helping Dr. Mooney tack his timeline onto the wall in STEWie's lab, I hurried back to the Hypatia House to make sure I had enough food for Kamal's defense and ran into Dean Braga just outside the building kitchenette. She was wearing what might be deemed a power suit and killer shoes and had stopped to grab a cold bottle of water from the vending machine on her way to her office. "Whoever decided that shoes with heels should be considered dress-up attire should be shot. I wonder if that's how men feel about suits and ties. What are those, Julia?"

I had been scrolling through the pictures of the runestone on my cell phone while I waited for the spinach dip to heat up. Dean Braga replaced her science dean's hat with her geologist one and looked over the photos. "The runestone, yes. It's nothing I've worked on personally... Has there been a STEWie run request from someone?"

"Uh, sort of. It's still the thing with my, uh, husband." Could I call Quinn my ex now that the divorce papers were signed and in the mail, or did I have to wait until they arrived on my doorstep? "There is a personal connection to the event on his side of the family. I went to Alexandria over the weekend to look at the runestone. What *is* graywacke anyway? I get the gray part—it's a gray slab of rock—but what about the wacke part?"

She shifted her weight from one uncomfortable shoe to the other. "It's a type of sandstone. Did you notice the striae on the back, from glacial action?" She zoomed in on the photo for a closer look. "There are some other lines here."

"From roots. The runestone was found under a tree."

"Right, that makes sense. The growing roots probably leached iron and magnesium out of the stone."

"How old does the inscription look to you? From what I've read, geologists seem to lean toward *yes* but historians and linguists strongly disagree."

She shook her head. "I can't tell you anything just from the photo. Before STEWie, I would have recommended further geological testing and peer review. As it is, if someone from Geology, History, or the Department of Linguistics writes up a well-funded proposal, it could make for a worthy STEWie run." Before I had the chance to tell her that Dr. Holm had tried and failed, she handed the phone back to me with a final remark that gave props to her own field of expertise. "Without a STEWie run, all I can say is this—given the choice between the soft sciences and the hard sciences, go with the hard sciences. Geological results can be double-checked and reproduced. Now if you'll excuse me, I really need to get out of these shoes."

∞

Food is the key to a well-run thesis defense. Let me repeat that. Food is key. Not for the defending PhD candidate, though I suppose it doesn't hurt to feed him or her either, but for the committee and audience members who might, if crabby and hungry, ask inconvenient questions that the candidate would be hard-pressed to answer. If well fed, the questions would still get asked, but more kindly. Before my time, the policy in the science departments had been that defending students provided their own refreshments, giving them yet another thing to worry about, but Dean Braga's predecessor had instituted a change. In the eight St. Sunniva science departments, from the Mary Anning Hall of Geology to the Maria Mitchell Astronomical Observatory on the main campus hill, the dean's office did the honors.

People were starting to trickle in as Oscar and I wheeled in drinks and snacks on a trolley. We parked it just inside the door, to one side of the podium, so that people could serve themselves as they entered. Xavier and Helen lingered by the side of the room while we were setting up.

"I'm surprised to see you here, Helen. I didn't know you had an interest in Neanderthal and Cro-Magnon interactions," I heard Xavier say.

"Neanderthal speech is something every linguist wonders about," Helen said calmly. Any questions she or the rest of the audience had for Kamal would have to wait until the end of his presentation, after which the room would clear out, and the committee would decide whether to give his work a thumbs up or a thumbs down as PhD-worthy material. "I don't see why we've concluded that they didn't have the ability to speak based on their more robust anatomy."

"It's not a conclusion," Xavier countered. "More like an assumption."

"Assumptions have no place in research."

"You won't get an argument from me there, but you have to start somewhere."

"I would prefer to give them the benefit of the doubt. Really, a five-minute recording ought to do it," Helen said. "Language should be easier to address than the question of why they went extinct."

"True enough, I suppose. Dinner at Ingrid's?"

"How about Panda Palace instead? Eight o'clock?"

"How about seven? Should I pick you up?"

"Let's meet there," Helen said, turning to the food trolley.

Their strong personalities had always grated on each other, but they had at last realized that it wasn't a sign that they shouldn't be together, merely that they shouldn't take disagreements personally. Helen had told me in confidence that she and Xavier were talking about moving back in together.

Oscar headed back to his post to point newcomers to the right classroom, and Dr. Mooney took a seat in the front row. I followed Helen up the auditorium stairs—I didn't stick around for every thesis defense, but would have for Kamal's even if I wasn't hiding from Quinn. The auditorium was the larger of the two TTE classrooms; the seating was stadium-style, with half desks attached to each seat. Although the Neanderthal story had yet to break widely (a press conference was planned for next week if Kamal passed his defense), rumors of lurid Neanderthal and Cro-Magnon footage had spread throughout campus, and people were steadily streaming into the room. Judging by what I had seen of Kamal's slides, unless anyone was fascinated by the technical issues regarding safe landing zones in the Neander Valley, most of the audience was going to be very disappointed.

Kamal stood fidgeting by the large Smart Board as he waited for the proceedings to begin. Dr. Mooney and Dr. Little were in the front row, level with the speaker's stand. Dr. Mooney was doodling on a napkin—many great scientific ideas sprang from idle thinking—while Dr. Little, clean-shaven and dressed in his trademark button-down vest, sat hunched over his laptop, his fingers moving furiously. Dr. Payne had yet to show. I hoped he hadn't forgotten about the defense—a faux pas not unheard of in the over-scheduled world of academia. I sent a small wave of encouragement in Kamal's direction, but he didn't notice. I muted my cell phone, which was just about the only thing I could do to help besides providing the food.

Dr. Payne hurried in at last, extinguishing his cigarette on his way in and flicking it into a wastebasket (I hoped it wouldn't cause a flare-up). He took a seat next to Dr. Mooney, who, as the chairing member, nodded at Kamal to begin. Dr. Little continued typing furiously for a bit, then closed his laptop and settled back into his seat.

His nervousness dissipating after a few minutes, Kamal slipped into what came naturally to him, speaking about a subject he loved. His nervousness had not sprung from a fear of public speaking, but from the fact that the three people seated closest to the podium would decide whether he would receive his PhD at the end of the semester. Most thesis defenses went well. Occasionally, a committee member would recommend additional research, and the student's graduation date and near-term job prospects would have to be adjusted accordingly. Rarely—I had only seen it once—a committee or audience member would spot a significant flaw in the work, something that made both the student and the mentoring professor, who in this case was Dr. Mooney, look bad. Dr. Little was already familiar with Kamal's work, so Dr. Payne was the only one likely to throw a wrench into the proceedings.

Kamal had started by explaining that stepping out of STEWie's basket into the land of our closest prehistoric relatives (and their chunkier cousins) presented its own set of risks, beyond the usual perils inherent to time travel like ghost zones and exposure to now-eradicated diseases. If you got time-stuck, the list of threats was long: hunger, thirst, the elements, wildlife, cannibalistic tribes—of both Neanderthals and early humans—and so on. Dr. B and Abigail, who were next door readying for their run to eighteenth-century France, could be reasonably sure they wouldn't be murdered by a thieving local or struck by lightning in a storm. There was a simple reason for that. Either scenario would expose the strangeness of the visitors from the future, from the manufactured undergarments under their period clothes to their unusually white teeth to the camera equipment and notebooks hidden in their satchels. But when you jumped thirty thousand years into the past and got hit by lightning, the most likely fate for your charred, injured body was that it would be consumed by an animal. Your hiking boots and clothes would decompose to nothing over the millennia, changing History not one bit.

All of which made Kamal sound like he was the wiry, hardy sort, when in fact he was, like I said before, what might be charitably described as slightly overweight and more fond of mental exercise than the physical variety. My guess was that he'd been attracted to research in extreme far-time because he wasn't expected to go near any of the locals, thus minimizing his chances of catching some exotic disease.

Helen sat up at one point when Kamal brought up one of the big questions—namely, *Did Neanderthals speak?* His team had heard shouts here and there as they took photos from afar, but whether these sounds could be classified as language or were mere grunts alerting others to danger or the presence of game, he couldn't say, nor was it his job to do so. That was Helen's specialty. I expected a request to land on my desk as early as the next morning for a STEWie run to one of Kamal's landing zones.

After a good twenty minutes of slides crammed with equations, during which I may or may not have dozed off for a bit, Kamal tossed up a couple of slides that sent a chuckle through the audience and I sat up. They were the ones I had seen when I previewed the presentation at his desk. He had used software which mimicked pencil drawing to sketch out some of the stills from his footage, giving the more salacious photos the feel of a cartoon—and protecting the privacy, even thirty thousand years into the future, of the individuals involved. I saw the corner of Xavier Mooney's mouth twitch as he turned back to glance at the audience, but he kept on his official committee member expression. It did seem like he was finally back to his normal self, and I was pretty sure Helen deserved much of the credit for that.

As Kamal neared the end of his presentation I leaned down to dig up my cell phone out of my shoulder bag to see if Dr. Holm had responded to my request for a second meeting—or if Quinn had been in touch. I flicked on the phone. There was a text message from Dr. Holm, but not the one I had expected. All it said was,

*HELP*

Before I could do more than raise a puzzled eyebrow, the auditorium door flew open. It was Dr. Baumgartner, Abigail's advising professor, and the clatter of her wooden clogs was amplified in the silence that suddenly descended on the room as Kamal stopped mid-sentence. A white bonnet covered the professor's blonde hair above her mushroom-colored bodice and drab, green ankle-length skirt. She struggled to get the words out. "STEWie's basket—they're gone—"

Dr. Mooney pushed himself to his feet. "Who's gone?"

The professor jerked the bonnet off her head. "Someone has hijacked STEWie."

Dammit, I thought. Quinn.

# 9

Drs. Mooney and Little hurried out of the classroom after Dr. B, leaving the thesis committee two short and Kamal openmouthed at the unexpected interruption to his defense. I scrambled down the auditorium stairs, following the three professors as they raced down the hallway to the double doors of STEWie's lab, where Oscar was standing, concern writ large on his usually tranquil features.

"I've called campus security," he said, stepping aside to let us pass. "They're on their way."

A single glance told us that all was not well at the lab. Abigail, dressed in period clothes similar to Dr. B's, was at a workstation frantically tapping keys. Nearby, a computer monitor and several lab notebooks had been knocked to the floor, as if someone had passed by in a hurry. The monitor had landed against a chair leg, its cable still plugged into the floor socket, its screen cracked. On the whiteboards behind the workstations, STEWie destination ideas and taped-up photos from past runs remained undisturbed. Beyond the whiteboards was STEWie's heart—a labyrinth of lasers and highly polished mirrors, some as small as a file folder and others almost grazing the lofty balloon roof of the building. Our view of the platform in the middle was concealed by one of the larger mirrors but residual heat from the STEWie send-off radiated from within.

I took in all of this as I registered snatches of conversation between the three professors and Abigail:

"They went in blind and didn't calibrate!"

"What's to be done?"

"We can't just follow them, can we?"

Then I heard Dr. Baumgartner's voice rise above the rest: "Why does stuff like this always happen just before *my* runs?"

How had Quinn done it?

One of the disturbed lab notebooks had fallen open to a page covered in spidery equations. A horseshoe-shaped object peeked out from underneath, sky blue and thin. I pushed the notebook off it with my foot and bent down to pick up the headband. It was Dr. Holm's.

"In here." It was Oscar, with Nate behind him and Officer Van Underberg bringing up the rear. The three professors turned to Nate and began to speak simultaneously.

"Unauthorized use of STEWie has occurred—"

"The basket is gone—"

"Someone who's not on the roster has taken off in STEWie's basket—"

Nate held up a hand. "Somebody fill me in," he said in his security chief voice, the one that got people listening. "Who is it and where have they gone?"

Abigail pushed through between the professors. Her outfit was a smaller version of the period-appropriate attire Dr. Baumgartner was wearing, down to the bonnet. Rather inappropriately under the circumstances, I wondered what color her hair was under her bonnet. I had gone to work before she and Sabina made an appearance for breakfast.

"Dr. B and I were in the travel apparel closet across the hall getting ready for our run to eighteenth-century France, the usual stuff, right? With us were two STEWie newbies who were coming along. Dr. B had to give them a rundown of History's rules, so I came into the lab to get everything ready. I found it like this." She shrugged at the mess on the floor as the cracked monitor let out a brief electrical buzz before dying for good. "I checked the log and saw that someone had just left on a run."

"Who was it? And where did they go?" Nate asked, his arms crossed over his campus security uniform. Next to him, Officer Lars Van Underberg was busy scribbling notes. Where Nate was lanky and reserved, his officer was short, stocky, and affable. He was partial to stroking his caramel-colored mustache nervously when in deep thought. The pencil and sharpener he'd used to carry to avoid getting ink stains on his uniform had long been replaced with the ballpoint pen he was scribbling with now.

Dr. B impatiently shuffled her clogs. "Where did they go? No idea. It's not like STEWie here has a large display with the time and date on it. Who was it? Two people is all we can tell you at the moment."

"Did the...uh, newbies, see anything?" Nate asked.

"They were still with me in the classroom when Abigail called. I've sent them to the grad student office to wait."

As Officer Van Underberg jotted all this down, I asked Oscar, "Did you see anyone suspicious enter the building?" I didn't want to bring Quinn into it if there was a chance that someone else—say, Dr. Holm herself—had hijacked STEWie. It was unlikely that she had done so, given the message she'd sent me, but I held on to the slim hope.

Oscar turned his palms upward. "You saw what it was like, Julia. All of those people came in for Kamal Ahmad's defense. They seemed like a normal school crowd." He was clearly distraught that this had happened on his watch. A wiry ex-Marine with a heart of gold, he spent more time at his post than off it. "None of them seemed out of place." He reconsidered for a moment, then added, "Except perhaps for a blond man who came in with a large backpack. But he said he knew Julia— called you Jules—so I figured it was okay."

Nate turned his square jaw in my direction. I went on talking to Oscar. "Did he have a tan?"

"Uh—yes. And a dark blue Hawaiian shirt, I think."

"Really?" This surprised me. The third rule of time travel was *Blend in*. A Hawaiian shirt, though a staple in Quinn's wardrobe, was surely the wrong thing to wear to either the finding or the carving of the runestone. Even Quinn should have known that. Maybe it wasn't him after all.

"Julia? Is he describing who I think he is?" Nate asked.

I sighed. There was no way around it. By now everyone in the room was looking in my direction, even Dr. Little, and it took a lot to wrest his attention away from a computer. After a quick glance at his superior, Officer Van Underberg cleared his throat and asked, "Ms. Olsen, you say you know the man in the Hawaiian shirt?"

"I'm pretty sure that it's my ex—that is, my husband. Quinn." I went on. "He has this crazy plan to prove that his grandfather told the truth when he said he witnessed the discovery of the Kensington Runestone as a boy. Have you all heard of it? I can tell you more about it later...Anyway, he thinks the stone is real."

As Nate opened his mouth to speak, I brought up the only reason left why this might *not* be Quinn's doing. "Wait, he wouldn't have had the door code to the TTE lab."

With Oscar around to keep an eye on things, the doors to the building were kept unlocked during the day, but the TTE lab itself was always secured. Only the TTE staff and students had the door code, along with researchers from other departments who were on the roster for the month. As soon as I said it, I realized that a door code would not have stopped Quinn. There were ways around that, from snooping around in my office to charming someone into letting him in. "There's more. I received a message from Dagmar Holm a few minutes ago. Here, take a look."

Nate raised two dark eyebrows at my cell phone. "She's the runic specialist you mentioned yesterday?"

"What does it say?" Abigail crowded in to look. "*Help.* What does that mean?"

"Also—this is Dr. Holm's headband. I found it on the floor." The headband had somehow found its way into my pocket.

Officer Van Underberg accepted the headband and placed it into a Ziploc bag he pulled from one of his uniform pockets. "Has anything else been disturbed, Ms. Olsen?" he asked quietly.

"Sorry. I should have left it in place. It's just—I can't figure out what happened."

Still in the same quiet voice, Van Underberg asked, "You think Mr. Olsen forced Dr. Holm to take him into—what year would it be?"

"1898, I imagine, the year the runestone was found. Or 1362, when it was supposedly carved. But this isn't how he operates."

"Does Mr. Olsen own a gun or a hunting rifle?"

"Does he own a *what*? Not to my knowledge. I don't understand," I said. "This makes no sense. If you told me Quinn had charmed Dagmar into an off-the books run, I'd believe it. But this…" I looked at the overturned monitor, lifeless and silent on the floor.

I saw Officer Van Underberg hunt around in his uniform for a second Ziploc bag and reached to take my phone back from Nate before the officer could bag it. I needed my phone. There was a seminar-scheduling conflict I had to resolve, not to mention several other office-related issues. Also, perhaps Quinn would call to tell me he was on his way back to Phoenix. Meaning that some other tanned, blond, Hawaiian-shirt-wearing individual with an interest in the runestone and a reality TV show would turn out to be the culprit.

Nate put his hand on his sidearm. "Van Underberg is right. We have to treat this as a possible kidnapping. We need to go after them and get them back. Van Underberg, let's go."

The pair headed toward STEWie's platform in the center of the mirror-laser array.

# PART TWO:
# KNEE-DEEP

# 10

"Hold it, Kirkland," Dr. Little demanded before Nate and his officer could do much more than step over the base of the nearest mirror. The young professor's tone was a shade sharp—he and Nate had been involved in a neighborly dispute over a rotted tree. The professor went on as he typed, still using that same brisk tone, "You can't get in the basket yet."

Nate said, "Wait here," to Officer Van Underberg and stepped back over the mirror base to where the rest of us were standing by the workstation. "And why is that, Dr. Little?"

"We don't know where they've gone."

"Can't you just keep the mirrors as they are and send us to the same place?"

"If you want to go in blindly, yes," Dr. Little said, like it didn't matter to him if Nate did just that. "But the generator will need to be recharged and the equipment cooled down before we send another basket." The specifics of STEWie's internal structure were above my pay grade, but I knew that a not insignificant dose of thorium was needed for the machine's massive power requirements.

"But that's not the only problem," Dr. Little added.

"Basket interference," Dr. Baumgartner said slowly. "Yes, it could very well be an issue."

Dr. Mooney, who had been silent up to this point, joined in the discussion. "Hmm, yes... Unless we make sure Chief Kirkland and his officer arrive far enough from the basket that's already there."

"We better get to work, then." Dr. B moused the other workstation to life and she and the other two professors launched into a technical discussion of the matter.

"Would someone please explain to me what basket interference is?" Nate asked.

"It's trouble," Abigail said. "Two STEWie baskets can't coexist in the same place and time. If we send you after them blindly, Chief Kirkland, your basket will return as soon as you step out of it and into—what were the years that you mentioned, Julia?"

"1898 or 1362."

"I get it," Nate said. "Our basket would no longer be needed since theirs is already there. And since baskets are invisible, we'll have no idea where theirs is, so we'll have to search for it—"

"—or rely on Julia's husband to bring you back," Dr. Little finished the sentence for Nate.

I winced. "Call him Quinn." He had wanted me to take him on a STEWie trip, but I'd refused. I should have realized that he would take matters into his own hands.

"And even if the basket interference thing weren't an issue," Dr. B said, "the prudent thing to do would be to check for ghost zones before anyone else steps into STEWie's basket. It's pretty clear that they didn't run the recommended safety checks—that's an overnight procedure. We *could* send the new WMR, I suppose."

Nate shook his head at the lab's wheeled mobile robot. "Sending the WMR ahead will take too long. Every minute that passes here is, what, half an hour there? We're wasting time talking. Professors, just get us somewhere close to them—but not too close—whatever the year and location."

This was a bad idea. If Nate ended up shooting Quinn, it would make for an awkward development in our relationship. More importantly, it would mean bad publicity for the school and unwanted attention on Sabina. Everything was just starting to get back to normal; this was the last thing any of us needed.

"I'm coming too," I said, raising a hand.

Nate shook his head at me without bothering to stop as he strode back over to the mirror-laser array. "Quinn has kidnapped Dr. Holm and hijacked STEWie like he was taking a car for a joyride, Julia. This is no longer a personal matter." He said it as if he thought it hadn't ever been a *personal matter*, and that I should have filled him in immediately. Well, perhaps he was right.

I hurried after him and pulled him aside. "Look, I don't know what happened, but if you really think Dr. Holm is in danger, you need me there to talk to Quinn. Having said that, I'm sure there's no chance of him harming her, so I don't think we need the guns." I wasn't used to seeing Nate with a sidearm, in his full campus security chief gear. School policy dictated no guns on campus, concealed or not, and campus security followed that rule until a more serious threat came up, which wasn't often. Most of the problems that merited their involvement had to do with pilfered lab items or stolen bicycles.

"I'm not leaving my sidearm behind, if that's what you're suggesting." Nate's voice wasn't exactly low and Dr. Little called out from the workstation, his fingers still busily moving, "I'm not sure a gun will work as you expect, Kirkland."

"It's the kind of thing that would draw attention to itself if you used it," Dr. B said. She and Dr. Little were side by side at the TTE workstations, she in her skirt and bodice, he in his vest and slacks—they were a mismatched pair if ever there was one. Dr. Mooney was pacing back and forth behind them as he pondered the problem of the double baskets.

What the professors were saying about modern devices was true enough—we had been able to use Abigail's Polaroid camera in Pompeii, but only discreetly. It had refused to come out of its leather bag on more than one occasion. We ourselves had not fitted in seamlessly either, managing to get time-stuck more often than not, forced to wait for History's paths to rearrange themselves.

"We *could* just wait them out," Dr. Baumgartner suggested without looking up from her workstation. "They'll have to come back soon enough. How many supplies could have been in that backpack? A few days worth?"

"It was a large backpack," Oscar said.

Still standing inside the mirror-laser array, Van Underberg rubbed his mustache and said pensively, "What if Mr. Olsen returns alone?"

"Exactly," Nate said. His hand was still on his sidearm. "With a sad story about Dr. Holm not making it back."

"Oh. He wouldn't do that, would he, Julia?" Abigail asked, patting me on the arm.

"No," I replied, more firmly than I felt all of a sudden. After all, I hadn't seen Quinn in what for him had been a whole year. People did change.

"What's going on here?"

It was Dean Braga. I hadn't thought to call her. Oscar must have gotten in touch with her after calling security. She had traded her power heels for the sneakers she kept in the mahogany cabinet of her office and looked winded from hurrying over from the Hypatia House. Dean Braga was too busy to attend every thesis defense, even one as newsworthy as Kamal's, but the call from Oscar had sent her running over to the TTE lab.

A sudden silence, interrupted only by the humming of the computer equipment, descended on the room as everyone waited for me to explain. I did, using as few words as possible. Except the threat to Sabina, I left nothing out. There was no hiding what had happened—not now.

Dean Braga seemed to think otherwise. "No word of this is to reach the media."

"Got it," said Nate, nodding at his officer.

"Everyone at Kamal's defense heard that something has gone wrong in STEWie's lab," I pointed out. "You might want to confiscate Jacob Jacobson's cell phone, Dean Braga. That is, if he already hasn't tweeted about this." Jacob's tweets had saved the day last time, in what I liked to think of as my first case with Nate, but this was a different matter entirely.

"I'll tell people it's a student prank. Let's stick to that story until proven otherwise," Dean Braga said, raising my level of admiration for her. Perhaps, micromanaging aside, she had the most important quality a dean could possess—the drive to put the good of the school first, no matter what. She added, "We can deal with correcting that mistaken impression later. If it *is* mistaken—are we sure, absolutely sure, that this isn't a prank?"

I nodded. "I wish it was."

She eyed the fallen monitor with its long crack as if estimating how much it would cost to replace. "Then for the time being let's try to control the flow of information as best as we can."

"There you are, Dr. Mooney," Dr. Payne said, peering through the propped-open doors of the TTE lab. "I've told your student that I have a couple of questions for him, but otherwise he can consider himself passed." Behind him, we could see people streaming out of the thesis defense classroom. I couldn't help but notice that everyone had chosen the longer route out of the building, which took them past the lab, rather than the more direct route via the other hallway. Several people had stopped by the open double doors and were looking in with frank curiosity. We were losing control of the situation.

Dean Braga sensed it as well and took charge. "Oscar, why don't you show everyone out and then remain at your post. If anyone asks, the building is closed for the day. Abigail, please go back to the graduate student office and make sure everyone knows not to tweet or text about this incident. Dr. Baumgartner, I think you might as well change out of those clothes. It doesn't look like you'll be going on a run today."

"No, I suppose not. But they might be, it sounds like." Dr. B nodded toward Nate. Officer Van Underberg was still standing by the mirrors, following our conversation from afar.

"What's this?" Dean Braga raised a thin eyebrow.

Nate explained, "Officer Van Underberg and I were about to go after them and bring them back."

"Bring whom back?" asked Dr. Payne, still leaning in through the door. "Who has gone where?"

Dean Braga nixed the security chief's plan without taking the time to explain the situation to the history professor. "Let's not be hasty and make a bad situation worse by blindly jumping into STEWie's basket. We need to put our heads together and see where we stand and what's to be done. Julia, explain to me about your husband again. But not here. Let's find a more private venue. And Dr. Payne..."

"Yes?"

"You might as well join us. It sounds like we may need your expertise."

$$\infty$$

Leaving Officer Van Underberg to guard the lab doors, his uniform lending a lie to the story that there was a student prank in progress, Nate and I faced three academics across the rectangular conference room table—Dean Braga, Dr. Mooney, and Dr. Payne. I usually brought refreshments for regularly scheduled meetings, and I fought the impulse to slip out to check whether there was anything left over from Kamal's thesis defense. Cookies would have probably made everyone feel better (even Nate, who usually didn't eat junk food, as he called it). I did pull out my yellow legal pad from my shoulder bag to start a list of what needed to be done.

The point Dean Braga brought up first surprised me. She suddenly looked worried. "If we decide that someone should go after them, it shouldn't be me. I need to stay here and oversee things on this end."

It was unlikely that anyone would have suggested otherwise— we needed the campus police, someone knowledgeable in time travel, and an expert in American history like Dr. Payne, who looked mildly interested in the proceedings. I watched Dean Braga nervously fiddle with the top button of her dark gray power suit, which is when I put the pieces together. It was well known in the science departments that Isobel Braga had what can only be described as a time travel phobia. I didn't blame her. She had entered the field of geology with the goal of studying Earth and its past with her feet planted firmly on it, poring over evidence etched into rocks and fossils and tectonic plates, not stepping into a whirlpool of warped light to make jumps measured in thousands of years. I suspected it was why she had sought out her position. She had no doubt been happy to leave behind the lab that had changed so much since she'd first stepped into it a good thirty years ago.

"We need you here, of course, Dean Braga. To oversee things," I said. Nate nodded shortly in agreement, and I watched Dean Braga's shoulders relax and the look of consternation disappear from her face. It was replaced by concern for Dr. Holm and the reputation of the TTE department and St. Sunniva University itself.

"As you know, I'm not supposed to travel," Dr. Mooney said glumly. "I'm sure either Dr. Baumgartner or Dr. Little will be pleased to offer their help."

"For what?" Dr. Payne asked, and I realized we had not filled him in yet. Dean Braga gestured at me, so I told him the story in a few sentences. The professor listened impassively, as if years of studying history had prepared him for all ranges of human behavior. When I had finished, he gave a little sniff but said nothing.

Dr. Mooney addressed Nate. "Wherever they have gone, whether it's the nineteenth century or the fourteenth, the new STEWie basket we send after them may very well return at once and leave you stranded. I'm not sure you understand the significance of that, Chief Kirkland. If they make it back to the STEWie basket first and leave you and Officer Van Underberg behind—"

"And me as well," I threw in.

"I suppose I could join, too, if you feel you need me," Dr. Payne said, "though I doubt that my expertise in the history of this continent, extensive as it is, would be of any use in chasing down Mr. Olsen and Dr. Holm."

"So we'd get stuck there for a while," Nate said. "But you'd know where to find us, Professor Mooney."

"Only if you stay in one place. You could be trapped for hours or days under unknown circumstances. If I were you, I wouldn't step into that basket without adequate food and water."

"It's not a good position to be in, but we'll deal with it."

"There is no way around it," Xavier said. "Unless—hold on, I've thought of something."

He pushed his chair back and left the room without another word. The conference room door closed behind him with a click.

"The student prank story won't hold long," Dean Braga said into the silence. "Julia, let's plan on releasing a statement explaining that there was a STEWie malfunction and that we're trying to locate the basket, which is lost somewhere in time. That's not inaccurate."

"I suppose not," I said. I liked this new side of her. If Dr. Payne hadn't been present, I would have told her the rest of the story then and there.

Dean Braga, noticeably more at ease now that she knew that she wouldn't be the one climbing into STEWie's basket, glanced in my direction again. "Did I understand correctly, Julia? Your husband wanted you to take him into the past? Is this why you were asking me about the runestone?"

Nate, too, was looking in my direction. It was hardly the moment to spill the beans about Quinn's attempt at blackmail, not in front of the others. I'd have to tell him about that part later. "I have no idea why he thought I would do it," I said. Which was true. How could Quinn have entertained the notion that I would sneak him into the TTE lab, even if it were in my power to do so?

Nate continued staring at me, then leaned back in his chair and said easily, "Perhaps he didn't realize that only researchers at the school are given STEWie roster spots."

"And that each run uses significant resources," Dean Braga added. "Most people don't seem to realize that." She was checking her phone to see if the news had leaked yet.

"You're a geologist," Nate said to her. "Is the runestone real or not? It looked real enough in the museum, but I'm no expert."

"It's a hoax," Dr. Payne answered for the dean, "and not a very good one at that. Being displayed in a museum does not make something of genuine value."

Dean Braga put her phone down, looking a little annoyed that Dr. Payne had given his opinion when hers had been sought. "Like I told Julia earlier, it's not anything I've worked on personally. But I believe that what little geological testing has been done has come down on the side of the farmer who found the stone. I tend to trust the hard sciences more, don't you, Dr. Payne? In any case, I'm not sure it matters at the moment," she added. "The important thing is to bring back Julia's husband and Dr. Holm safely before word of this gets out. At the very least, we'll need to revisit our security procedures."

"It matters," Nate said. "If this thing is real, the stakes are higher."

Dr. Payne leaned forward and rapped the table with a bony fist. "We *could* debate the lines and cut of each rune on that stone. If I pointed out that it's unprecedented to find pentadic numbers and Hindu-Arabic place value notation on a fourteenth-century runestone, you would counter by saying that the Norsemen had learned these things from their travels to the far corners of the Old World. If I pointed out that it wasn't typical to put a date on a runestone at all, you would tell me that this is the atypical case that proves the rule. I could say there is no evidence in the form of other artifacts, and you would tell me we need to look harder. So the argument I like to make is the simplest." He gave a smoker's cough and brought up one of the counter-arguments on the list in my shoulder bag. "It's too much of a shiny coincidence for a runestone supposedly carved by Scandinavians to be found by a Scandinavian immigrant. Had an Italian or Chinese immigrant been the one to make the discovery, I'd have been more open to entertaining its validity."

No one had asked for my input, but, carried away by Dr. Payne's zeal, I found myself giving it anyway. "I'm no expert, but it seems like there is a simple argument for the other side of the matter as well. Vikings reached North America in the eleventh century and built a brief settlement at L'Anse aux Meadows." I hoped Dr. Payne and the others would be a tad impressed that I knew about Lansey Meadows. "Isn't it not only possible but likely that they went farther inland? All they would have needed is a boat and some luck."

"It would hardly have been a simple matter, Julia. Besides, the preponderance of evidence must come from the side wanting to change history books. The runes on the stone—"

"I was going to ask Dr. Holm to explain the issues with the runes, but now...I guess she'll get to see what really happened. And Quinn will tape it for his TV show."

"What TV show?" Nate asked. "I thought you said this had to do with Quinn's grandfather."

"Didn't I mention it?" I slapped myself on the forehead and explained about the reality show, adding, "I have no doubt that Quinn brought a video camera along to shoot footage for the pilot. That was his plan."

"If he's going to be the star of the show, wouldn't he need someone else to film *him*?" Dean Braga seemed pleased with a scenario that didn't involve kidnapping. She suggested, "Perhaps that's why Dr. Holm came along. Could he have promised her a spot on the show?"

"It's possible," I said. "He offered me a spot."

"It doesn't explain the text message asking for help," Nate pointed out curtly.

Behind him, the door to the room opened and shut.

"It's gone," Dr. Mooney said, sliding back into his chair. "They've taken it."

"What's gone?" Nate asked, his voice implying that he really didn't need any more bad news.

"The Slingshot. I left it on a utility table in the lab. They must have taken it with them. You know what that means."

"The Slingshot?" Dr. Payne asked.

"The portable version of STEWie. I've been working on it all summer."

"Right, right. I've only used the lab proper myself."

Nate pushed his chair back and got to his feet. "Professor Mooney?"

"It means they'll be able to jump around in the past without us knowing where." Dr. Mooney took a deep breath. "Wherever STEWie's coordinates point to, they're probably not there anymore."

Which explained what Dr. Baumgartner said when she hurried into the room a moment later, Dr. Little on the heels of her clogs. "This is really strange—they're neither in 1362 or 1898. They have gone to Woodstock."

# 11

I suppose if you needed a location to use as a stepping-stone in time, where suddenly appearing out of thin air would not draw much notice, the infamous 1969 music festival was the place to do it.

"Well, that certainly covers their tracks. No point in looking for them at Woodstock." Nate tapped the table hard, rattling my yellow legal pad, which was still blank. "If Julia's right about Quinn's motives, they must have only been there for a brief period of time."

"If I were them, I would have stayed to hear Janis Joplin, The Who, the Grateful Dead...oh, and Sha Na Na—" I said, with another of those inappropriate stabs of envy.

"Well, you're not them," Nate interrupted me.

He was right, although he didn't have to be quite so rude about it. No, I hadn't told him Quinn's real reason for being in town. Yes, there had been a secret motive when I'd asked him to go look at the runestone with me. Well, I wasn't perfect. I was new to being an aunt and having a young person under my roof. It seemed to have screwed up my priorities.

"Fine," I said. "Woodstock doesn't matter because I know where we'll find them. In 1898 on Olof Ohman's farm."

∞

"Why are you sure that they went to 1898 first and not 1362?" Nate wanted to know.

We were back in the TTE lab. Dr. Baumgartner had gone to change out of her period attire, and Dean Braga to the mid-afternoon unveiling of the new telescope at the Maria Mitchell Observatory. (The Maria part of the name was pronounced *Ma-rye-ah,* and the new telescope, mounted on the roof of the observatory, was the first large—that is, expensive—item purchased with the funds Dean Braga had procured in her new capacity as science dean. The unveiling was supposed to be a signal that we were starting to put behind us all of the bad publicity following the previous dean's arrest for attempted murder. Leave it to Quinn to throw the Science Quad back into upheaval, I thought.)

"Why do I think they went to 1898? Because..." I waved my arms in the air, trying to decide how to explain it best. "Magnus—Quinn grandfather—died when Quinn was just a toddler. He never got the chance to tell him he believed him. How could he *not* go there first?"

"I concur," Dr. Little said from his workstation. At first I thought he was agreeing with me merely to spite Nate, but he went on. "That's what I would do if I were in his place and there was some sort of family connection. You go to see the family member, find out what they were like. You carry their genes, right?" he said, sounding as young as Abigail for a moment. I was used to thinking of him in the faculty category, but the junior professor wasn't much older than his own grad students. I noticed that he had bags under his eyes and made a mental note to ask him if his young daughter, Piper, was sleeping through the night yet.

Dr. Little went on, "Who hasn't wondered what their parents were like when they were young, or their grandparents, or their favorite movie or sports star? I'm not a sports or movie aficionado, but if I could tie my research into it somehow, I wouldn't mind going back in time to see Charles Babbage design his Analytical Engine, or the Polish and British codebreakers in action in World War II on the Enigma machine...We all have our own interests." It was somewhat of a long and personal speech for the young professor, who was usually so focused on work. He had gone on a few runs, but for the most part his research involved running STEWie computer simulations that touched upon logistical issues for time travelers—for example, as a result of his research we knew that you couldn't travel to a time period in which you existed already, and (relevant to our current situation) that two baskets couldn't be present side by side in the same time period.

"I think everybody in the lab has had to fight the impulse to use STEWie for personal reasons," Dr. Mooney said. "Don't say it," he added into the sudden silence. "I know I lost that battle. But I only had good intentions at heart. I thought I could be of more use by moving into the past and dedicating myself to documenting life in the Roman Empire than by sitting idle at my desk."

I realized, right then and there, that I was no longer satisfied with being holed up in my office fielding other people's requests for STEWie runs. I had gotten my shoes dusty in Pompeii, and I wanted to get them dusty again. There was only one problem. I didn't know how I was going to make that happen. I couldn't keep waiting for crimes to take place. I bent down to gather the scattered notebooks from the lab floor. "I don't think we can credit Quinn with any altruistic motives."

Dr. Payne had somewhat unexpectedly followed us back into the TTE lab. "If you ask me, to investigate this rune-stone affair properly, one wouldn't jump to 1362 *or* to 1898. A true historian doesn't follow rumor and legend, only artifacts and verified written accounts. Trash sites, in particular, can be very illuminating. A proper investigation would begin at L'Anse aux Meadows, since that's the only confirmed pre-Columbian site."

"I thought Dr. Holm wrote up a proposal for a run to L'Anse aux Meadows," I said.

"She wrote up a *linguistics* one. A historical run must come first. We should not use STEWie as a short cut to proper research—"

Dr. Little interrupted him, not rudely, but in an effort to get things back on track. "Let's say they did jump from Woodstock to the nineteenth century. Keep in mind that terms like 'first' and 'later' lose their meaning when you're talking about time travel—it doesn't matter if they went to the fourteenth century first to look for the carvers of the stone or to the nineteenth to see it dug up, or vice versa, as long as they ended up in 1898 at some point—"

"Dr. Little?" Nate, in turn, interrupted him.

"Yes, Kirkland?"

"Get us to 1898, then. If nothing else, I want to watch this damned stone come out of the ground. If Quinn and Dr. Holm are there, all the better. If they aren't, we'll come back, regroup, and look for them in 1362. It's unfortunate that they have the Slingshot." He turned to where the gray-haired professor was, at the utility table that had held his creation. "Dr. Mooney, can you build another one?"

"Certainly, certainly."

"Good. How long will it take?"

"A couple of weeks." Then, at our reaction, "Well, it's not like the parts are prefabricated and sitting on a shelf, are they?" The professor waved at the tools and instruments that covered the utility table except for an empty spot in its middle, as if to make it clear that everything he'd built, he'd built from scratch and that he was the only one in the world who could do so.

"Will they need to come back to recharge the Slingshot?" I asked. "I don't remember battery life being a problem on our ride back from Pompeii. We did, what, five jumps?"

Dr. Mooney shook his head. "That was different. Let's just say power could be an issue, especially if they jump all over the place."

"Wait, I want to understand. Give me the one-minute spiel, please," Nate said.

I could see Dr. Mooney considering how to frame his words in a way that would make sense to non-physicists like Nate and me. "When we were coming back from Pompeii, we were going *with* the arrow of time. Think of it as stepping off a plane. Gravity gets you home, but you need a parachute to slow and control your descent. The Slingshot served as our parachute, controlling our return to the present—badly, I know—but it got us home. The new version I've been tinkering with—Slingshot 2.0, if you will—is a step up. It can go *with* or *against* the arrow of time. It uses a little something the engineering department came up with as its power source. I presented the new design at the conference last week, but wasn't ready to demonstrate it just yet, not until I worked out the final kinks. I don't know how Dr. Holm knew that I had a workable device, or what she may have told Quinn—"

"Everybody knows," said Dr. B, who was back, having changed out of the period attire. "You've gone from—if I may be blunt—drooping around the lab to humming in the hallways. We've all seen you testing the new Slingshot around campus, jumping from one side of the lake to the other."

Nate had turned to Dr. Payne. "Are you up for this?"

"Oh, you want me to come along? I suppose, yes, though I have a class lecture to prepare."

"Cancel it. We need a historian to help us find our bearings and weigh in on the stone finding. Julia, if you're really coming along—"

I didn't bother answering; instead, reflecting on how different Dr. B looked in her beige slacks and short-sleeve shirt from the eighteenth-century outfit she had been wearing, I asked Dr. Payne, "Should we change into nineteenth-century immigrant apparel?"

"We could," Dr. Payne said, "if we wanted to blend in and interact with the locals. But if all we want to do is hide behind farmer Ohman's barn and watch him pretend to find the stone, we're fine as we are."

∞

"Julia and Nate, you remember History's rules?" Dr. Baumgartner asked as Dr. Little readied our coordinates.

How could we forget? I quickly rattled off the four rules of time travel: "One hour in the past equals 133 seconds here. History protects itself, not us. We should try and blend in, but even so, we may find ourselves time-stuck. And—there's always a way back."

The last one held—unless you encountered a ghost zone.

"We'll need a fourth," said Dr. Payne, who had returned with a folder full of relevant articles and notes that he'd gathered from his office. He had a video camera slung across one shoulder.

"A fourth rule?" I asked, confused. "The fourth rule is *There's always a way back.*"

"While that's correct, Julia, I meant that we need a fourth person to come along." He swung his folder through the air with a flourish. "I'm a historian. While I've been on quite a few STEWie runs, that hardly makes me an expert on the ins and outs of time travel—it sounds like we may be dealing with some unexplored territory here. Plus, what if the runestone turns out to be authentic and I drop dead from a heart attack?" The professor gave a mirthless laugh to show he was joking. "Another knowledgeable person should come along."

I decided to overlook the implied insult. Nate and I had only been on one STEWie run, but it had been a doozy. Still, it hardly made us experts.

Dr. Baumgartner raised her hand. "I volunteer. To put it plainly, they messed up my run and I'd like to do something about it."

That was certainly plain enough. I saw Nate throw her a look of understanding, mixed—perhaps—with a touch of admiration. I swept a hand through my hair and looked away.

"And let's bring Jacob Jacobson along," Dr. B suggested.

Nate didn't seem so thrilled about *that* idea. I was with him on that. "I'm not sure we should be bringing students along. It might not be safe," I said as Dr. B pulled out her cell phone to send a text to Jacob. She had been mentoring the second-year grad student while Dr. Rojas was on his sabbatical. I thought Nate would back me up on my "no students" idea, but he said, "I thought you told us there's no chance that Quinn's dangerous, Julia."

"There isn't. The worst I can say about him is that he's a person who doesn't like hard work. Or any work. He's always looking for shortcuts." I added, "I was thinking of other dangers. We may get marooned because of the double basket thing—you said, Dr. Mooney, that we could get stuck for a while."

Dr. Mooney turned his palms upward. "Don't look at me. Except on the very first runs that Gabriel and I did, I always brought students along, no matter what the destination."

"Exactly. This is a university," said Dr. B, reaching for the Callback, the calculator-size device that would send us home at the touch of a few knobs. "Every STEWie run is a learning opportunity. Jacob needs to pick a thesis topic soon, and he hasn't been on a run yet. This will be a good opportunity for him to get his feet wet."

This time Nate definitely gave the professor an approving look. I felt a small tinge of irritation. That was easy for Dr. Baumgartner to say—she wouldn't have to answer to Dean Braga if anything went wrong.

"Somebody get me a map of—what town would it be?" Dr. Little barked out from the workstation.

"Solem Township, near Kensington," Dr. Payne answered with the alacrity of one well versed on the subject, not because of any intrinsic interest in it, but for the pleasure of debunking it. He rifled through his folder and pulled out a copy of an old plat map of farmer Olof Ohman's rural neighborhood. It was dated 1890. "The area hasn't changed much. Current population, two hundred thirty-nine souls. The stone was planted and 'discovered' on the hill where this X marks the spot—"

Dr. Baumgartner had pulled up a modern map of the site on the workstation next to Dr. Little's. "The coordinates of the hill are...North 45 degrees, 48 minutes, 40 seconds...West 95 degrees, 39 minutes, 40 seconds."

Nate leaned toward the monitor to get a look at the modern map. He pointed. "There. That teardrop-shaped pond. Get us right by it. I expect that the deep grass and reeds will provide some cover."

Dr. Little threw a look in our direction. "Can all of you swim? I always like to ask that before sending anyone near water."

We nodded.

"What day and time?" Dr. Little wanted to know next.

"The day the stone was dug up. That's where we'll find them," I said. "There's a date listed on the affidavit that Olof Ohman gave. August, I think. Do you have the document in your folder, Dr. Payne?"

Dr. Payne snickered. "Have you been reading popular books on the subject, Julia? The affidavit was given eleven years after the fact and the date in it was just approximate. It differs in various versions of the story. August, September, and November are the months mentioned most often by supposed witnesses."

"We don't know which month?" I said disbelievingly. If the witnesses couldn't even agree on a month, that did not bode well for the stone's authenticity—or for finding Quinn and Dr. Holm easily.

Nate seemed to take the matter in stride. "Witnesses are like that. If you question them about a break-in, about half will say they noticed a tall stranger on foot in the neighborhood, the other half will say the culprit was short and on a bicycle, and there'll always be the odd person who claims he did it himself, but didn't really." He shrugged. "If anything, it's a point in the favor of the runestone. When witness accounts are all identical, I tend to find them less credible."

Dr. Payne's only answer to this was an affronted sniff.

"That must be why Quinn and Dr. Holm took the Slingshot, so that they could jump around until they found the correct day," I hazarded a guess.

Nate turned to Dr. Payne. "So we have August through November to work with? Let's look for them one day at a time, then, all one hundred and twenty days if need be."

"August 1 to November 30 is one hundred twenty-*two* days," said Dr. Little, who liked to pounce when someone spoke with imprecision.

"We could cross-reference with weather data from the time period and rule out rainy days," I suggested. "Do farmers clear land in the rain? If not, that would narrow it down a bit."

"There's a better way to look for a mark in time," Dr. B said, beating Dr. Little to it. "We jump to the halfway point—October first. If the stone has been dug up already, that tells us that we need to look *before* that day; if it hasn't, then *after*. Depending on which it is, we next jump to either September first or November first, and find out whether we need to look later in that month or in the previous one. Then to the fifteenth of whichever month, and so on. I imagine it won't take more than a handful of tries."

"That would be the way to do it, a binary search," said Dr. Little, as if Dr. B's suggestion should have been obvious to everyone without her long explanation.

I heard the lab doors open and shut. Jacob Jacobson had hurried over to join us in response to Dr. B's message.

"Can you swim?" Dr. Little asked him.

"Yes," Jacob answered breathlessly.

"I'm still not sure about bringing students along," I said, giving him a long look.

There was no one to back me up. Dean Braga was at the observatory, and Dr. Mooney had left to begin the process of ordering the parts he needed to build the new Slingshot.

"Why are you so concerned, Julia?" Dr. B asked from where she was printing out a map of the Runestone Hill area for us to take along. "The worst we'll probably encounter are mosquitoes."

Abigail had come back in with Jacob. "Are we going to go look for Quinn and Dr. Holm? I volunteer to come along."

"Me too," said Kamal, who was still in his thesis-defense suit and math tie, looking more uncomfortable and out of place than Abigail, who hadn't changed out of her period attire yet.

"I volunteer too." This from Jacob. "What did I just volunteer for?"

Loudly enough to be heard over their voices, I said, "I was just anticipating Dean Braga's objections to the matter. As to the nature of the run—we're headed to an immigrant farm in the year 1898. In Solem Township, not too far from here," I said to the students and quickly added, "Geographically speaking, that is," before the three of them could remind me that STEWie calculations had to take into account everything from the movement of the Earth in space to rising ground levels. It would take Dr. Little some time to ready our coordinates.

"Huh, 1898," said Kamal. "I'm afraid I don't know much about Minnesota history. Will it be dangerous? You know, Indians and such?"

Dr. Payne looked at Kamal like he was considering revoking his positive thesis defense vote on the spot. "Young man, the year 1898 was just about forty years after Minnesota had become the thirty-second state. The Dakota War and the Civil War had come and gone, the grasshopper plagues that had devastated the crops of the local farmers were over, and the Great Northern Railway link from St. Paul to Seattle had been completed. The state population was skyrocketing, with European immigrants pouring in, drawn by farming opportunities and the thriving lumber and milling industries—"

"And, incidentally," Dr. Baumgartner interrupted, "a girl's school had been founded just about then by an immigrant couple, Knut and Agnes Hegge. Julia, the building where you work is the only one remaining of the three that originally comprised the campus, other than the church. It had a different name then, and the dormitory that stood next door is no longer there."

"It would be nice to see what the school was like in the past," Abigail said, "before we went co-ed."

"It must have been kind of odd," Kamal said. "Girls only, I mean."

"I'd like to see the school—or anything else, really. I just want to go on a run. Any run," Jacob said. During his first year, he had struggled with his graduate studies, but he finally seemed to have found his footing. I noticed that he was wearing a T-shirt with a Star Wars motif on it—a light saber–wielding Yoda hovered above the words *Pass on what you have learned*, making me think that a professorship down the road might be the right path for this student.

Kamal tugged at his math tie. "If you need me, I'd be happy to change out of this suit—"

"What's going on?"

"And can we come along?"

"Wow, that's a big mirror!"

Three more TTE students had walked in: Tammy, Sergei, and a new arrival whom I didn't recognize, all eager to volunteer their services. It made me think we needed to be more restrictive about giving out the door code.

"All right, everyone out," Nate commanded. "Except for you, Jacob. We're going as is, no need for anyone to change. Dr. Little, are we good to go?"

"Just a bit longer. Don't want you arriving in the middle of the pond."

The five of us—Dr. Baumgartner, Dr. Payne, Nate, Jacob (looking like he couldn't believe his luck), and yours truly—headed past the workstation where the monitor still lay on the floor, no one having had the time to deal with it, and to STEWie's platform in the middle of the mirror-laser array. We scrambled onto the elevated platform and squeezed everybody in. Around us, like a wall-less elevator, a metal frame defined the limits of STEWie's basket.

After the promised few minutes, the equipment in the lab started to come to life, and the mirrors began to pirouette into place in a slow, well-oiled dance. I knew what to expect: Once the mirrors had inched into place, STEWie's generator would warm up enough for the cryogenic coolers under the floor to kick in, and it would soon get very noisy and very bright.

"What are we going to go see?" Jacob asked, his voice high with excitement.

"A runestone," I said.

"We'll be outside?" He pulled something out of his pocket. "Anyone want suntan lotion? I burn easily. I grabbed some insect repellant too."

"Well, don't spray it in here," Nate said. "We'd all get a noseful."

"I think I've heard of this runestone," Jacob said as he slathered lotion on his nose and cheeks, having put the bug spray back in his pocket. "Chiseled by the Vikings, right?"

"If it's authentic," I said, "it will be proof of pre-Columbian exploration in North America by the Vik   by Norse explorers."

"If we prove it's real, can that be my thesis topic?" Jacob's sneakered foot trod on mine. "Sorry, Julia, I'm just so excited. Can I tweet about this and take pictures for my blog? Everyone will want to know about it."

"Not a chance. Put the phone away."

"I could snap a few pics, write it up, and that would be that— a PhD with flying colors."

Dr. Payne looked down his nose at him, as if Jacob had meant it seriously, which he may have. "A PhD requires more than just a few photographs, young man, even if the stone were genuine, which it's not. You'd have to tell the whole story—who carved it, why they carved it, and how they happened to be there in the first place. Also what route they took inland, with whom they came in contact…I don't believe coming along with us for the ride will count for much."

"If it did, I could write up a thesis myself," I said, raising my voice over the increasing rumble of STEWie's generator. The last of the mirrors, the one that almost touched the balloon ceiling, came to a grinding halt. As Dr. Little called out from the workstation to remind us to cover our eyes, I asked Nate, who was on one side of me, "Isn't Officer Van Underberg coming with us? We should be able to squeeze in one more."

The officer was by Dr. Little's workstation. He just seemed to be standing there doing nothing.

Nate shielded his eyes with a lanky hand. "I decided that he should stay here so that there are no surprises like last time."

Before I could point out that the officer would hardly be able to tell by looking over Dr. Little's shoulder where the professor was about to send us, we were on our way.

# 12

Jacob Jacobson got his feet wet, figuratively and literally.

Because what came next was a series of runs, a blur of light each time, followed by a cold splash as we arrived knee-deep in water among the reeds of what was not the small teardrop-shaped pond that the modern map had shown but an extensive marshland out of which several small hills sprouted. On our first jump, icy rain fell on our heads, the trees were half-bare, and the hillside on Olof Ohman's land had been cleared for planting; on our second, it was hot and humid, the land was green and lush, mosquitoes were biting, and the runestone hill was fully wooded. One run was a total dud—somebody must have been in or around the pond, because we landed instead in the middle of a heavily wooded, impenetrable area. As we jumped back and forth between the past and present, our feet got wetter and wetter and we watched the township farmers go about their business, on foot or horse and buggy. Sometimes we saw things out of sequence, which was a bit odd. Runestone Hill on Olof Ohman's farm was cleared of trees and pulled into service as a field, then it was woodsy, then it was somewhat cleared...

It took me a moment to get my bearings the first few jumps. The park that Nate and I had visited, with its picnic area and paved roads, was gone, replaced with spread-out farmhouses and barns and planted fields. Olof Ohman's white farmhouse was not visible from our vantage point in the reeds, but even as limited as our view from the pond was, one thing was instantly clear— unlike the steady-state, modern Kensington area that Nate and I had visited, this was a place of *change*. Rightly or wrongly, sleeves rolled up, the newcomers were painstakingly shaping the land so that it resembled the European farms that they'd left behind in the old country. Acre by acre, marshland and woods were being transformed into farmland. This was a land in the grips of a transition—a deep, rapid, profound reshaping—and we were witnessing a small bit of it.

On the sixth jump we struck gold, so to speak.

Fall had come early to the Solem Township, and shafts of afternoon light broke through yellow aspen leaves, dancing around the farmer as he cleared his land. Occasionally he stopped to wipe his brow while digging beneath a mature aspen whose roots obviously extended deep into the soil. The five of us crouched in the lake reeds, unseen and unnoticed.

The pocket of my slacks hid the list of pros and cons that I had jotted down in the library. I had been very sure that I would be able to spot at once whether Olof Ohman was about to perpetrate a hoax on his neighbors and the world at large. The problem was, *because* I knew what was going to happen, it all looked pre-scripted, like I was part of an audience watching a play acted out onstage. If Helen had been present, she would have quoted the Bard in my ear: *All the world's a stage, and all the men and women merely players* . . . which would not have helped at all in clearing up the issue. I was aware that a suspension of disbelief on my part might merely mean that the lights had been dimmed and the play had begun.

Pre-scripted or not, nothing was happening very fast.

Olof dug around the base of the old tree to loosen the soil, using his foot to push the spade into the ground. Even in the crisp fall air, clearing the field must have been hard work and the farmer's brawny, begrimed arms tensed and strained under his shirt and overalls as he worked the dirt. To one side, a couple of trees had already been cleared, leaving gaping holes in the ground. Farther down the hillside, a wooden fence separated Olof's farm from his neighbor's, and beyond that was a second farmhouse, where a hatted figure worked the land, his back to us.

After a few minutes of digging around the base of the tree, Olof Ohman started to look—for want of a better word—irritated at some kind of obstruction. Pausing to wipe his brow, he set the spade aside and picked up an axe. He proceeded to hack at the roots of the tree, loosening them further for the felling that was about to happen.

That was when I noticed the boys. There were three of them, and two—Olof Jr. and Edward—were alike enough to be twins, except for the difference in their height. The third was a smaller boy, blond and thin. He could only be Magnus Olsen; a golden-haired ragamuffin of a child, he looked so much like Quinn that I was momentarily thunderstruck. All three were wearing overalls and caps, and it looked like they were helping Olof clear out some of the underbrush. Realizing that he was about to pull down the aspen, they abandoned what they were doing and ran over to watch. No kid of any century passes up the opportunity to see a tree get cut down.

Olof gave the roots one last whack with his axe, then waved the boys to one side, out of harm's way. They obeyed without argument. The farmer set the axe aside and readied a winch of some kind, which was connected to the tree with a thick rope. He turned the crank on it.

I could feel the tension creep up my arms like a sudden chill in the air, the anticipation hard to bear. This was it. A strand of History was about to unravel, the stone would be under the tree or it wouldn't, and either Dr. Payne or Quinn would be proven right.

Olof turned the crank harder.

Nate elbowed me in the side.

"Ow. What was that for?" I whispered to him.

He nodded toward Dr. B, whose beige slacks had been darkened to just below her knees in the water, and who had the Callback out. She was moving it left and right, scanning for something, a frown on her face. Next to her, Dr. Payne's eyes were glued to the action on the hill, his facial expression one of disdain as he recorded the event with the video camera in his hand. Jacob, in front of me, seemed dumbfounded by the experience of time traveling. He kept pinching the reeds nervously as if checking whether they were real. We hadn't lingered long on the other runs, so this was his first chance to *feel* the past.

Nate nodded toward Dr. B again. Was there an issue with the basket? Had it returned to the lab, and did that mean Quinn and Dr. Holm were here? I glanced around to see if I could spot Quinn's blue eyes and blond hair peeking out from behind a barn, but didn't see anything. I sent a small shrug in Nate's direction and returned my attention to the hillside. It was impossible not to.

The winch rope had tightened and the aspen was teetering, as if deciding whether it wanted to fall. After a moment of indecision, like everything was happening in slow motion, gravity took over and, with a great crack and a thud that carried over to where we were crouching, the aspen came crashing down, roots and all. Involuntarily I took a step forward in the water. A gray object had emerged from the ground, still clasped in the tree's roots, its face now turned to the sky. Root and rock had come out in a single earthen lump, and I realized that the sensation that I was watching a play had vanished the moment the stone emerged from its resting place. It seemed like it had been underground forever.

Olof Ohman stood back and wiped his hands on his overalls, giving us our first full look of his face as he took off his cap for a moment to cool off. I caught a glimpse of a strong chin and bushy eyebrows above a walrus mustache before the cap went back on.

"I'll be damned," I heard Nate whisper next to me. "He was telling the truth. He did dig it up."

Olof had returned with the axe to hack away the roots, then used a grubbing hoe to flip the stone aside with one large heave. Once that was done, he wiped his forehead and focused his attention on detaching the winch from the fallen tree. Meanwhile, the boys took turns trying out the stone as a seat.

There was laughter and jostling for a position on the rectangular slab.

I wished I had a watch so I could check whether time had really stopped moving or whether it just seemed that way because I was impatient for the boys to notice the runic writing.

The younger of the Ohman sons was scraping clay off the stone with his foot when he suddenly started shouting, his excitement carrying over to where we were hiding in the reeds. All three boys went down on their knees, sweeping away more clay and dirt, but now with purpose. Young Magnus Olsen had taken off his cap and his blond bangs slid onto his forehead, like Quinn's were given to doing, as he helped the Ohman sons wipe off the stone, using his cap to accomplish his part. A conversation was held and the boys called for Olof Ohman, who was prepping the base of the next tree. They made room to let the farmer take a look. He bent down for a long moment, then straightened up and said something to the older of his sons. The boy fetched water from what looked like the remains of the farmer's lunch on a nearby tree stump. It was poured onto the stone to further dislodge the dirt and expose what was underneath.

Farmer Ohman stood still for a moment, clearly at a loss. Finally, with a shake of his head, he turned and, cupping his hands, called out to the hatted figure working on the neighboring farm. The neighbor didn't hear him at first, so Olof Ohman called out again, louder, what sounded like a name: *Niiiils*. This time the neighbor heard and, seeming happy enough to take a break from working on his own field, clambered over the short wooden fence that separated his land from Olof's. The new arrival took off his wide-brimmed hat, peered at the stone, touched it. He checked out the downed aspen and bent to look at the hole the tree and stone had left in the ground, shaking his head in wonder. The two men stood stroking their identical walrus mustaches, mulling over the matter in a reserved, classically Scandinavian kind of way. We could not hear what was being said.

A thought occurred to me, an odd one, unconnected to the play we were watching. We were a small group from the future, observing and recording an event as it unfolded, and none of the participants were aware of our presence. Five of us, five of them. Audience and actors. Who was to say that someone from farther along in the future wasn't around watching *us* watch Olof Ohman and his sons and neighbors? A traveler from a thousand years into the future using some sleek version of STEWie that documented *all* of the world's past for future generations, chronicling every word, every action, every flutter of History's pages in some overwhelmingly large database. I shook off the thought. I suspected that if I did this long enough, I would acquire the habit of looking over my shoulder to check for STEWie travelers from the future. Not that my life was overly interesting, but you never knew.

Dr. Payne adjusted his position to get a better view of the hilltop with his video camera, and the gentle rustling of the reeds broke through my reverie. I noticed that Nate, standing near me, was staring intently at something, his body perfectly still, only his eyes moving. I elbowed him back, almost causing him to lose his balance.

"Sorry," I whispered. "What do you see?"

"There."

I followed the line of his arm to a sturdy oak in an as-yet-uncleared bit of land. Behind the autumn-hued leaves rustling in the still afternoon, I saw a flash of blue among the thick brown branches. How had I missed them? I even recognized the shirt, which Quinn had worn the morning we eloped on a beach in San Diego—it was dark blue, like Oscar had mentioned, with parrots on it. Above him, one branch up, a petite figure clung to the trunk. I had been too preoccupied with what was happening on the hill to notice them before.

They didn't seem to have spotted us yet.

Nate and I both tried to make a move, but we were only able to take a few halting steps in the water before we were forced to a stop. History, protecting itself. Had we charged out of the lake in the direction of the oak and its two visitors, the men and boys on the hill would have seen us, and it would have taken their day in a completely different direction. Being prevented from moving by an invisible barrier was an odd sensation, but I knew that it wouldn't last, so I made an effort to relax. In the worst case, we would be stuck until Olof Ohman finished for the day and could make our move then.

Still, I hoped we wouldn't have to wait long. I was itching to confront Quinn over the problems he had caused me at work.

Not to mention that my feet and socks were sopping wet inside my shoes. I felt something brush against my leg and hoped it was a small fish and not a snake.

The men on the hill had come to some sort of a decision, which seemed to be that they would put aside the stone and get back to work. The neighbor—Nils Flaaten, I suddenly remembered from my library reading—headed back to his own farm with a friendly wave to Olof.

Another call came, I couldn't see from where, and the golden-haired child, Magnus Olsen, left for home, too. The last we saw of him, he was trying to clean the dirt off his cap by rubbing it on his pant leg as he sauntered along.

I wondered if Quinn was glad he'd come. What was I thinking? Of course he was glad. He had been proven right.

In front of me Jacob, who was snapping pictures with his cell phone, jumped as if something had grazed his leg, probably another of the small fish. Nate and I both shot out a hand to steady him, but not before Jacob's arm splashed the surface of the water, loudly, and his phone sank out of sight.

I don't know if it was the movement or the sound that alerted Quinn and Dr. Holm to our presence, or if the two had already gotten the footage they wanted and were ready to leave. In any case, we saw a rustle of blue on the oak where they were perched, a flash of light like sunbeams reflecting off fresh snow . . . and then the two figures up the tree were gone, leaving the orange leaves stirring behind them as if in a sudden wind.

Nate turned to Dr. B and asked in a hard whisper, "Are we stuck here? Did our basket leave?"

We watched Dr. B press a sequence of keys on the Callback as if she was double-checking something she already knew.

Nothing happened.

"Bad luck," she said. "We'll have to wait for Steven to send another one."

I hoped Dr. Little would be quick about it. I felt a sneeze coming on, and what with the chill in the air and my damp feet, I didn't want to catch a cold. And we had seen what, or rather who, we had come to see and had not been able to do anything about it.

Dr. Payne looked a little shaken, and my guess was that it wasn't over the basket issue. "We could try to, uh, explore a bit...though I doubt that History would let us. Not dressed like this, anyway. She'll probably pin us in place."

Jacob tried to push through the reeds and of the water, but something stopped him short.

"History doesn't want us wandering around in the nineteenth century. My hat's off to her," Nate said. "Let's not anger her by leaving anything behind." Pondering the question of whether History really was a *she*, like an extension of Mother Nature, I shook off my chill and joined Nate in trying to help Jacob find his phone. We stuck our arms into the cold water and groped the bottom of the marshy lake.

But the cell phone was gone, lost in the muddy, weedy bottom. There was nothing to be done but take a last look at the hill, where the day had reverted to ordinary, squeeze the excess water from our sleeves, and wait to be rescued.

We had found out this much, however—Dr. Payne had been wrong and Quinn had been right. I gritted my teeth at the development. At least we had guessed correctly where our missing pair had gone...and we had a good idea of where to look for them next.

# 13

"And then the farmer pulled the tree out of the ground, and out came the roots and the stone, dirt flying..."

I was relaying the day's events between bites of takeout from Panda Palace. Helen had joined us at the house for a late dinner, eager to hear the story. She and Abigail had suggested that we might as well tell Sabina about Quinn's blackmail threat, since the newest developments did not involve her, but I suspected that I already knew what her reaction would be. Sabina was as headstrong as her father, who had opted to stay in Pompeii and face the eruption on the off chance that he could save his mother and his shop. She'd probably make a curse tablet with Quinn's name on it—or a replica with pen and paper. I wanted to discourage that sort of thing.

"I hate to say it, but it looks like Quinn was right about the runestone." I was utterly famished and still chilled to the bone. Dr. Little had sent another basket as soon as ours returned empty, but the bare minimum of time required for the equipment to cool off was fifteen minutes, which had translated into almost seven hours for us in 1898. At least after the first four had passed we had been able to squelch out of the water and wait out the remaining three on dry land in the fading light. My toes were still pruney.

The first thing I had done once we had made it back to the present—that is, after a hot shower and coffee—was to add one more item on the *Pro* side of my list about the runestone. I had seen it come out of the ground with my own eyes. As had Quinn and Dr. Holm. Their next stop would be the fourteenth century. In the morning, we would regroup and come up with a strategy to find them. I pushed the thought aside and continued to describe for my audience the day's adventure, Sabina interrupting between mouthfuls to have a word explained—marshland, aspen, overalls, walrus mustache.

"We watched Olof Ohman pull the tree down, an old one—he would have hardly needed a winch otherwise. That's a big crank that you turn by hand," I added for Sabina's benefit. "The roots were tightly wrapped around the stone, like it had been in the ground for a long time."

"So it's real." Abigail gave a little sigh of satisfaction. Having been brought up in a string of foster families, Abigail had a bit of a romantic streak and a soft spot for happy endings. Still, I felt compelled to reply, "Well, it might not be. Doctor Payne still thinks that Olof Ohman could have buried it under the tree, only to 'discover' it several years later."

"He would. I kind of want it to be true—oh, sorry." Her cell phone had beeped. I belatedly remembered that I had meant to ask everyone to turn off their phones for the duration of the meal. I wanted to set a good example for Sabina.

Abigail checked the message. "It's Jacob—huh, he bought a new cell phone, he says. I wonder what happened to his old one."

"He dropped it into the lake on Olof Ohman's farm," I explained. "We couldn't find it. He bought a new one somewhere this late?" It was almost ten by the kitchen clock, but much later for me. I fought a jaw-stretching yawn.

"The Emporium was still open." This was Thornberg's carry-all store.

"There is a word for that." Helen did something she rarely did, scrunched up her nose; she wasn't exactly a Luddite—without technology, there would be no STEWie—but she wasn't the biggest fan of modern gadgets either. "*Nomophobia*. Anxiety experienced by cell phone users when they forget their phone at home or the battery dies and they are out of contact with friends and family. The term is a shortened version of *no-mobile-phone-phobia*. Researchers have found that the stress levels are similar to those experienced on a dentist visit."

Sabina scrunched up her nose. "Dentist, I no like."

"And Jacob no like being without his cell phone," said Abigail, who was exchanging a series of text messages with her fellow grad student. "I don't either...or without my laptop. Does that mean I have *lapophobia*? Jacob says he's going to go borrow his parents' car tomorrow so that he can go back to the lake to see if he can find his old phone." Unlike most of his office mates, who had rooms in graduate residences, Jacob lived at home and biked to campus. His parents ran a combination bookstore/antique shop in town.

"There's no reason for him to retrieve the phone from the bottom of the lake, not from the point of view of History," Helen said. "It's already been there for over a hundred years without drawing any attention."

"And the warranty must have expired by now, right?" Abigail said with a snicker as another arriving text message beeped. "I think he has hopes of retrieving his list of contacts from it. He says he's heard that if your cell phone gets wet and stops working, all you have to do is place the phone into a bag of uncooked rice overnight and the problem is solved...A bit optimistic, if you ask me, since his phone has been lying at the bottom of a muddy lake for more than a century."

Sabina leaned over to look as Abigail texted Jacob back, and I was momentarily amused by how quickly she had accepted cell phones. Really, if you thought about it, it was quite astonishing how Abigail's typed letters turned into invisible waves that bounced off cell towers and into Jacob's new phone, then became letters again.

"Anyone want the last potsticker?" I asked as Abigail put the phone away. Celer, who was dozing in one corner of the kitchen, twitched in his sleep as if experiencing a pleasant dog dream. The potsticker was waved in my direction and I proceeded to dig into it.

After Abigail and Sabina had cleared the table and taken the dishes into the kitchen, Helen said, "So Dagmar will take Quinn into the fourteenth century."

"Presumably." Then Helen's phrasing sank in. "Helen, you don't believe Quinn made her go at gunpoint either, do you? Officer Van Underberg suggested it, and Nate seems to think it's a real possibility given the text message she sent me." Why had she sent it to me and not the police or someone in her own department? Had she grabbed her phone and texted blindly, sending the message to the most recent number in her history? I didn't like the thought.

"I don't know if he made her go or not," Helen said. "Even if he didn't, I think that our Chief Kirkland will always be bothered by anything your ex does . . . except, perhaps, if Quinn leaves town for good."

I waved off her last comment. "I wish you had been with us today. I can't tell if Dr. Payne is being contrary because he wants to be proven right, or if he's just being cautious with the evidence at hand, as an academic should be. 'Further runs are obviously warranted,'" I said, mimicking Dr. Payne's snippy tone. "He spent most of the seven hours we were stuck in the mud explaining his position to us. And he wasn't talking about Quinn and Dr. Holm. I don't know how historians coped before STEWie, really I don't." It was maddening that we still didn't know for sure if the stone was real after all we'd been through. "Relying only on documents and what's left behind in the dirt—not being able to check things directly, in person—that would drive me crazy."

"Trying to figure out what really happened...well, that's half the fun, Julia. STEWie is only a tool that helps us do that. As you found out, even something that you see with your own eyes needs to be interpreted and put into context."

There was a lot of truth to her words. If Quinn hadn't been involved, I suspected that I would have greatly enjoyed solving the mystery of the runestone.

"But yes, STEWie is a wondrous thing, there is no denying that," Helen added. "Xavier's certainly having fun. He's up to his elbows in electronic parts and whatnot, building another Slingshot. Kamal is helping him."

"Nate asked him to hurry. We are all a little nervous about relying on STEWie alone and getting stuck in the fourteenth century after what happened tonight."

"Why don't we just leave Quinn in the past?" Abigail called out from the kitchen. We could hear the clink of cups and plates as she and Sabina loaded the dishwasher. "Problem solved."

"Well, I think Dr. Mooney wants his Slingshot back. And we all want Dr. Holm to return safe and sound, don't we?" I called back.

Helen helped me sweep the crumbs off the table and into a napkin. "Speaking of Chief Kirkland..."

"Were we?"

"Why didn't he join us for dinner? I would have liked to hear his impressions of the events on Olof Ohman's farm."

Why hadn't Nate joined us for dinner? For one thing, I hadn't invited him. For another, I'd gotten a vibe. Nate seemed to be annoyed that I wasn't more angry at Quinn. Which wasn't exactly right—I was *furious* with Quinn. But I still wasn't convinced that he had kidnapped Dr. Holm. I wondered if the shrimp curry dinner on Friday night was still on. To my surprise, I suddenly realized that I had rather been looking forward to it.

I didn't want to explain all that to Helen, so instead I let a yawn escape and said, "He had to get home to feed and walk Wanda."

"I should let you get to bed," Helen said, rising to her feet. "You've had a long day."

"Helen, want to come along with us to 1362?" I asked as I walked her to the door.

"I don't know that my presence would help much. My work is with language, letters, manuscripts—and yes, the runestone is a document and falls into that category. But I'm neither an expert in runic linguistics nor in the pre-Columbian history of the Americas. Ironically, the person you need is Dr. Holm herself. I wonder what she thought of seeing the stone come to light."

I had wondered that too.

# 14

*Ten men, red from blood and dead.*

"You do realize what that sounds like?" Nate said as I repeated the ominous snippet of text from the runestone.

Of course I realized. That was why I had brought it up.

"It sounds like a ghost zone," Dr. Baumgartner said, hurrying into the meeting Dean Braga had called in her office. Dr. B slid her tall frame into a chair, a coffee cup in one hand. "Sorry I'm late, I overslept. What did I miss?" Like the rest of us who had gone on yesterday's run, she looked jet-lagged—our more than seven-hour stay in the past had felt like the equivalent of a plane hop west, time zone change and all.

"Dr. Payne thinks that it's a waste of time for us to look for them at all, that it would take too many runs and tie up the lab indefinitely. The rest of us disagree," Nate summarized for her.

Dean Braga gave a harried sigh. "Not to seem heartless, but the department's emergency funds only go so far. It *does* sound like a lot of extra runs with no guarantee of success."

"Quite correct, Dean Braga. Other researchers," Dr. Payne said, meaning himself, "need access to STEWie. We all have work that needs to get done, not to mention article deadlines. The Norsemen never came, so this is all a waste of everyone's time."

Dr. Payne, if anything, had dug his heels in even more now that he'd had a chance to process everything. I assumed that the only reason he had bothered to come to the meeting at all was to argue for the lab to be opened up again.

"If the Norsemen never came, yes, that would be a problem." Dr. B said. She took a long sip of the coffee. "Because the point in time where we'll most likely find Quinn and Dr. Holm is when the stone carvers were there."

"And if they never were?" I asked, even though I knew the answer.

"Then we'll be jumping around in time endlessly looking for our missing pair while they jump around in time endlessly looking for the Norsemen."

It was becoming clear that going into the fourteenth century would be no simple matter. I shifted where I was, standing with my back against the wall of Dean Braga's office. There was the question of when and where—Dr. B's binary search method had yielded excellent results in 1898, but was not as straightforward if a moving target was involved. There was a good chance we would be bouncing around the fourteenth century like unsuccessful billiard balls, draining the TTE lab resources and Dean Braga's patience.

Dr. B added, "That's not the only problem, Chief Kirkland. If both parties—our team and the missing pair—do manage to converge on the Norsemen's visit—if they came," she added for Dr. Payne's benefit, "—we will face the same problem we encountered in 1898. We'd have to stay hidden. We wouldn't be able to confront Quinn and rescue Dr. Holm in the presence of the Norsemen."

The whole thing was rather circular. We were most likely to find Quinn and Dr. Holm in the vicinity of the Norsemen, but that was exactly where we wouldn't be able to take action.

And that was assuming that the Norsemen had come at all, as Dr. Payne kept reminding us.

Nate crossed his arms over his chest and sat back in his chair. "Quinn has burned his bridges. The only way this comes out all right is if he comes back a hero, the great explorer, the first person to find conclusive evidence of Norse presence in the US. He is not simply going to sit on a hilltop and wait. I know you still believe that the runestone's a hoax, Dr. Payne, but I doubt that's Quinn's opinion."

"I agree," I said, and they all turned in their seats to look at me, like they had forgotten I was present. Well, I wasn't just going to sit in my office while this mess was going on. "Quinn—and Dr. Holm—well, you don't go to all that trouble without being convinced that what you're seeking is real. Which means he needs the whole deal—the Norse ships, the men, and whatever deadly event they encountered...their ghost zone."

"It's not technically a ghost zone," Dr. B said, "since the Norsemen belong to that time period and aren't time travelers."

"It might as well be if it killed ten of them at once," I said.

Dean Braga brought up the most economical option and the one guaranteed to satisfy the university researchers who had been deluging her office asking when STEWie runs would resume. "Again, I don't want to sound heartless, but we *could* just wait for them to come back and let the lab get back to its normal schedule in the meantime. After all, they can't do any harm to History. Let them search for the carver or carvers of the stone."

A law enforcement officer's frown furrowed Nate's eyebrows. "What if Dr. Holm is in danger from Quinn?"

"Or their battery power runs out?" Dr. B said. "Dr. Holm has sat in on a couple of time-travel workshops, but she's green when it comes to practical issues that pop up on runs. What if they *can't* come back?"

"Like I said, I think Nate is right," I said into the sudden silence. "Quinn wants to return with footage to seed a reality show, so it'll have to include more than just a lone chiseler on a hilltop. That, I think we can all agree, is an activity that's pretty low on the action scale as far as TV audiences go."

How much better (for TV ratings) to score footage of a Norse vessel gliding into the New World, its woolen sails taut in the wind, its prow proudly pointing landward. I imagined Quinn and Dr. Holm shooting close-ups of the ship's crew from shore, capturing for eternity the wind-chiseled, bearded faces of the Gotlanders and Norwegians. It occurred to me that unless there was some form of hierarchy present, a Gotlander must have carved the stone. They were listed first on the runestone, after all.

"I imagine," I continued, "they'll want footage of the Norsemen's ships sailing into the cold waters of Lake Superior—"

"Or Hudson Bay, to the north," Dr. Payne interjected. "The probability of one is as high as the probability of the other, that is, almost zero."

"And of the explorers on their journey farther inland—"

"They wouldn't have passed unnoticed. It wasn't a wilderness they were heading into. There were people living there," Dr. Payne said.

"I know," Nate said. I thought I detected a new note of irritation in his voice, one that had nothing to do with me this time. "I'm related to them."

"Oh, are you, Chief Kirkland?"

"One of my grandmothers is Dakota."

"Well, there you have it. They would have run into some of your ancestors. Here's something to wrap your mind around— like Columbus, they would have thought they were in Asia," he said, echoing what Dr. Holm had told me back in the Coffey Library.

His words made me wonder how much of our modern world-view was completely and utterly wrong. Like all past cultures, we held certain beliefs based on nothing but assumption. How soon before someone new came along, like Copernicus and Einstein had in the past, to adjust our worldview?

"Perhaps the Dakota watched from the shore as the Norse vessels sailed in, wondering what to make of the strange arrival," I said.

Dr. Payne shook his head at once. "The Norse kept up a presence on the coast of Canada from the turn of the millennium onward. They wouldn't have been unexpected visitors. Word of their ships would probably have spread west. There was a trade network in place." He went on, "Look, I know you all think that I'm a crotchety old man, and it's true. But that's not the issue here. I represent the Department of American History," he said rather grandiosely. "When I tell acquaintances that, they always assume that my research interests start with the Pilgrims landing at Plymouth Rock. Not so. The group I lead, well, we've been sharpening our time travel skills on events in near time, such as the Battle of Antietam, before venturing deeper into the Americas' past. Without fail, my grad students and postdocs always have silly ideas they think will make them famous. Your estranged husband would fit right in with my students, Julia." He gave a small, back-of-the-throat laugh. "We're almost at the point where we are ready to tackle far time. Far time! I don't want to waste roster spots looking for needles in the haystack of History. Just think of all the wonderful things that you could document for posterity—and we plan to do it! The Incas building their suspension bridges across deep mountain gorges and constructing a stone road system that rivaled that of Rome; the Chinchorro creating History's first mummies; Cahokia, the biggest population center to the north of the Rio Grande before the floods and the earthquake—"

"Professor," Nate interrupted him, "I agree with you. But that's not the issue facing us."

"Humor me for just a moment longer, Chief Kirkland. Do any of you know who the closest genetic relatives to Native Americans are?"

Clearly impatient to return to the problem at hand, Nate surprised me by answering, "Siberians."

"That's right, indigenous Siberians. How wonderful it would be to find out when their ancestors crossed the Bering Strait. Did they continue inland and south on foot, or did they build boats and follow the Pacific coastline? I don't know which one it was. No one does. My money is on the boat route. What do *you* think, Chief Kirkland?"

"I—well, I would probably say boats, too."

"You and I both know that finding out the answer wouldn't make for great television or an easily financed STEWie run, don't we? The real mysteries in the world's past usually do not. Here's another one—maize was domesticated in Mesoamerica from the wild grass teosinte, but when and how? I'd probably generate more interest in the media if I put about a rumor that I suspected that aliens had brought the first corn kernels to Earth." The professor gathered his things and got to his feet. "Bear all that in mind as you decide what we should do, Dean Braga. Now if you'll excuse me, I have essay topics to come up with..."

After the professor had left, mumbling to himself about the book he was planning to write ("A monumental work—*The Rise and Fall of the Mayan Empire*—why *did* they abandon their cities? We must find out, and make another attempt to rescue more of their codices...And in the sequel, I could decipher the Inka *khipu*..."), Dean Braga turned to the rest of us and said reluctantly, "One run. That's all I can give you. Dr. Mooney is still a couple of days from finishing up the new Slingshot so plan your run for Friday. I don't like the forced wait any more than you do, Chief, but I think it's the prudent thing to do."

We needed Dr. Mooney's Slingshot to correct our position once we were in the fourteenth century and as backup in case we got stuck there because of the double basket problem. Going to a mapped nineteenth-century farm was one thing, but blindly traipsing around in the fourteenth century was a different kettle of fish.

"And if we're lucky," she added, "that will give Dr. Holm and Mr. Olsen enough time to return of their own accord."

Nate caught my arm as we left Dean Braga's office together. "Can you meet me in my office later? I know a history expert I'd like to consult before we head into this supposed ghost zone. Her name is Mary Kirkland. She's my grandmother."

∞

"There you are," Nate said as I walked into his office just before noon, having run a couple of errands first. "Do you want some coffee before we go? I'm still a bit groggy from last night."

"Sure."

He headed into the large front room of the campus security office and returned with two Styrofoam cups. He handed me one. "Sorry, it's really not that good. Cream? Sugar? Neither will help."

I hadn't been in the security office in the main campus administration building since Dan Anderson, our previous security chief, had retired. A hallway led from the small parking lot at the back of the building, where three or four security cars waited, past Officer Van Underberg, who was typing up an incident report, and another officer I knew only slightly, ending at Nate's desk.

I stirred a small cup of powdered creamer into the coffee. As always, I had a box of cookies in my shoulder bag for dealing with any emergencies that arose in my capacity as dean's assistant. It was no secret that Nate was more of a fan of freshly made food, with no preservatives, additives, or corn syrup, but I offered him the macadamia chocolate chip cookies anyway. He took one.

I took two. I was stressed by how long we had to wait before going after Quinn, not to mention an embarrassing conversation I'd had before coming to Nate's office. And I felt guilty and awkward about having kept Quinn's blackmail attempt from Nate. In hindsight, I realized that I should have confided in him. The fact that he *hadn't* said, *You could have trusted me, Julia,* rather proved that I could have.

After a moment of uncomfortable silence during which he seemed disinclined to speak, I asked between cookie bites, "Why aren't they back yet? It's been weeks. For them, I mean."

Quinn and Dr. Holm had taken off at around 4:00 yesterday afternoon. The pair had been gone twenty hours, which, assuming they had stayed in the past that whole time, meant that three weeks had passed for them. *Three weeks.* What had they been doing all that time? And what were they doing for food, I wondered as I munched on another of the cookies. Hunting, fishing, eating granola bars? Quinn hated granola bars.

There were too many questions and not enough answers.

"We're not giving up on finding them. We just have to be smart about it." Nate shifted in his chair, causing it to creak. It looked a little small for his lanky frame. "As for why they aren't back yet, I can think of several reasons."

He dipped the cookie I had given him into his coffee, looked at it with suspicion, and then put the whole thing in his mouth. "All right," he said after a moment. "One, they could be camped out on Runestone Hill in 1362, waiting for the Norsemen to show up. Two, they got what they needed but overshot the present like we did coming back from Pompeii, and can't do anything about it because they drained their Slingshot. They might show up out of thin air in a few weeks. Three, they're finding the Slingshot difficult to control, and they've ended up someplace completely unexpected. Even Dr. Mooney admits that his Slingshot 2.0 still needs some work." He rubbed his chin, which had stubble on it, as if he hadn't bothered with a morning shave. It looked good that way. "Four, it hasn't really been three weeks because they're jumping back and forth between the past and the present to replenish their supplies. For all we know they could have had dinner last night and, uh, spent the night in Quinn's hotel room, or in Dr. Holm's apartment." I thought I heard him gnash his teeth at the possibility that they'd been so close. "That occurred to me this morning, and I drove out to check both places. No trace of them. The manager at Lena's Lodge hasn't seen Quinn since yesterday, but that's about it. I've asked the town police to keep an eye out on both places."

"I never would have thought of checking the hotel." I added, considering his words, "It sounds like you're starting to give Quinn the benefit of the doubt. If they're having dinner at Dr. Holm's apartment, she can hardly have been forced into it."

"Like you say, it's been three weeks. She may have very well succumbed to Stockholm syndrome and become invested in helping Quinn."

"Oh."

"There is one last possibility I can think of," he added, shifting uncomfortably in the chair again.

"Which is?"

He offered me one of the cookies from the box I had set on the desk, taking another for himself. "If the Slingshot *did* send them into a ghost zone, they might be dead."

He said it carefully, as if the thought of Quinn's death might disturb me. I almost said, *You clearly haven't spent much time around divorced people*, but didn't think he was in the mood for humor. Besides, I didn't belong to that group yet—the signed divorce papers still hadn't arrived. I was keeping my fingers crossed that tomorrow's mail would bring them, or Thursday's at the latest, unless Quinn had completely forgotten to mail them in the excitement of planning his jaunt into the past. I washed the cookies down with some of the weak coffee.

Dr. Holm's role in the whole thing still puzzled me. If she had gone willingly, there was no explanation for the disturbance in the lab or the text message she had sent me. If it hadn't been for those two things, I would have pegged the most likely scenario as being (a) Quinn charms Dr. Holm, (b) Dr. Holm agrees to take him into the past, jeopardizing her career, which might have been stalled anyway, and (c) they steal their way into STEWie's basket, with the goal of filming the carving of the runestone.

On the other hand, Quinn had tried to blackmail me, charmingly or not. Maybe there was a dark side to his personality that he'd kept hidden under all his charm, a side I hadn't picked up on before. I considered myself a good judge of people, but only fools assumed they were never wrong. And I liked to think that I wasn't a fool.

Realizing that Nate was watching me, I brought up another question. "So what do we know about Dr. Holm?"

"I've spent the morning on the phone with her colleagues, relatives, and neighbors." He stopped to take a sip of his coffee.

I was happy to hear that he wasn't taking her innocence for granted. "Did she pack a bag?"

He looked up from the cup. "What?"

"Oscar saw Quinn go into the TTE building with a backpack, right? What about Dr. Holm?"

He sat quietly sipping his coffee for a moment, as if weighing something. It dawned on me what that something was. He was questioning not only Dr. Holm's colleagues and relatives but also *Quinn's* colleagues and relatives, of which I was one. He was considering which category to place me into—person of interest, witness, or (I hoped) ally.

He leaned back in the chair, as if satisfied, and said, "Oscar remembers seeing Dr. Holm around the TTE building— apparently she's taken a couple of Dr. Mooney's STEWie orientation courses—but he wasn't sure if she came by the day of Kamal's defense." He quoted Oscar, and I could picture the doorman saying the words in his raspy voice: "'A lot of people came to Kamal Ahmad's defense because of the Neanderthal mating thing, and, this being a school, they all had backpacks.' She would not have stood out."

So Oscar was a dead end.

"Dr. Holm lives alone," Nate continued. "No roommate, and—as far as we could tell—she's not dating anyone at the moment. Her landlord let me in. Nothing seemed amiss at the apartment, but, to answer your question, we have no way of telling if one of her suitcases was missing, or any clothing beyond what she was wearing. We showed the picture of Quinn you gave us to the landlord and around the building. No one recognized him. Several people on campus remember seeing him in Dr. Holm's office on Friday, however."

"I sent him there. After he came to my office that morning."

This seemed to be news to him. "You did? Why?"

"Helen suggested that an expert might be able to explain to him why his plan was so unrealistic."

"It doesn't seem to have worked out that way."

"No."

"Suppose Quinn got into the TTE lab on a pretext, maybe asked Dr. Holm to give him a tour. I've been told she didn't have the door code to the lab?"

"She wasn't on the authorized list. In the workshops that she attended, the students would have gotten hands-on experience in the lab, but they certainly would not have been given the door code."

"I'll ask around to see if anybody gave the code to either of them. In any case, they got in somehow, and Quinn would have needed Dr. Holm to program the Woodstock coordinates. Willingly or unwillingly, she did, and then she got into the basket with him. What did he say to you exactly? On the phone when he called during Sabina's party?"

I tried to do my best to remember Quinn's words. "When he popped into my office out of the blue, he said that he had evidence of Sabina's secret and would reveal it to the world—plaster it all over the Internet, I believe were his exact words—unless I got him into the TTE lab. He, uh, also hinted that he'd hold off on signing the divorce papers if I didn't arrange the STEWie run for him, although he seems to have changed his mind about that. He didn't seem too bothered by my refusal and gave me until after the weekend to think about it. I sent him to talk to Dr. Holm."

"Then what?"

"Then *I* went to talk to Dr. Holm."

He glanced at me quickly. He hadn't been aware of that either. I hoped that all my disclosures wouldn't shift me out of the ally category.

"Mostly she and I talked about the stone and what it said," I explained. "She showed me a poster of the runestone in the Coffey Library. When Quinn called later that day, during Sabina's party, he said he had signed the divorce papers and put them in the mail. Also..."

"Go on."

"He implied that he had a date that night. He was meeting someone at Ingrid's over on Lakeshore."

"And you think that might have been Dr. Holm. We can check. I'll send Officer Van Underberg."

"I just got back from Ingrid's."

He frowned, and I felt myself slip further out of the ally category. "What did Ingrid say?"

"That it was Dr. Holm."

The whole thing had been somewhat embarrassing. When I showed up before the restaurant opened to ask questions about Quinn's date, kindly, motherly Ingrid had assumed I was jealous. After all, Quinn and I were still married, so it was only natural that I'd want to know about his love life. Swinging her ample hips from side to side, she had led me to a table away from the kitchen, then fetched us both slices of lingonberry pie. She didn't know Dr. Holm by name, but she recognized the photo I pulled up on the English Department website. According to Ingrid, the pair had stayed for two hours and had gone through as many bottles of wine. The leggings and Viking-themed shirt that Dr. Holm had worn to the library earlier in the day had been replaced with a black dress, low cut in the back. And dangly earrings, Ingrid had added, as if that made Dr. Holm even more of a home-wrecker. In order to keep up the fiction of being a jilted woman, I felt like I should pretend to be put off by the lingonberry pie. I ate my slice anyway.

As I told him about my sit down with Ingrid, Nate jotted a few sentences down on the pad in front of him. I wondered if he would send Officer Van Underberg to talk to Ingrid to double check what I had told him. He was a police officer, and it was his job not to take anything at face value, though I hoped he knew me better then that. There was the matter of his unfortunate experience with the pyromaniac, which had undoubtedly made him distrustful of people—especially people he had a personal interest in? Or was that side of it wholly my imagination? I pushed my coffee cup away and sat up straighter in the chair, suddenly feeling like I was at a job interview and not chatting with a friend in his office.

Officer Van Underberg stuck his head in the door. "Chief, I think you ought to see this."

Nate left the room and I slumped back down, taking the opportunity to pull out my cell phone to check my email and do a quick Internet search on Sabina's name, which I did every so often to see if any rumors about her past had started to seep out online. Sabina didn't have what we might call a last name, so she had appended Abigail's to hers—Sabina Secunda (after her father) Tanner.

There were no hits, and I heaved a sigh of relief.

As I was putting the cell phone away, Nate came in and slid into his seat across from me. "Did Quinn say anything about what he's been doing in Phoenix?"

"Only that he had a couple of rundown properties he was flipping so he could sell them for a profit."

"I've had Officer Van Underberg do a bit of research. Quinn obtained mortgage financing with no money down and bought three fixer-uppers. The work on all of them seems to have stalled because he stopped paying the contractors. Julia, he is deep in debt...which means he's even more desperate than we thought."

There wasn't much to say to that.

"You didn't find anything in his hotel room, did you?" I asked.

"Like what?"

"The signed divorce papers. I thought he might have left them there." If I wasn't feeling embarrassed and awkward before, I was now, but I had to know. I needed those papers. I was desperate for my connection to Quinn to be officially severed—especially now.

Nate wrote something down on his notepad and said, without looking up, "I'll check. You might want to talk to your lawyer. If you two are still married, you might be liable for Quinn's debts."

"Lovely."

"One more thing. His car. He flew into MSP—adding to the debt on his credit card—and rented a vehicle at the airport. The rental isn't in the parking lot at Lena's Lodge."

"Is it somewhere on campus?"

He shook his head. "No. We check all vehicles left overnight for campus parking stickers."

"Well, that's odd. I have no idea where it could be. I'd have expected it to be either in the campus visitor lot or at Quinn's hotel. What *did* you find in his room at Lena's Lodge?"

He paused long enough for me to wonder if he was thinking of going back to calling me Ms. Olsen since this was official business and I had connections to his prime suspect, then answered, "A suitcase, half-empty. Receipts for a large backpack, a flashlight, two sleeping bags, a water filter, freeze-dried meals, and other camping gear. And—a receipt for a hunting handgun." He said it evenly, without changing his expression.

"Oh. And Dr. Holm?"

"No similar purchases on her credit card statement. No one at the Emporium remembers seeing her. Quinn bought enough supplies for two. Julia, why are you so reluctant to see him in an unfavorable light?"

Was I? It just didn't seem characteristic of Quinn, who seemed much too lazy to concoct such an elaborate plan. I wasn't sure how to communicate that to Nate, though, so I tried another tack.

"About Dr. Holm—the text message of hers asking for help—"

"What about it?"

"It was all in capital letters. It's hard to believe that someone who was panicked would stop to hit the caps lock button, if her phone even has one. I know it's a very small thing—"

"It is."

"You know this is her third postdoc, right? I looked up her university employment record. Before coming here, she was at Berkeley for two years, and before that, she spent eighteen months at Groningen University in Netherlands. Maybe she got tired of postdoc limbo, of waiting for a STEWie spot and an offer of a professorship. Quinn's appearance may have been just the catalyst that she was waiting for."

"And the overturned table, the text message asking for help?"

"To throw us off her track and focus our suspicions on Quinn."

"So you think *he* is the one in danger."

I hadn't thought of it that way, not until Nate said it.

"Honestly, I have no idea what's going on," I admitted. "I just think we shouldn't take things at face value."

"I never do."

"Uh—good. In the meantime, Dean Braga's trying to think of the best way to spin this."

"It's a big problem. Two people, a civilian and a postdoc, missing somewhere in the past on her watch. I wouldn't want to be in her shoes. Let's hope the problem solves itself and Quinn and Dr. Holm return of their own accord before Friday." Nate checked his watch and got to his feet. "Ready? My grandmother said that we should come at one."

I gave the rest of the cookies to Officer Van Underberg on the way out.

# 15

A one-hour drive in Nate's Jeep, Wanda in the back seat, brought us to a craftsman-style house with a wide front porch. It was painted a warm blue, and it sat sandwiched between two houses bordering on MacMansionism on a bluff overlooking the Mississippi River just south of St. Paul. We parked on the street out front. Wanda raced up the steps as if she was a frequent visitor to the house and gave a short bark. The door opened before Nate and I had a chance to reach the front stoop.

I had expected Nate's grandmother, Mary Kirkland, to be a lot like him, that is to say, tall, lean, and a bit reserved in speech. She was none of those things. She was short and stocky in a denim dress, and, as I was about to find out, quite free with her opinions.

She rubbed Wanda's ears, gave Nate a bear hug, which he returned somewhat awkwardly, and then turned to me. "And this is...?"

"This is Julia. Remember, Kunshi, I explained on the phone—"

"Nothing wrong with my memory. You two are here to ask me about the runestone. C'mon in."

Wanda ran in ahead of us and we followed Mary down a hallway lined with photos of a life lived to the fullest. A husband who had passed away—Nate's grandfather, Duncan, who appeared to be the source of Nate's strong jaw and cheekbones. I counted seven children, three girls and four boys, some with their own progeny. There was a cute picture of what had to be Nate with a plastic spatula in one hand and a toddler-size chef's hat on his head, helping Mary attend to a pair of roasting turkeys at a family picnic. I wondered if the picnic where Mary and Duncan had first met had started an annual tradition in the family—there were many picnic photos. In the middle of them, there was one showing Mary Kirkland handling a library book during her career as a cataloger at the Minnesota Historical Society, her long black hair streaming down her back.

Suddenly my own accomplishments, few as they were, took on an even more meager hue. I had one failed marriage (almost) behind me; a bungalow that I had inherited from my parents when they moved to Florida; and I was probably on the hook for loans defaulted on by Quinn. On the plus side, I did like my job, which, I'd come to realize, was a rare thing—it brought me joy to see young faces come to St. Sunniva University eager and idealistic about doing science and then leave four-to-six years later with a PhD in their pocket, a little wiser and more seasoned. Still, I couldn't help wishing for something more; the STEWie bug had bitten me. I had caught the desire to feel the dust of other places and times under my fingernails and toes.

My eyes stopped at another photo on the wall. "Hey," I said. "Julia?"

"That's my Mom! How funny. I don't know who's with her, though." My mother Missy, looking unbelievably young, was smiling at the camera next to another woman of about the same age; both were carrying an armful of textbooks and had large hairdos.

Nate came back into the hallway and Mary turned on the lamp on a corner table so that we could all see better.

"That's my daughter-in-law Gigi. Nate's mother," Mary explained of the woman in the photo next to my mother.

"It's a small world," I said. "They must have been friends at school. I didn't know your mother attended St. Sunniva."

"It was one of the reasons I applied for the campus security job at the school."

"They were at the school in the seventies, just after it turned co-ed. It must have been an interesting time. I'll have to ask my mother about it when she and Dad get back." I thought it would be rude to say that my mother had never mentioned her friend Gigi from college. I would have remembered the name. But parents, I had come to understand in my job, rarely seemed to tell their kids much about their own college and graduate school experiences, other than how hard they studied for all their classes and how few parties they attended, busy as they were studying.

"You should ask Gigi about it," Mary said to Nate as we followed her into the kitchen.

"I will. Julia, you said your parents now live in Florida?"

"They're in charge of a retirement community in Fort Myers. They're all gone, though."

"I'm sorry?" Nate said.

"My parents, with their retirees. They went on a Caribbean cruise. It's one of *those* cruises," I added.

"Which?" Nate said with a nervous glance at his grandmother, like I was about to reveal that my parents were swingers or something. I suspected that not much would shock Mary Kirkland. Her hair, the black now streaked with gray, was tied back into a neat bun that framed a face weathered by life and crisscrossed with deep lines, more of them carved by laughter than sorrow.

"The cruise? It's one where no tech gadgets are allowed," I explained. "A complete, blissful disconnect from the hectic pace of modern life. I'm quoting the brochure there. No cell phones, no laptops, no emails, no text messages. Ship-to-shore communication only for emergencies, should one of the cruise guests come down with severe seasickness or worse. Apparently all the retirees happily signed on to the idea of no electronics. My parents said they might mail me a postcard when they went ashore to sightsee. I haven't received one yet."

I had never been on a cruise, electronic gadgets or not, but I figured that I'd get bored after twenty minutes of lying in a leisure chair on the ship deck, even with the onboard pool and shuffleboard and whatever else cruisers did to keep themselves entertained. The sightseeing, on the other hand, I would have enjoyed quite a bit.

"Sounds lovely," Mary said from the fridge, where Wanda was waiting, her tongue hanging out in an unseemly manner.

"I've heard the cuisine on these cruises is good," Nate said in the voice of one who would be uncomfortable in anything larger than a canoe, unless he was in charge of it.

Mary had taken eggs and a container with some kind of chunky white cheese out of the fridge. She scooped half of the cheese out, let Wanda have the rest, and headed for the stove. "Speaking of food, how about I make you kids something to eat?"

∞

Mary sat us down at the large kitchen island that doubled as an informal eating area. Behind her, a grand cooking range held the spot of honor. Copper pots and pans hung suspended above the range, well-thumbed cookbooks lined a nearby shelf, and a rack with spices hung to one side of it. She was clearly a much more seasoned cook than I was.

Mary expertly cracked four eggs, added a dollop of creamy milk, and whipped up the combination while the pan heated up. I tried to reconcile her forthright manner with what Nate had told me about her life. She had been born in the Lower Sioux Community, on the banks of the Minnesota River, and then sent away to Pipestone Indian school at age six, where she had acquired her Americanized first name. (Her parents named her Yellow Bird.) Some of her friends had gone back to their Dakota names later in life, but Mary hadn't. As I was starting to realize, she was a woman who did not do what was expected of her. I liked her very much.

According to Nate, her life philosophy was *You don't hide your scars.*

Mary set some polenta slices onto a griddle to brown and asked Nate to make a salad. She poured the eggs into the pan, and, as the omelet sizzled, crumbled in the white cheese and added prosciutto and some parsley. She folded the omelet after a minute or two and turned it, not with the spatula, but by flipping it into the air. If I had tried a move like that, the omelet would have stuck in the pan, or, more likely, the ceiling. Maybe all it took was a firm hand and an equally firm belief that the omelet would obey the chef.

Accompanied by the polenta and the salad Nate had put together, the omelet was delicious. You would have thought that I'd be full after the lingonberry pie at Ingrid's and the macadamia cookies in Nate's office, but I was still making up for the seven hours we had been stuck without food or water in 1898. Next to me Nate, too, was digging into the food.

"What is this?" I asked, licking the softened white cheese off my fork. The taste was vaguely familiar.

"Feta cheese," Mary explained. "I've been on a Mediterranean kick this month for my cooking blog."

I had come across feta before in finger foods I'd organized for school events, in spinach and cheese pastries, but never in its natural state. "You have a cooking blog?" I asked between bites.

"Just something to keep me busy in my retirement."

I wondered if it would be rude to invite myself over to Mary Kirkland's house more often. It was obvious where Nate had gotten his gourmet palate.

Mary watched us bolt down the food and added a second helping to our plates. "Don't they feed you at St. Sunniva? Don't mind me, I'm not hungry," she added and set a coffeemaker brewing, then pulled up a chair. "You wanted to know about the stone."

I swallowed a forkful of omelet and launched into the story of what had happened, holding nothing back. I had not planned to mention Sabina but somehow it all came tumbling out—Pompeii, Sabina, Quinn and Officer Jones, Quinn's debts, seeing the stone disinterred, everything. Mary Kirkland listened, nodding occasionally. After I finished, she got up to attend to the coffee. She filled three mugs, pushed one in my direction, along with the milk and sugar, and said, "I'd like to meet this Sabina. She sounds like quite a young lady."

I glanced at Nate. "We could bring her by sometime, couldn't we? She hasn't seen the Twin Cities yet, so we could make it a day of sightseeing." I didn't mean the traditional kind, where you might take a guest from out of town to see the caribou at the Minnesota Zoo or to shop at the Mall of America, but the kind where you wandered around on foot, just *looking*. I paused for another bite, then went on, "Mary, we were wondering if you had any insights about the runestone, either from your years at the Historical Society or from oral histories in your family."

"About white explorers who might have made it to Dakota land in the middle of the fourteenth century?" She gave a deep sigh. "You'll have to remind me of some of the details. You say they came on ships from Vinland?"

"Twenty two Norwegians and eight Gotlanders, the stone said. Ten stayed with the ships 'by the sea' and ten died."

"How did they die—does the stone say?"

I scooped up the last of the omelet while I thought about how to delicately describe the most likely scenario. Nate shrugged. "A run-in with the Dakota or another local tribe, probably. One that didn't end well."

I remembered that I had read about another possibility. "Plague carried on the Norsemen's own clothing or effects might have flared up. But I'm not sure it could have killed ten in a single day, unless the group that had been left behind was already ill."

Mary sighed and set her coffee mug down. "I haven't heard anything about the plague, but smallpox killed its fair share."

We waited for her to go on.

"If I had your time machine, I wouldn't look for a small party of explorers. I'd sweep down the land, from the ice-gripped Arctic lands all the way south to Cape Horn where the Pacific and the Atlantic meet. And I would count..."

Nate looked uncomfortable.

"I would count the dead," Mary said. "When the Europeans came to the Americas, starting with Columbus, they unknowingly brought the virus with them. It swept through the land in lethal waves, like they had set a slow, unstoppable brushfire to clear their route for them. It spread from person to person, village to village, and community to community. Estimates vary—you'd be hard-pressed to find two historians who agree on the matter—but it's possible that in the first hundred years of contact smallpox and other diseases killed every other person in the Americas, perhaps as much as ninety percent of the population. No one really knows the true number. Those are just guesses in the dark."

I had put my fork down long ago. The plague—the Black Death—came up on occasion as a topic of discussion during planning meetings for STEWie runs to medieval Europe and Asia, and I knew that in that case the culprit was the *Y. Pestis* bacterium, carried by rat fleas. Our researchers were protected against it by a vaccine, and they also received vaccines for smallpox and other defeated diseases. But even the outbreaks of the Black Death had not been as deadly as what Mary was talking about. "What made it so bad?" I asked.

"The continent was a blank canvas for the disease. No one had any immunity to it, no genetic resistance...In the Old World, dense populations had lived in close contact with each other and livestock for centuries, experiencing waves of epidemics: smallpox, measles, the flu, tuberculosis...When de Soto's ships came ashore in Florida in 1539, they carried a herd of pigs onboard, one of which may have been infected—Julia, is something wrong with the coffee?"

The coffee was delicious. That wasn't it. I felt a shiver pass through me. "I don't even like the thought of it. It makes me glad I'm up to date on all my vaccines."

Perhaps Mary sensed that there was more to it than that. She topped off my coffee and said, "Land claims aside, we are all immigrants, you know, all of us. The world is a fluid place and Nate is living proof of that. You should bring Julia to one of our family picnics, Nate dear." She smiled at him, then continued, "Why, my neighbors down the street are from Somalia. That's the largest immigrant group to Minnesota these days, with Ethiopians being the second—did you know that? Nate's grandfather Duncan came over as a child from Scotland back in 1935. At the turn of the century, Scandinavians and Germans were the largest immigrant groups."

"My great-grandparents came on a ship from Norway," I said.

"Here's a statistic to keep in mind about the nineteenth century, about your great-grandparents, about the farmer who found the stone. In 1850, Minnesota had about six thousand souls, at least according to the census. By the turn of the century—just fifty years later—the number was 1.75 million. There wasn't a gold rush or anything to make that happen—far from it. The newcomers wanted a better life and were willing to work hard for it."

"Still," I said. "They displaced people who were already here."

"Yes. For some of us…well, our roots go all the way down to the bedrock. Thousands of years ago, my own ancestors crossed a land bridge that formed when water froze into ice sheets and the ocean levels fell. Fifty miles as the crow flies separates Asia from Alaska. Put that way it doesn't sound like a very long distance, does it? My point is this—" She leaned forward and patted my hand. "We all of us—stand on the shoulders of our parents, and they on the shoulders of theirs, and so on."

I caught myself wondering if we at St. Sunniva University had been guilty of bias in our explorations of history. Early on, it had been decided that STEWie could never be used to settle the "big" questions anyway, such as which people had a more valid claim to a certain territory, or which side had fired the first shot that started the battle that started the war. There was no way to correct historical wrongs. Still, I felt embarrassed that I had come to ask Mary about a stone that had been carved by newcomers (whether it had happened in the nineteenth or fourteenth century), when her own ancestors had made a life on this land for thousands of years.

We were entering our third year of STEWie runs, and most of the slots had been devoted to researching the figures that anchored history books, which was how it went with funding priorities and public interest. STEWie had been the brainchild of the science departments, so a significant number of runs had been devoted to those on whose shoulders the current crop of scientists stood, legends like Marie Curie. Clandestine visits to her lab and home—starting in the 1890s, the decade when farmer Olof Ohman had found his stone—required radiation suits. The radiation on her papers and personal things still lingered into the present. It was all circular, in a way. We already knew more about Europe's past than that of the Americas, so it was easier for our researchers to prepare for runs to the Old World and obey time travel's third rule, *Blend in*. Places and peoples that had been lost to time and textbooks were a lot harder to tackle.

I took a sip of Mary's rich, aromatic coffee; the one that Nate had given me in his office was just a pale, distant cousin to it. I had been worried that Mary might not welcome the idea of people sneaking a look at her ancestors, that it was disrespectful on some level. But it sounded like she felt just the opposite about it, that it might be good to know more.

Mary stood up to take our dishes to the sink.

"You should drop by and talk to Dr. Payne sometime," I said, rising to my feet to help her. "He's a bit—well, grumpy—but I think you might agree on a lot of things."

When Nate took Wanda outside into the yard to let her stretch her legs, Mary refilled my coffee cup. "Are you two kids dating?" she asked abruptly.

"I beg your pardon?"

"Nate didn't explain one way or the other over the phone, but I've known him all his life. Sometimes his silences speak volumes."

"We're just colleagues," I evaded, "collaborating on this incident at the school. As the science dean's assistant, I help out when a problem arises in one of our eight science departments. And my ex taking STEWie on a joyride, well, it's definitely a problem."

"Spouses will do that. Embarrassing things, I mean."

"Usually not *this* embarrassing."

"Duncan and I were married for fifty-four years. A lot can happen over that much time, most of it good, once in a while bad, sometimes just strange. Nate has always been a bit hard to read," she added in somewhat of a non sequitur. "Did he tell you about what happened at Boundary Waters and why he left?"

I nodded.

"He hasn't gotten over it yet. I think it's made his already cautious nature even more cautious. Well, you're young, both of you. I will tell you one thing: At your age, I wouldn't have let a little thing like an estranged husband on the lam stop me. Life's an adventure. Do you and Quinn have any children?"

I shook my head. "I'm not the motherly type. I can't even keep a potted cactus alive. And Quinn—well, he's not a home-body either."

"Not everyone is cut out for it, I suppose."

"Thanks for not saying the opposite."

"Which?"

"That once I hold my own offspring in my arms I'll suddenly discover some hidden, primal Julia who knows exactly what to do about poopy diapers and runny noses. I wouldn't. I'm much better with them once they're young adults. I feel like the students in the science departments are all mine to take care of, in a way."

"And Nate keeps peace and order on campus. Yes, I see."

Wondering what it was she saw, I leaned forward on my elbows, the coffee cup between them. All I could see was that my life was in a bit of a muddle. I wondered if she—and Nate—thought that I still had feelings for Quinn. It wasn't black and white. Very few things in life were. I certainly didn't love Quinn anymore, but I didn't hate him either...and I didn't want to. Hate was a feeling that weighed you down, making it harder to walk through life. It was like being time-stuck in History.

When Nate came back inside, he asked his grandmother the question that had brought us here. "Kunshi, the rune-stone...Real or not?"

Smiling at him, she considered the question. "The Minnesota Historical Society did offer an opinion, a favorable one, back in 1910, you know. As for me—I think I'd prefer to give the man who found it the benefit of the doubt."

"Olof Ohman," I supplied.

"Olof Ohman, that's right. I figure it's like being on a jury. We have to assume Olof was innocent until he's proven guilty."

"That's not how it is in academia," I said, conscious of sounding like Dr. Payne. "The burden of proof is on the presenter of new evidence, especially if the claim is an extraordinary one."

"I know. That's why I never went for a higher degree. Too confining, I felt. As for the stone—there is an account in Dakota history. I may not be the best person to tell it, but I know a couple of people who are...If you need someone knowledgeable to come along with you to the fourteenth century, they fit the bill. They know a lot about a lot of things. You'll like Ron. And Ruth-Ann, well, she's a younger version of me. Make sure to ask her about the Good Earth Woman's story."

I already had my yellow pad out. "The Good Earth Woman...Ron and Ruth-Ann, you said?"

"Ron and Ruth-Ann Tuttle. They can be a bit hard to reach, but let me get you their number."

# 16

The names of the wife and husband pair who had been recommended by Nate's grandmother sounded familiar—I remembered
leafing through their book in the library. Ruth-Ann and Ron
Tuttle were amateur historians and archeologists. Their book had
been sandwiched between a thick tome whose flowery academic
prose I couldn't tolerate for more than a few pages and another
that I also put back immediately, though for different reasons. (It
claimed to offer proof that aliens built the pyramids of Egypt and
Mesoamerica. This was a theory that showed up often in emails
and letters sent to the dean's office; any evidence to the contrary
brought back from STEWie runs in the form of photos or footage
was deemed fake.) The Tuttles' privately published book occupied
the sweet spot between academic tome and conspiracy fluff in its
content as well. I had found it very readable. They seemed to be
the all-around experts in everything runestone-related.

Once I got back to my office, I called the number Mary
had given me but the line had been disconnected. Mary had
also mentioned a website, so I looked there and sent an email
to the address listed, hoping that wherever they were they had
access to a computer. I lingered on the website after sending off
the email. It seemed to have a bit of everything—there were
pages devoted to Native American petroglyphs as well as a

section on the Kensington runestone and other finds of possible Norse origin. Like their book, *Runestone: Rock Solid,* the website had maps of potential Norse routes inland and copies of documents, including the letter written in Olof Ohman's own hand. One thing had me scratching my head. Neither the book nor the website gave the authors' opinions of the stone's provenance. The "Rock Solid" part of the title appeared to refer to the natural hardness of graywacke, not the preponderance of evidence in favor of the runestone's legitimacy. I wondered what the Tuttles would make of the footage we had taken of the farmer unearthing the stone.

I hoped they'd get back to me before Friday's run.

In the meantime, I went to talk to Dr. Payne. I found him in the courtyard of the History building. He was sitting on a bench with his back to the lake, grading papers on one knee and enjoying a cigarette.

"Sorry to interrupt you, Dr. Payne. I came to ask—thanks." He had made room for me on the bench. "I came to ask if you wanted to come along with us to 1362."

I hoped he would say no. The thought of spending a few days essentially camping with the chain-smoking professor did not appeal to me. Still, I felt that the dean's office had to extend the invitation since the Americas were his playground, research-wise, even though he had voted against the run.

The idea of bringing him along hadn't appealed to Nate either. When we discussed it on the drive back from his grandmother's house, he had said, "I'm not sure he's physically fit enough. We don't know how much walking we'll have to do. There'll be backpacks to carry. And if it takes a while or we get time-stuck, we might have to hunt for food—"

"You're kidding, right?"

"Buffalo, elk, deer, beaver, otter, whatever we can find."

"Ugh. Aren't you a parks person? Can't we just fish? I think I can handle fish."

"Nothing wrong with hunting if you follow the park rules. But no, I wasn't serious. We'll bring along freeze-dried meals and energy bars. Though if we really wanted to blend into the era, we would have to do just that—hunt and fish and pick berries and so on."

"Well, then I'm happy that we have no hope of blending in. I don't mind roughing it, but I draw a line at shooting animals."

"But fish would be okay?"

"Yes. They're cold and slippery."

∞

Dr. Payne puffed on his cigarette and answered my question about whether he wanted to come along with a single syllable. "No."

"Why not?" I felt compelled to ask. "You don't think we have a hope of finding them?"

"It's not that. I've already wasted enough time on this, time I should be spending on my own work. Yes, I know that a week in the fourteenth century would amount to only an afternoon here, but it's a week in *my* lifetime, and I don't feel like I have that many left." He took a deep drag off the cigarette with no apparent sense of irony. "Besides, why do you need me to come along?"

"The Americas—"

"Are two big continents whose history spans thousands of years. You need an expert whose interests are specific to that time period and area. Someone who is, shall we say...as *obsessed* with the runestone as your Mr. Olsen."

"I have contacted someone, as a matter of fact."

"Well, there you go. And I suppose what you bring to the table is your expertise on Quinn."

I decided not to take offense.

He went on, "Who's paying for all the runs we did to 1898 and this final one? And whose roster spot are you going to take?"

"Chancellor Evans assured Dean Braga that the school will cover expenses, within reason. One of our postdocs is missing, after all."

He didn't deem that worthy of comment.

"Dr. Payne? Do you think we should get the Black Death vaccine before we go?"

"You're unlikely to catch anything from fourteenth-century Native Americans, and certainly not the bubonic plague."

The converse—us passing on a European disease—was impossible because of History's constraints. Neither were what I was worried about. "There's a theory that the Black Death carried on their own clothing or effects killed the ten Norsemen."

"Ah. *That* theory. Well, I would ask Dr. May about it, but I believe that the vaccine is a multi-dose one, administered during the course of a few weeks. I suppose you could get the first dose. In any case, antibiotics will come to the rescue if you come back covered in boils."

I couldn't tell if he was serious or if he was making fun of the Black Death theory. I got to my feet. "The fourteenth century— any advice, professor?"

I meant in terms of bringing items like bug spray or night vision goggles, but he stabbed out the cigarette on the bench and said, "Bring me back photos. Of everything you see."

∞

The phone rang on Wednesday afternoon while I was dealing with a stack of conference travel receipts. "Science Dean's offices, Julia Olsen speaking, how can I help you?"

A hearty female voice said, "You're the person I'm looking for. That is, if you're the one who sent a message to the authors of *Runestone: Rock Solid?*"

I admitted as much.

"That'd be me and Ron. Did you enjoy the book?"

I admitted that I had, and she asked, "Did you want Ron and me to come in and sign some copies? We also do workshops where we teach the lost art of runic carving. It's best for ages ten and up, what with the possibility of injury from the chisel—"

"It's nothing like that," I interrupted her, deciding to return her forthrightness by being forthright myself. "Care to come along to the fourteenth century?"

"I'm sorry, where did you say you worked?"

"St. Sunniva University. I'm the assistant to the science dean. There's an ongoing matter in the Time Travel Engineering department on which we could use your help and expertise."

She gave a throaty peal of delight. "The Time Machine is real? Ron will be pleased. We thought it was, but you never can tell with the media. All those photos of British coronations and footage of Elvis concerts, it was hard to tell if the whole thing was just a big hoax."

I cringed. The footage that made it into the news wasn't exactly representative of what we were trying to accomplish with STEWie.

"It's real enough. If you do decide to come with us...well, I should let you know that there's probably an element of danger involved."

She didn't miss a beat. "Well, it is time travel. I wouldn't expect it to be a walk in the park."

"It's not just the time travel part of it—we have a situation on our hands. How soon can you be here? It would be more prudent to discuss the details in person."

"Would the morning suit you? That will give us time to finish up here and drive up."

Then she asked me a long list questions. All were insightful, and some raised important issues that I hadn't thought of myself. I hung up the phone thinking that our amateur enthusiasts might turn out to be more helpful than I had anticipated.

∞

I watched as a white recreational vehicle twice the length of a car and with an overhang above the cab pulled into the campus parking lot. The RV body was plastered with informational ads regarding the Tuttles' books and workshops. I had come out to meet them since first-time visitors tended to find the campus's circular layout confusing. Two chunky, smiling figures descended the three steps of the RV into the crisp mid-September morning and greeted me. They had left before sunrise to take the two-hour drive north to St. Sunniva University.

Ruth-Ann gave me a bear hug—she smelled of lavender shampoo and freshly baked pastries—and said, "Thanks for inviting us, hon. The campus looks lovely. Want a tour of our abode? C'mon in."

As we all filed back into the RV, she explained that she and her husband took turns driving and that the kitchen/living area expanded at the touch of a button. She proceeded to demonstrate. The RV was now their home, she said. "We sold the business and the house and bought the bus so that we could drive to sites and stay as long as we like." They earned money from selling books, teaching workshops, and accepting donations from historically minded citizens, she said, adding that I had reached them at the Jeffers Petroglyphs site, where they had spent the past month researching a new book about pre-Contact Native American petroglyphs.

"We like painted and carved rocks," Ron said from behind me, the first sentence I'd heard him speak other than *Hello*. Ron's light-brown beard was braided into three sections, giving him somewhat of a Viking look. It had colorful beads woven into it. He was wearing a lime-green T-shirt, worn jeans, and hiking boots.

"Want an orange juice and something to eat, hon? I just pulled some muffins out of the oven." Ruth-Ann lifted the foil off a plate. Blueberry. She reached for a napkin and placed a muffin on it for me. She, too, was wearing jeans, hiking boots, and a T-shirt. Hers was a pale pink.

We ate the muffins standing, since the table seemed to serve as more of an office than an eating area; the reference books, petroglyph sketches, and photos that covered it had spread to the couch, the main seating option. A half-finished sketch of a turtle from the Jeffers site caught my eye. Ruth-Ann explained that Ron was the one with the artistic talent and that before turning their hand to amateur archeology they had run an interior decorating business—she had done the books, he the decorating—which explained the pleasing hues of the interior of the RV, reds and blues that complimented the steel frame of the vehicle.

I returned Ruth-Ann and Ron's hospitality by giving them a tour of STEWie's lab. Dr. Mooney was there, at the workbench in one corner, painstakingly building his Slingshot 3.0 from scratch. "I'm close, Julia. Just waiting on some custom-made parts on a rush order. They promised delivery by the end of the day." He wiped his hands on his apron and shook Ruth-Ann and Ron's hands enthusiastically. "You're going with Julia and the others tomorrow?"

He set his tools aside to show the Tuttles around the lab. Ruth-Ann was very taken with all the photographs of people and places of the past that covered the walls. Ron, for his part, kept looking up at the largest mirror as if impressed by its size. Most visitors were.

"Ah, that was the problematic one," Dr. Mooney explained fondly. "We discovered a kink in its shape just after it was mounted in the lab. We had to take it down, fix it, and remount it."

"I'm not sure what we can pay you," I said as we finished the circuit of the lab and returned to Dr. Mooney's workbench. "I'll have to check with Dean Braga to see if she'll approve a consulting fee. Any photographs you take will be yours to do with as you wish, of course."

"Anything you can spare, hon. The bus could use an update to its plumbing system. Where are we going exactly?"

I met the professor's eyes over their head. "That's something we'll need your professional opinion on. Let me show you the footage."

Ron and Ruth-Ann pulled up chairs and I brought out my laptop. For the next few minutes Dr. Mooney and I had the pleasure of watching the wonder on their faces as they watched the video Dr. Payne had taken on Runestone Hill. It made me forget about Quinn for a moment, at least until we got to the end of the tape and I had to explain what had prompted our run into 1898.

"It's the fourteenth century that we need to focus on now, because that's where they would have gone next. Sorry, let me just check this." I had noticed that there was a voice message on my cell, which I had turned off during the tour. It was from Nate. He never called my cell unless it was urgent.

While Dr. Mooney took the opportunity to explain to the Tuttles about the new Slingshot, I stepped aside and listened to the message. I returned the phone to my shoulder bag and turned to hear the professor say, "—and that approach seems to have succeeded in keeping the stability problem under control. Like I said, if the last of the parts arrive as promised, you'll be able to take Slingshot 3.0 with you in case you need to adjust your position in spacetime. Now, Julia, you were saying that we need Ruth-Ann's and Ron's opinion on when and where to aim our fourteenth century jump…"

I didn't answer. I had a bigger problem on my hands. Sabina was missing. She had not shown up for her afternoon classes.

# 17

"Sabina, you can't just decide to leave school in the middle of the day."

"*So-ree.*"

"I'm just glad Officer Van Underberg found you. Don't forget to apologize to Abigail when she gets here. And to Nate the next time you see him. We were all worried sick."

Abigail, who had been out looking for Sabina on her bike, wasn't back yet. Nate and Officer Van Underberg had taken separate cars to increase their odds of finding her. The officer had finally spotted Sabina on Eagle Creek Road, walking in the direction of the highway, Celer trudging along behind her. All the good-natured officer could get out of her was that she had not gone back to class after lunch. Instead, she had marched out of the high school building and gone home to fetch Celer. The officer had dropped off the pair at the house before heading back to the campus security office.

"Did someone say something at lunch?" I asked, pacing around the kitchen table. Sabina sat at one end of it looking like a stereotypical sullen teenager. Celer had lapped up some water and then headed into the living room to settle in behind the TV for what he no doubt considered a well-earned nap.

"No thing." She pronounced it as two words.

"Did they bully you or call you a name?"

"No."

"It's not because of tomorrow's dentist appointment, is it?"

She didn't even deem that worthy of a reply. I tried another tack. "Where were you headed?"

"No where."

"You must have had some place in mind."

"To big road, then big water—*At-lan-tic*—then boat. Boat to home."

Her words came out haltingly and I felt a lump in my throat.

When she had asked where Pompeii was in regards to St. Sunniva's, we had drawn a map for her. She wasn't too enthusiastic about the prospect of flying, so she had decided that she would one day cross the Atlantic by boat. Of course, there was no real home for Sabina to return to, not really.

"Sabina, there you are!"

Abigail had burst into the house. She rushed over to give Sabina a hug. "I'm glad you're okay, I was *so* worried. Now, what happened? Tell you what—let's make some hot chocolate and you can tell me all about it."

I left the kitchen to give them some space and sat down at the dining room table with my laptop—I had to get back to campus but didn't want to leave until I was sure Sabina was all right. Thinking that Abigail might need to explain just how far the Atlantic Ocean was from Minnesota, and also about passports and things, I gave my attention to catching up on the day's emails and tried to look as if I wasn't listening to what was being said in the kitchen. Unfortunately for me, the two switched to Latin at once, probably because it was easier for Abigail to coax the story out of Sabina that way.

My fingers, of their own accord, took me from my work inbox to a website stocked with Pompeii photos, where I had gone a few times just to look. I scrolled through them now with a different eye. If Sabina had managed to make it there, she would have found the stone streets and houses eerily empty, bereft of life and laughter, except for the tourist kind. Sabina's father's garum store was not in any of the photos. It lay in the still-unexcavated part of town, undisturbed.

I thought at one point that I overheard my name being said in the kitchen, and also the word STEWie (which Sabina pronounced with a long vowel, *STOO-eee*, like she was calling a pig).

As I continued to scroll through the Pompeii website, an idea popped into my mind. Who was to say that Sabina couldn't go back for a visit when she was a bit older? Not on an ocean liner to the tourist Pompeii, but via STEWie into the proud merchant town of the past. She could never return to Pompeii of her childhood because she was already there in that time period—History wouldn't allow it—but perhaps a few years before she was born, say 50 or 60 AD, just to take a look around for a bit?

We had come a long way since STEWie's mirrors had first inched into place to send Drs. Mooney and Rojas to 1903 to watch Wilbur and Orville Wright make aviation history near the town of Kitty Hawk. I hoped that once the technology improved and time travel was cheap and safe, it would be opened up to tourists. I would be first in line, and I had a feeling that Sabina would be by my side.

I heard Abigail say something at the kitchen table, where the pair had been sipping on hot chocolate. She repeated it in English. "You can tell Julia, it's all right."

I gave up the pretense of working and went back into the kitchen to hear Sabina's story. She had put two and two together about what was going on in the TTE lab and had jumped to the conclusion that I was going to be fired from the dean's office because I hadn't reported Quinn's plan to steal STEWie. And that it all had something to do with her. She had decided that the best thing for everybody would be if she left.

"Nonsense," I said firmly. "No one is going to get fired. The only one in trouble is Quinn."

"You protect me?"

"I was protecting all of us, and that wasn't how it went down anyway." I drew up a chair, giving myself a mental kick for keeping Sabina in the dark for so long. Abigail had been right. Determined not to keep anything else from the girl, I launched into the whole story—how Quinn and I first met, his sudden move to Arizona, why he was back. Sabina interrupted me once to clarify a word—"*EEE*-lope, what this?"—but said nothing else as I recounted Quinn's threat to expose her. "But I didn't know he would hijack Dr. Baumgartner's STEWie run or take Dr. Holm along," I hurried to explain.

When I came to the end of my story, Sabina stayed silent. She shook the whipped cream container, which had been emptied to top the hot chocolates, and got up to drop it into the trash with obvious reluctance—she hated wasting things that might be reused. She wiped her hands and turned back to Abigail and me. "Secrets—no good. We tell people, yes?"

She was right, of course—secrets were no good. And Mary Kirkland was right, too, in her life philosophy—you don't hide your scars. It was just that I—all of us—wanted Sabina to be at ease with the ordinary things in modern life, like tossing out empty whipped cream containers, before we threw her to the wolves. And Quinn was damned well not going to decide on the timing for us.

I glanced at Abigail. "Let's tell everyone once this dies down, or better yet, at the end of the school year," I suggested. "Anyone want a slice of the apple pie? I think we still have some left."

The pie we had made with the Zestars the girls had picked at the orchard had turned out pretty well. There was a quarter of it left.

"That's probably enough sweets for Sabina for now," Abigail said. "We don't want her ruining her dinner, Julia. She'll need a good meal after all that exercise she got walking around town."

Was there a note of testiness in Abigail's usually cheerful voice? She was Sabina's legal guardian, of course. I was just Aunt Julia, which was how it should be. I hoped she didn't resent me making the occasional suggestion. "Sounds like you have things under control. I'll take a slice back to the office with me."

On my way out, I heard her say, "Sabina, do you have any homework for tomorrow? Math? Here, you work on that and I'll get some research done, and we can make something for dinner after that. I bet Celer is hungry, too…Celer? Where are you? He's somewhere napping, isn't he?"

∞

"According to the directions on the stone, we'll find the Norse camp a day's journey to the north from Runestone Hill. Seems simple enough," Nate said. It was late and we had all gathered in the TTE lab. Dr. Mooney was at his workbench, and the occasional whirr of a drill or clink of a hammer interrupted the discussion.

"The Norse camp will be near two landmarks," Ron said.

Nate turned to him. "Yes, I wanted to ask about that. What are they?"

"Unfortunately, no one knows. If the rune word in question is read as *skjar*, it might refer to a pair of skerries—small rocky reefs or islands—in which case we should look for the camp on a body of water like a lake or a river."

Nate frowned. "But the stone says that ten men stayed behind at the camp while the others went fishing. It doesn't sound like the camp itself was on a body of water."

"Could be that they happened to pick an unusually poor fishing ground. Or the word might stand for two natural shelters of some kind...or something else altogether."

Nate had pulled out a modern map of our area and spread it open on the empty workstation whose monitor had been knocked to the ground the afternoon Quinn and Dr. Holm had left. "A camp a day's journey from Runestone Hill...On foot or by boat? Let's say that it was a combination of the two—rowing and portage."

I had never done one, but I knew a portage was when you carried your boat and gear from one lake to another. The term went back to early French fur traders, also known as Voyageurs.

"We need to estimate the distance they would have been able to cover in a single day. This sea where the Norsemen left their ships is a fourteen-day journey from the stone according to the directions on it—"

"Surely they would not have meant the Atlantic Ocean," Ron interrupted Nate. "It had to be a closer body of water. If their route brought them from the east, up the St. Lawrence River and into the Great Lakes, the sea would probably be Lake Superior. If they came from the north and sailed into Hudson Bay, that would be the sea they refer to. From there they would have followed the Nelson River or the Hayes River to Red River and into Minnesota. Neither route would have been easy or straightforward—imagine having to portage Niagara Falls!— but the Norsemen had plenty of experience. Their eastern trade route followed riverways all the way to Constantinople and reached as far east as Baghdad.

"The third possibility," he added, "is that they came from the south, from the Gulf of Mexico and up the Mississippi, but no one takes that suggestion seriously. Which leaves the eastern and the northern options. We can talk more about it later—"

"Pick one," Nate said.

"The eastern route, to Duluth. It's the one early French explorers took."

"Hmm. Well, Duluth to St. Sunniva University is a drive I've done a few times now."

Named after the French explorer Daniel Greysolon, Le Sieur du Luth, the seaport town on the western tip of Lake Superior was Nate's birthplace and his parents lived there. "It's two hundred and twenty miles by car odometer, so about as many to Runestone Hill, then. If we divide that distance by the fourteen days it took them, it means they covered, what, fifteen, sixteen miles a day? We can use that as our measuring stick." He took a pencil compass from the lab catch-all bin and widened it to fifteen miles according to the legend on the map. Then he stabbed the point end of it on Runestone Hill and drew a short arc to the north before adding two lines radiating to it from the hill. "There. Fifteen miles from Runestone Hill takes us past Highway 94 on a line to Evansville and the Balgaard Wildlife Management Area. We should look for the camp in this triangle to the north."

"Where do we want to land? Should we aim for the teardrop-shaped pond again?" Dr. B asked from the other workstation, where she was readying our coordinates. As with the last time we'd used STEWie, we were skipping the typical check for ghost zones.

Nate shook his head. "We've already gotten our feet wet enough this week. Plan for sending us to the top of Runestone Hill. I think we can assume that at least will be dry."

"What month?" Dr. B asked next.

This was a bit of a thorny point. We knew that seasons would not be that different in the fourteenth century: winters—white and frigid, with the occasional blizzard; spring—crisp, wondrous, and brief as the land burst back to life; summers—green and humid, with the occasional thunderstorm; and autumn, a kaleidoscope of color. If we arrived on Runestone Hill early in the spring, it was possible that we would encounter lingering snow. If we waited until the summer, there was a risk we could miss the stone carvers—and therefore Quinn and Dr. Holm—entirely.

Ron considered the matter. "The Norsemen waited out the winter in Vinland, then readied their boats after the spring melt-off. Factor in a couple of weeks for river travel, then another two on foot or canoe to the Kensington area... It's not likely that they would have gotten here before the end of May. Probably not until well into the summer."

Nate had furrowed his brow. "I'd rather be too early than too late."

"For the stone carvers?" I asked.

"For Dr. Holm. Quinn is looking for the stone carvers. We're looking for them. Let's make it mid-May, Dr. Baumgartner... And a full moon would be helpful."

"How long are we giving it?" I asked.

Nate turned to me. "Giving what?"

"Ourselves to find them. I want to know how much snack food to bring along."

He rubbed his eyes as if it had been a long day, or week. "We'll have enough supplies for four days."

At the computer, Dr. B was talking to herself. "Checking the moon phase calendar for the fourteenth century... full moon, the Julian calendar... May 9..." She looked up briefly. "Julia and Chief, can you give the Tuttles a quick rundown of History's rules and tell them what to expect tomorrow?"

"Will do," Nate said. "And professor?"

"Yes?"

"Get us there just before dusk."

Over at Dr. Mooney's workstation there was a loud clank, followed by a short hiss and a muffled oath. Something was clearly not going the professor's way.

"Keep your fingers crossed that I can finish this by morning," he called out. "Otherwise, you'll be on your own."

# 18

Dr. Baumgartner had lent me her backup gear—she always kept a pair of bags ready in the travel apparel closet across the hall from the TTE lab. I had driven to campus in my jeans, hiking boots, and yellow St. Sunniva University sweatshirt, with a rain jacket and a sun hat on the passenger seat by my side. I had gotten up early enough to do one more thing on my way to STEWie's basket.

The Department of Classical, Medieval, and Modern Languages (incorrectly but irreversibly known as the English Department) occupied a two-story building by the bend in Sunniva Lake, a five-minute walk from my office, which I took at a hurried clip in the hiking boots. The building had been constructed in the (mercifully) brief period when cement and boxiness were all the rage in campus architecture. I waited briefly outside the revolving doors as a student struggled to push his bicycle through, then went inside. I found Rosco in the basement, where he was tending to the building's air system.

Rosco was the English Department's custodian and the younger brother of Oscar, the security guard in the TTE building; their parents had given their sons names that were almost palindromes. Rosco explained that the building's air system was never off—either the heating or the air-conditioning had to be running at all times, which meant that it was always too hot or too cold. The cycle was on the heating half at the moment, and beads of sweat had broken out all over his forehead as he attended to the furnace.

I explained that I needed to get into Dr. Holm's office.

Looking happy to have any excuse to get out of the hot basement, Rosco led me up two flights of stairs. I considered how unalike he and Oscar were—whereas Oscar never slept, Rosco always looked like he'd inherited all of his older brother's sleeping hours plus some, with deep bags under his eyes and constant, mouth-stretching yawns. Or maybe it was the quiet atmosphere that pervaded the English Department. There were no classrooms here, only offices for professors, visiting fellows, and postdocs.

As he unlocked Dr. Holm's office for me, Rosco explained that her officemate's research fellowship had expired at the end of the summer but he hadn't gotten around to taking the extra nameplate down. One of the two desks stood empty. On the other, journals and books sat next to a computer, organized into orderly stacks in a fashion that warmed my office administrator's heart.

"Lock up behind you when you're done, Julia. I'll be in the basement," Rosco said, heading off with a yawn.

I unzipped my sweatshirt and took it off, rubbing my shoulder where I had received the starting dose of the plague vaccine. I dropped into Dr. Holm's desk chair and suddenly felt weird about violating her workspace. But if she had been abducted, she would certainly want us to do everything we could to help. And if she had gone with Quinn willingly, she had committed a breach of university protocol, and we had every right to look through her things. I compromised by deciding to look only at whatever was sitting out in the open, and not to rummage through any of the desk drawers.

To make the whole thing seem official in case anybody asked, I sent Nate a quick email telling him where I was, figuring he wouldn't see it until after we got back.

The books sitting on the desk were thick academic tomes on Germanic languages. I leafed through one quickly. It was a dictionary listing words and their pronunciations, the latter marked with those peculiar little symbols that linguists use in copious amounts, dots and other accent marks and such. The journals stacked next to the books were thinner but equally dense to the untrained eye. One article had a sticky note attached to it, and I pounced on it, but it was merely one about the Kingittorsuaq Runestone, the one in Greenland that Dr. Holm had mentioned. Curious about what that one might have to say—the runestone, that is, not the article—I found a translation on the third page. Apparently one Erling Sighvatsson, along with his buddies Bjarni and Eindridi, had built a cairn on a rocky island in the northern hunting grounds on a Saturday. Well, that was a rather mundane bit of business, unless you were one of the three gentlemen involved.

I turned my attention to Dr. Holm's computer (which, after all, sat openly on her desk), but it was password protected.

I glanced around the small office. Textbooks and reference books lined the shelves, but there was not much in the way of personal belongings. Dr. Holm's appointment was in its second year and would be running out soon, I knew. She probably had hopes of being offered a tenure-track junior professorship and a better office. According to Helen, the funding just wasn't there at the moment.

I caught sight of something in the recycling bin to one side of Dr. Holm's desk. And by caught sight of, I mean I dumped the paper bin onto the carpet, thankful that the cleaning staff hadn't gotten around to emptying it yet. Wondering if Nate or one of his officers had already done this while searching the office, I shuffled the papers around until a stapled set of pages caught my attention. Dr. Holm had printed out a research proposal. Here and there sentences had been crossed out or reworded in red as she toiled on proposal number fifty in an effort to raise her batting average of three out of forty-nine.

I checked the time and quickly looked over the proposal. This was more like it. The introductory section touched on ideas that had been proven correct after being initially greeted with raised eyebrows. The theory of plate tectonics was mentioned, the finding of Troy, and the well-known but as yet unverified quote from Galileo—*Eppur si muove* ("And yet it moves")— about Earth circling the Sun rather than the other way around. Dr. Holm stated boldly that the Kensington Runestone was a solid lead to proving a Norse presence in the Americas, before getting to the crux of the matter: Vinland. She wanted to find it and had a plan for doing so.

Back when she had shown me the runestone poster in the library, I had been left with the impression that the idea had already been turned down by Dr. Payne and that that was the end of it. But here was an all-or-nothing stab at a proposal—it looked like she had intended to circumvent Dr. Payne and seek funding from private donors. It was the right move on her part, as non-academic sponsors tended to be more motivated to support unorthodox research topics. She would still have needed Dean Braga's approval to obtain a STEWie roster spot to look for the place she described in her proposal as being the land of "grapes and Leif Erikson's footsteps" and the site of the first "Norse encounters with the Skraelings," whoever they were—

I sat up abruptly.

Quinn wanted to find the runestone carvers. Dr. Holm wanted to find Vinland.

I quickly leafed through the rest of the proposal. Here was the plan set down in black-and-white, complete with a section titled *Strategy for Finding Vinland* and a color map. Dashed lines led from L'Anse aux Meadows inland and south to New England. She had planned to start at the settlement and see where the Vikings went.

I wondered if Quinn knew that she had her hopes pinned on a much bigger prize than the Kensington Runestone.

I tore off the page with the map, set the recycling bin upright, and remembered to grab my sweatshirt on my way out.

$$\infty$$

Helen spotted me through her open office door as I hurried down the hallway to return the key to Rosco. "Julia, come in. It's my office hours," she called out, inviting me to take the empty chair opposite her desk.

"Well—all right, but I only have a moment," I said, remaining standing and stuffing Dagmar's map into my pocket. "We're leaving in ten minutes. Did you know that Dagmar Holm wants to find Vinland?"

"Who doesn't? Do you want some coffee?" I shook my head. "I don't know why I bother having coffee on hand...or why I bother with office hours at all for that matter. Students never come by in person anymore. I keep my cell phone number private, but they email me questions—most often in the middle of the night—and expect a prompt reply! And even then, they never seem to read past the first line. Never mind that. Who's coming with you and Nate this time?"

"Ron and Ruth-Ann Tuttle—you haven't met them yet, but they're our experts in Dakota and Norse history. And Dr. B and Jacob. Are you sure you don't want to come along to lend your opinion?"

"Julia, if you find a stone in the fourteenth century with runes chiseled into it, it will be authentic. You won't need me there. Bring back pictures," she said, echoing Dr. Payne's words. "By the way," she added, "how's Sabina doing after yesterday's adventure?"

"She's back in school today. When we find Quinn, he's going to have to answer to me for making her life more difficult than it already is. Speaking of which—" I glanced at the time on my cell phone and held up the postdoc office keys. "Can you do me a favor and give these back to Rosco? I think I need to run."

# PART THREE:
# IN THE FUNNEL

# 19

The fourteenth century. Nate and I had already visited Runestone Hill in two time periods—in its present form as a serene state park, and at the end of the nineteenth century, when the land had undergone a major transformation from wild terrain to farmland. Now we would be going six hundred and fifty years into the past, zipping past an unbroken chain of twenty-some generations in Mary Kirkland's family, to arrive in the place where her forefathers and foremothers had lived. There was no concern on my part that we would be stepping into a ghost zone—it was a small hill in a marshy area—but I still felt a twinge of unease. My great-grandparents, contemporaries of Olof Ohman and his neighbors, had come to North America looking for a better life and found it. But the price had been paid by others.

"Thanks for joining us, Julia," Dr. Little commented dryly as I ran into the lab, nodded at him, then hurried to squeeze onto STEWie's platform. Dr. B, Nate, the Tuttles, and Jacob were already there and made room for me. Everyone was wearing hiking shoes, layered clothing, and rain jackets. Nate had changed out of his uniform into more practical hiking gear and had a compass on his belt. I couldn't help but notice that he had stuck with his plan to bring a firearm. He was also holding a large yellow mass made of rubber.

"What is *that?*" I asked.

"Since we can't fit a real canoe in here, these two inflatable kayaks will have to do."

"Will we really need them? They look cumbersome to carry, and they're not exactly subtle."

"They'll come in handy if there are any big lakes we need to cross. Once they're inflated, they're pretty easy to portage."

He thought for a moment before adding, "Sorry, I should have asked this before—can everyone swim? I didn't bring lifejackets."

He was addressing the Tuttles; Dr. B, Jacob, and I had already answered the question before we did the 1898 runs.

They both nodded.

"Are we sure we don't need to make an effort to blend in?" Jacob asked a little apprehensively as Dr. Little entered the coordinates Dr. B had set for us and the mirrors started to inch into place.

"It doesn't matter what we wear, Jacob," Dr. B explained. "We will move like shadows, stealthily." I figured she might be having a bit of fun with the young student.

"We could dress like Indians," Jacob suggested.

Ruth-Ann shook her head. "Chief Kirkland, I hear that you're part Dakota—"

"On my grandmother's side."

"Then you'll know that we are about to enter the domain of the woodland dwellers—hunters, harvesters of wild rice, experts on the land, the sky, and plant and animal life. I don't know a thing about time travel, but I imagine that even if you and I dressed in deerskin and moccasins, it wouldn't make a difference because we don't have a clue about how to behave in a way befitting the fourteenth century. Plus—your hair is too short." Nate's hair was shoulder length, which apparently wouldn't cut it, so to speak, in the fourteenth century. "So that's your answer, young man," she said to Jacob.

"We could dress up like the Norsemen?" Jacob suggested next.

Ron shook his head. "But we wouldn't know how to interact with Norsemen any more than we would with Indians."

Dr. B agreed. "Any contact with either group would impact history to a large degree. It just can't happen."

Though I wouldn't have minded a face-to-face meeting with one of Mary Kirkland's ancestors or the Norsemen of the stone, I knew Dr. B was right. Which explained why Nate had felt confident enough to pack rubber kayaks instead of trying to squeeze authentic dugout canoes onto STEWie's platform. If History allowed us to travel by boat, it would be because no one was close enough to see us.

Dagmar Holm's map was burning a hole in my pocket, but it didn't seem like the right time to bring it up, or her possible alliance with Quinn.

And so it was that we arrived on the top of a small, rocky hill in a cluster—the six of us and two inflatable kayaks. It took a moment for my eyes to adjust to the new surroundings after the brightness of the TTE lab. The sun, red and large, was about to dip below the horizon. In the fading light, I could see that the trees on the hill had just sprung their buds. I breathed in the raw, sweet aroma of spring. A quick glance around told me that there was no runestone... at least not in our immediate vicinity.

Nate had put the uninflated rubber kayaks down and was making a circle of the hill, pushing at the dirt here and there with the toe of his hiking boots. "Well, I'd say there is no stone propped up for all to see, or even freshly buried."

Dr. B was concerned with other matters. Scanning around with the Callback, our link to home, she let out a sigh of relief. "Our basket didn't leave. They're not here yet."

STEWie's basket had once been imaginatively described by Abigail as silver Jell-o floating midair in large clumps, if only you could see it. Dr. B's instruments could—fragments of the basket hung all around where each of us had arrived.

"Good. We have the upper hand, then," Nate said. "If Quinn and Dr. Holm jump here, the only way they'll be able to leave the fourteenth century is with us."

Dr. B went down on her knees to slide a thin probe into the soil. I assumed she was doing some kind of testing for the stone, but when I came over to look, she explained, "It's a beacon, Julia. We learned pretty early on in the STEWie program how a place without familiar landmarks can be. This way, if we get lost, we can find our way back to the hill and STEWie's basket by following the signal the beacon sends out."

"I'm planning on navigating the more old-fashioned way," Nate said, tapping the compass that hung from his belt. "Though I admit it will be odd not to have GPS. But you need satellites for GPS to work, and the nearest one is more than six centuries away."

I mused that terms like *old-fashioned* and *modern* had loose meanings when it came to time travel.

He was repeating his circuit of the hill, this time looking all around us rather than down at the ground. The look of satisfaction he had because we'd arrived here before Quinn and Dr. Holm slowly melted from his face. I left Dr. B to her beacon and went to see what was wrong.

There was water all around us, serene and unrippling in the sunset. Runestone Hill was an island.

# 20

"I don't know why everyone is surprised. The runestone very clearly says *Have ten men by the sea to look after our ships fourteen days' journey from this island.* And we found an island." Ron Tuttle bent down and felt a boulder with his calloused hand. "It would have been bigger than this one," he muttered, "since the side part was chipped off before carving. And this one's too knobby...hmm...this one's too small, and so is this one..." He continued examining the rocks, turning over some of the smaller ones and kneeling down by the bigger ones to feel their surface with the palm of his hand. "Wait a minute—that stone lying on its side between those two trees. I think that's the one. Oof— What on earth?"

He had been stopped in his tracks. He put his hand up in front of him, as if checking for some kind of invisible wall, and found it. Not even his hand would go through. Ron's mouth fell open slightly—nothing in his fifty-some years of experience had prepared him for this. He tugged at his beard in puzzlement.

"What's going on?" Ruth-Ann asked a little anxiously.

"It's the oddest thing," her husband said slowly. "Ruth-Ann, come and see this. That's the graywacke boulder, I'm certain— just lying there between those two trees, but I can't get any closer."

"You're time-stuck," said Dr. B, who was double-checking that the beacon was operational.

"But I'm not planning on disturbing the stone," Ron protested. "I was going to turn it over, and then put it back exactly as I found it."

"Even the smallest of changes can affect future events. Besides, History can't read your mind."

"Are there runes on it? Can you tell?" I asked the Tuttles.

Ruth-Ann balanced on the tips of her hiking shoes, one arm on Ron's shoulder for support. "The stone is face down, so I can't tell if there's any writing on it... Can you see any better, Ron?"

"I'm pretty sure it's blank. Yes, that side—the one facing us—that's where it will say, *Ten men by the sea.*"

Jacob had joined Ron and Ruth-Ann and was pushing at the invisible wall of History. "Awesome," he said, clearly enjoying the sensation of being prevented from falling by an invisible force, even though he'd already experienced it back in 1898. "I expect I'll have quite a story to tell on my blog when we get back home."

"I'm not sure we want the details plastered all over the Internet," I said to Jacob.

"But Julia, we'll be heroes. We're playing a game with History itself, and we're going to win. We'll rescue Dr. Holm, arrest Mr. Olsen, and find the Norse explorers..."

"Only if it all turns out as planned," Nate said with the concern of a seasoned time traveler. "Let's hope that's the only way we can't go. Never mind the stone clearly waiting to be carved. We should inflate the kayaks and get going. I don't want to stay here tonight. I'm worried that if we wait until morning, we'll be too exposed to travel across the water in the boats. We could get time stuck here for days if we're not careful."

"We're not just going to wait here for the Norsemen?" Jacob asked.

Nate shook his head, then, as if a thought had struck him, turned to Dr. B. "What would happen, Professor?"

"Sorry, Chief Kirkland?" Dr. B asked.

"If we camped out here and the Norsemen suddenly showed up. How would History prevent us from running into each other?"

"Ah." Dr. B chuckled. "Since we're the ones who don't belong, History would make us leave. We would feel ourselves become boxed in, squeezed into a space shrinking so rapidly that we would soon barely be able to draw breath, the pressure on our bodies so immense that all our bones would be at risk of shattering. Or at least, we think that's what it would be like. No one has ever stuck around long enough to find out. Everyone leaves along whatever path History permits or gets back into STEWie's basket real quick."

I had heard whispers about this phenomenon in the TTE hallways. It was said that the experience was akin to drowning at the bottom of the ocean, only without the water. I had never experienced anything close to it and wanted to keep it that way.

Nate checked his compass, which had a small light attached to it. "We'll paddle in that direction," he pointed. "North, like the text on the runestone instructs—will instruct—oh, you know what I mean. I'm not looking to put a lot of distance between us and the island, just enough that we can get moving in the morning. We can camp in those woods over there. They should provide good cover."

Jacob went over to help him untangle the two kayaks as Dr. B readied the foot pump. I left them to it and squinted at the cluster of trees on the side of the hill where Ron had been stopped by History's hand. Now he sat on a boulder, sketching the island in the rapidly fading light. The stone wasn't to be disturbed, not today. But my interest was caught by something else. What

I had assumed to be a random collection of trees, distracted as I was by our first look at the runestone, revealed itself upon closer examination to be an orchard. The grove of what I guessed were black walnut trees, going by their gray, furrowed bark and pointy leaves, was shadowy now but would attract plentiful light on sunny days. It was not a modern, fenced-in orchard, but it was an orchard nevertheless. This place had caretakers.

"You want to switch, Dr. Baumgartner?" I heard Nate ask. He took over the foot pump to give the professor a break. I hadn't realized that inflating a boat was such a slow business. Dr. B had filled in the floor compartment, and I watched the first of the kayaks expand into its slim, double-pointed shape as Nate pumped air first into one of the side tubes, then the other. "Oars?" I asked, not seeing any.

"The paddles are attached to my backpack and Chief Kirkland's." Dr. B nodded at the backpacks lying in a heap to one side. "Two for each kayak."

Ruth-Ann and I set upon detaching the telescoping paddles and expanding them out to their full length. "Who goes in which kayak?" Ruth-Ann asked brightly. "Ron and I both have kayaking experience." She and Ron were in their early fifties and a bit—well, stocky—but thinness did not equate to physical strength and agility, and the opposite was true as well.

Dr. B, who was in good shape and enjoyed outdoor activities like jogging and cross-country skiing, said, "I have kayaking experience, too."

I didn't. Nor, I guessed, did Jacob.

Nate moved the pump to the other kayak and eyed us all in turn as if to gauge our weight. Jacob, who could best be described as scrawny, hadn't taken off his backpack; it seemed like it was liable to tip him over as he practiced using one of the paddles in the air.

After a moment's consideration, Nate said, "Uh—Jacob, why don't you and the Tuttles go in one kayak. Dr. Baumgartner and Julia and I will take the other."

As we carried the kayaks down to the water, Nate seemed to be considering something. "What?" I asked.

"Just a logistics problem. I would prefer to go in the first kayak and lead, but I want to be able to keep an eye on the other one. It would be bad if they got time-stuck behind us and we got separated. Not to mention that our flashlights have to stay off."

In the end, after warning them not to get to far ahead, he let the Tuttles' kayak go first, with Jacob firmly ensconced between the two amateur archeologists.

"Here." He handed Jacob a two-way radio. "Let's hope these work. I'll tell you when to pull ashore, then we can set up camp. Try not to tip the kayaks over, everyone. We don't want to lose a backpack."

∞

After some creative placement of backpacks so that the kayak was well-balanced, we set out in a smooth glide, Dr. B and Nate expertly paddling us forward. The others were just ahead of us. The rising full moon seemed bigger than usual, like a round, pock-marked face keeping an eye on us from above.

I couldn't shake the feeling that we were being watched, and I wasn't talking about the moon. I knew it was almost certainly an illusion from being out on the water at night with our flashlights off and rowing as quietly as possible. Still, I glanced toward the tree-lined shore once or twice to see if anyone—or anything—was visible.

"There," Nate hissed. "By those reeds. That looks like a good spot."

He radioed ahead to Jacob, who had been put in charge of communication while the Tuttles paddled. Luckily the radios worked just fine and Nate was able to instruct the other kayak to hold back and let us approach shore first. We glided in, catching a few reeds as we did, which halted our progress. Nate got out of the kayak and into the water, almost tipping us over. He guided the kayak through the reeds and mud onto a small beach, then helped Dr. B and me out.

Ron Tuttle was about to get into the water to lead the other kayak ashore, but Nate waved him off. "I'm already wet. Can't get any wetter," he said in a loud whisper. He waded back in and guided the Tuttles' kayak next to ours, steadying it as it ran aground.

"Careful," he said in the same low voice as Ron Tuttle hopped out to help him with the final bit. "There are some sharp rocks. We can't afford to lose a kayak so soon."

Once everyone was out, we carried the kayaks through some underbrush and stumbled into a clearing between several pine trees where the accumulated pine needles had kept plant growth to a minimum. "Seems like it's as good of a spot as any to camp for the night," Nate said. "I think we can chance the flashlights."

It was all very well for him to think so, but History had other ideas. We tried all of the flashlights in turn, but one by one they refused to click on.

"Okay, then," Nate said. "No flashlights."

"Lucky for us we chose a full moon," Ruth-Ann said brightly as she detached her sleeping bag from her backpack.

Nate was still frowning at the uncooperative flashlight in his hand. "I was hoping to light a small fire to dry off my boots. I've already spent too much time with my feet wet this week."

"Maybe a fire will work since it's not anachronistic like the flashlights," I suggested. "Let's try it after we set up."

"Bear in mind," he added, "that if we don't get the fire or the stoves going, we can't heat up the water and rehydrate our meals. Unless you want them cold and chunky and still half-dried."

He and the Tuttles had brought tiny lightweight stoves in their backpacks. We had all brought sleeping bags, but not tents, just individual bivy sacks in case we got caught in the rain. Dr. B had instructed me to add as few items as possible to the bag she had given me. ("After the first hour, your backpack is going to get heavier by the minute.") I had added my own water bottle and a few small items, one of them being Dagmar's map.

After giving us all a crash course on wilderness protocol, like putting our food in a bag and hanging it on a tree branch to avoid midnight visits from black bears, Nate turned his attention to making a fire. He gathered some fallen sticks and branches onto a small pile and readied his lighter and a handful of dry pine needles. "Here we go."

I had pulled out my sleeping bag and was looking around for a good place to lay it out. I heard Nate swear under his breath, but didn't need to turn around to figure out what the problem was. Ron tried a match and the stove, but that was a no-go either. History clearly had a firm opinion on the matter, but Nate and Ron were equally stubborn and took turns rubbing two dry sticks together. All they got in return were blisters. Whether the procedure itself was close to impossible for newbies like us, or whether History's hand would have been equally persistent in blocking any attempts to produce fire, there was no way to know.

"It could be something simple, like that the smell of our warmed up food is foreign to this century," Dr. B said. "Freeze-dried lasagna and beef stew hardly belong here."

Nate stuck the lighter back in his pocket and squelched away from the stacked wood to set up his sleeping bag on a small rise some distance from us. Meanwhile, Ron turned his attention to using a broom-like twig to sweep sticks and small rocks from the spot he and Ruth-Ann had chosen. He placed their sleeping bags side by side. A voice behind me spoke up as I started unrolling my own sleeping bag. "Do you mind if I bunk with you, Julia?"

"Not at all, Dr. B."

I made room for her sleeping bag and looked around to see where Jacob had found a spot.

He was nowhere to be seen.

# 21

"Jacob," I called, perhaps a touch more loudly than I'd intended, causing Dr. B to drop the granola bar she had just taken out of her backpack. She grabbed it before it had time to gather any dirt. "Is something wrong, Julia?"

"I don't see Jacob."

I scrambled to my feet. I had promised Dean Braga I would keep an eye on the student and here we had already lost him. I'd happened to be in her office with some paperwork she needed for a tenure meeting when Jacob had popped in to ask if he could go. Clutching his backpack, in which he had swapped his books and lab notebooks for so many camping items that the zipper across the top couldn't be closed, the ginger-haired student had pointed out politely that Dr. B had already said he could come along and he only needed Dean Braga's okay because of the unorthodox nature of the situation. Besides, we had already allowed him go to 1898. And if she thought it best, he promised not to bring his new cell phone, although it would come handy for taking pictures, and was it really that different from a camera?

Dean Braga had finally given in and waved him away.

I remembered thinking that it might be good for Jacob to see that the Internet would do just fine without him for a whole week.

Given the way that time travel worked, though, it wouldn't really be that long for the Internet, just for Jacob.

Now I felt bad for my cavalier attitude and was about to alert Nate to the young student's disappearance when Jacob emerged from behind a tree. He had his sleeping bag in his arms—a Star Wars–themed one, it looked like, though in the darkness I couldn't really tell—and was glancing around uncertainly.

"Ah, there he is," said Dr. B and went back to eating her granola bar.

I dropped back down to the ground and let out a sigh of relief. The feeling that we were being watched was still with me, and I had been sure that Jacob had wondered off and gotten into trouble—though how or from whom, I couldn't say. I was about to chastise him for disappearing on us for so long, but I realized what the problem was as he continued to look around uncertainly. He was the only student in the group. Ruth-Ann and Ron were already snug in their sleeping bags and had pulled out matching e-readers and settled in to read, using their backpacks as pillows, their faces feebly illuminated. I found it amusing that while we hadn't been able to start a fire or light the camping stoves, the e-readers' artificial lights, tinny and scentless, worked just fine. I hadn't thought to bring one because there was no room in my backpack, and also because it had seemed prudent to leave modern devices behind. Perhaps we should have done a better job of explaining History's rules to the Tuttles, I thought.

In any case, the pair seemed like they didn't need a third. Nate wasn't exactly sending off the vibe that he wanted company either. Having taken off his socks, he was drying his feet with a small towel. That left me and Dr. B, and I could tell that Jacob thought it would be weird to bunk next to his advisor.

"Jacob," I said firmly.

Jacob eyed me. "Yes, Julia?"

"Unless you want to bunk with Chief Kirkland up there—"

"I'm not sure…uh, that there's enough room."

"Then here." I pointed to the ground next to me, on the opposite side from Dr. B.

Jacob sent me a grateful look and set up his sleeping bag, which I now could see was covered in small green Yodas, before disappearing again behind the pine tree. I made myself comfortable and, since we were out of luck as far as hot food went, dug some crackers out of my backpack. I offered a few to Dr. B, but she shook her head.

"No thanks, Julia, I'm good." She finished off her granola bar as if that constituted an adequate dinner and washed it down with a swig from her water bottle. After digging around in her backpack, she took out a tiny toothbrush and squeezed a minimal amount of toothpaste on it. Brush in mouth, she said, "There's one in your backpack as well."

"Thanks."

I wondered what Ruth-Ann and Ron were reading, if they were looking at maps and planning our itinerary for tomorrow, or if perhaps one of them was a fan of whodunits and the other of steamy romances. I rather pegged Ron as a closet romance reader, maybe because the colorful beads in his beard made him seem like he had an unexpected side to his personality.

Nate passed by wearing a dry pair of hiking socks on his way to the food bag. I noticed him raise an eyebrow at the Tuttles' e-readers.

"Don't worry, Julia," Dr. B spoke up quietly from beside me. She slid her toothbrush back into its case and put it away. "No one blames you for this incident or for Quinn's behavior."

I bit into another cracker and, chewing it, said, "Thanks, but I feel I should have foreseen this." I realized that Erika and I had never talked about anything personal. All our interactions had been limited to school business. It occurred to me that she and I were about the same age. "Uh—how's the other Dr. Baumgartner doing?"

This was Soren, Erika's husband, who was a professor of modern poetry. Rumor had it that their marriage was on the rocks, which seemed to be going around. Both wife and husband were extremely busy with their tenure-track positions, hers being a joint one in TTE and History of Science and Soren's being in the Creative Writing Department.

"Soren?" Dr. B busied herself with the contents of her backpack, unnecessarily unfolding and refolding a spare shirt. "He's going on a sabbatical starting in November. Japan. Six months."

I hadn't heard *that*.

"Sorry," I said.

Erika smoothed out imaginary wrinkles in the shirt. "If you don't mind my asking, Julia, do you find that between work and love, work is often easier to manage?"

"Yes."

She chuckled. "I didn't mean the current situation with Quinn. I meant as a general rule."

I considered the question again. "It can be—but I think I stumbled into a job that was a good fit for me and a marriage that wasn't. It's probably the other way around for many people. And if you're *really* lucky, maybe you do well in both." Then I added in a lower voice, "Ruth-Ann and Ron seem like they've found a good balance, wouldn't you say?"

Ron was helping Ruth-Ann adjust her backpack in its capacity as a pillow so that she would be more comfortable.

"The nomadic lifestyle in the RV does seem to suit them," Erika said. "I don't know how I'd feel about not having a steady paycheck."

"There is that," I allowed.

She rolled the shirt into a cylinder and stuffed it back into her bag. "Well, maybe it will do Soren and me some good to spend a few months apart. What about you? There's a rumor going around about you, Chief Kirkland, and Pompeii."

I suppose it was only fair that there were campus rumors about me as well. "Really? I don't know where people get their ideas. We're not dating or anything."

"So you're not interested in him?"

Where was Jacob? He seemed to be positively wedded to that tree.

"I have a lot on my plate at the moment," I said.

"Just curious. He is rather good looking, isn't he?"

"Is he?" My voice sounded a little funny even to my own ears.

"He's a bit reserved, though. I can't seem to get him to call me Erika. Even Dr. B would be better."

"He prefers to keep things formal on all official business," I said, quoting what Nate had told me back when he still used to call me Ms. Olsen. "In his book, anything that happens on campus, including in the TTE lab and wherever STEWie's basket happens to go, is official business."

Jacob shuffled back, a bag of pretzels in hand.

"We thought you'd gotten lost on your way back," I said.

"Sorry. No, I was just—oh, it's no good. I can't keep a secret. I was looking at my phone."

"There's no Wi-Fi or 3G in the fourteenth century," I pointed out.

"I was just catching up on tweets. I didn't get a chance to do that earlier because I was so busy getting my gear together. The tweets stop at nine this morning."

This was when we had left.

"It's something you're going to have to get used to if you want to stay in this field," Dr. B reminded her student, curling up in her sleeping bag. "Time travel means being out of touch for hours, days on occasion."

"I guess." Jacob plopped down on his sleeping bag, pulled open the pretzel bag, and started munching.

"Well?" I said. "Anything interesting in the world of the Internet?"

I had meant it as a gentle poke at his nomophobia, but I also had an underlying concern, my usual one. I was worried that one day he would come by to tell me that Sabina's name was trending worldwide. Jacob knew the whole story, having been the first to greet us when we'd returned with Sabina, all of us covered with ash from Vesuvius.

Jacob offered us some of the pretzels; Dr. B shook her head, but and I took a handful and offered him some of the crackers in return. "Not much that you'd find interesting," he said of the Twitter news. "Yesterday was Scooby-Doo's birthday."

"I beg your pardon?"

"In home time, I mean. September was when the show's first episode aired in 1969—it was called *What a Night for a Knight.*"

"I did not know that," I said.

"Can't say that I did either," Dr. B said. "Are you a Scooby-Doo fan, too?" she said, with a glance at his sleeping bag.

"Never seen the show in my life," Jacob confided. "I don't watch much TV. I just saw it mentioned on Twitter. Is it about a big dog?"

"Something like that," I said, suddenly feeling old.

We drifted off into silence. It was nowhere near night in home time—in jumping from morning to dusk we had undergone more of the time travel version of jet lag, like we had traveled east a dozen time zones—but given the inoperability of our flashlights and the lack of a fire, everybody was soon snug in their sleeping bags.

Not having been on a camping trip since childhood, I had forgotten the cacophony of sounds that lie over the woods like a soft blanket—the crunching and squeaking and the occasional hoot of an owl—all of them amplified in the darkness. As I already knew from the Pompeii run, the night sky of the past was something to behold, a treat. I spent a while looking up at it, admiring the starry dome undulled by smog or light pollution from malls and parking lot lights. Countless bright stars surrounded the rising full moon, its cratered surface scarred by millions of years of one asteroid hit after another. The faint light of the Tuttles' e-readers only added to the sensation of yours truly being a very small mortal in a very large universe.

The fourteenth century. We were really here.

The Woodlands. It had been the homeland of the Dakota, Ruth-Ann had said, before their later migrations to the plains and prairie, before they started riding horses, and before they were called the Sioux by French fur traders.

I turned to one side. I had never been one for roughing it in the great outdoors, but this wasn't too bad—the ground was relatively level and devoid of rocks. Tomorrow, with any luck, we would find Quinn and Dr. Holm and the whole incident would be over. I slid farther down into my sleeping bag, pulling the zipper up as far as it would go. It seemed like it was going to be a cool May night here in the woods.

Jacob, on one side of me, was already gently snoring amidst the Yodas.

# 22

A hand on my shoulder woke me up, making me gasp in surprise.

It was Nate and it was just before dawn. He held his finger to his lips and beckoned, for some reason pointing to the rise where he had slept. Dr. B stirred next to me. On the other side, Jacob was still fast asleep, his mouth slightly open. Without thinking, I reached for my phone to see what time it was before realizing that I didn't have it. I yawned and fought my way out of the sleeping bag, managing to get the zipper tangled in a stray bit of string. I had spent most of the night tossing and turning, I was chilled to the bone, and I was sure that I had terrible sleeping-bag hair. Dr. B had unzipped herself from her sleeping bag and was on her feet, stretching to touch her toes several times. Her blonde hair, straight and thin, looked just fine. I ran my fingers through my own, wondered if the backpack she had given me included a comb in the little pocket of toiletries, and decided something right then and there. I was here to help bring Quinn and Dr. Holm back. I couldn't worry about the way I looked.

Nate had gone over to shake the Tuttles awake and was still insistently pointing to the rise. Dr. B and I shrugged at each other and followed him. Rather oddly, just before he reached the top of the rise, Nate threw himself on the ground and began crawling forward.

Dr. B grabbed my shoulder and indicated that we should do the same. I dropped to my knees and inched up to where Nate was peering over the rise. Ruth-Ann and Ron were right behind us.

The trees were blackened silhouettes, and the sun hugging the horizon had dyed the sky a brilliant orange that was reflected in the sprawling lake below us. And beyond its still waters, on the far shore...

"The Psinomani," Ruth-Ann whispered.

# 23

The village—living history before our eyes—lay spread out on high ground on the shore of a large, pear-shaped lake. A protective wooden palisade encircled a roomy cluster of birch-bark houses of varying sizes; there were cultivated garden beds both within and outside the palisade, as well as a row of burial mounds to one side of the village. The lake was not the one we had traveled on the night before, but its neighbor, whose still waters sparkled in the shafts of dawn light. Minnesota meant "the place where the sky tints the water," and even I knew the name came from the Dakota language.

We lay motionless as morning broke over the land and the sun turned its eye on the lakes, streams, hills, woodland, and, somewhere just to the west, the tall grass of the prairie. Soon figures started emerging from the bark houses, first just one, a stooped old woman, then a few more, all unaware of our presence across the water and in the trees.

Something soon stuck me as odd. Mary Kirkland had mentioned that there were healthy Dakota populations in the pre-Columbian times, but unless most of the village was still fast asleep, there weren't a whole lot of people there. The old woman and a couple of other figures bent over with age slowly attended to morning tasks, curious toddlers played in the dirt, and a handful of young women, clearly the caretakers of the two other groups, were engaged in the task of lighting a morning fire. Two men who seemed to be serving as village guards were positioned at opposite ends of the village. Judging from their relaxed poses, they didn't look like they were expecting trouble anytime soon, if at all. I glanced at Ruth-Ann and saw her face scrunch up in puzzlement. Where was everyone?

Just as quietly as we had crept up the rise, we crept back down. Jacob had to be firmly shaken awake, but he seemed to instantly understand the need for silence. If we were in danger of being seen or heard, our options would diminish, and we might even get pinned in place. We gathered our things, remembered the food bag that we had left suspended from a tree branch, and carried the kayaks back down to our lake.

"What did you think?" Dr. B asked as she and Nate paddled across the water. The old-growth trees watched us silently from the lakeshore. Beads of dew glittered on the light-green spring leaves, reflecting the warming rays of the morning sun.

"Of what?" I yawned and stretched, careful not to tip the kayak over. It was morning here but nighttime according to my body's internal clock.

"Of the Psinomani village." That was what Ruth-Ann had called her woodland ancestors, gatherers of *psinh*, wild rice.

"That I would have paddled across the lake to meet them," I said.

Nate said nothing. The others were behind us and I could hear Jacob regaling the Tuttles with stories of ghost zones in an excited whisper, not that he'd ever been to one. But the topic made it possible for me to pose the question without actually asking it. "The village seemed—rather empty. Only kids, old people, and caretakers."

Dr. B, paddling with ease in the front of the kayak, without turning around said, "Hard to say what it means, if anything. We did drop into a single morning in the villagers' lives and history, after all. Chances are it's a perfectly ordinary day."

"I wonder when Quinn and Dr. Holm will get here," I said.

Dr. B nodded in thought. "I've been wondering if they're basing their search on the runestone text only, like we are, or if they have a piece of information we don't."

"*I* have a piece of information that the rest of you don't have yet," I said.

"Julia?" Nate asked without breaking his smooth paddle stroke.

"I found a map in Dagmar's office."

"Oh?"

"It was sitting out in the open." Inside a recycling bin, anyway. "I'll dig it out of my backpack the next time we go ashore. Dr. Holm is after a bigger prize. She wants to find Vinland."

I couldn't tell if Nate already knew that or not, but he didn't sound particularly surprised. "Does she? How?"

"I read a proposal she wrote. It's for a STEWie run to L'Anse aux Meadows, which she's assuming was a ship-repair station and a gateway to Vinland." I cocked my head to one side. "Now that I think about it, this could be a problem. Because what if Quinn and Dr. Holm never come here? What if the place to look for them isn't here at all, but on a Canadian island at around 1000 AD? Dean Braga said we only had one run. I suppose it's a good thing we have the Slingshot 3.0, so we can jump there if we need to."

"You didn't tell her?" Dr. B said, glancing over her shoulder at Nate.

"Tell me what?"

"We did bring along the Slingshot," Dr. B explained, "but not the 3.0. Dr. Mooney worked well into the night, but one of the laser casings that arrived yesterday was the wrong size. He didn't get to finish."

"You brought along Slingshot 1.0?" I sat up in the kayak, almost tipping it over. Once I had regained my balance, I said, "The device that sent us into five ghost zones, one after the other, on our way back from Pompeii? You're kidding, right?"

"It was my idea," Nate said. "All three professors— Dr. Mooney, Dr. Little, and Dr. Baumgartner here—assured me that nothing like that could happen again."

"Julia, when all of you were in far time, Xavier had no way of calculating a safe trajectory to home. The Slingshot, left to its own devices, sent you along an easy route—that is to say, it sent you along a chain of ghost zones. Luckily, we can calculate where we need to jump. I brought my laptop. It's in a waterproof pouch in my backpack."

I was sandwiched rather snugly between our three backpacks, which made me wonder what other unexpected items each of us had brought. Jacob had his cell phone, I had Dagmar's map, Dr. B a laptop, Ron a sketching notebook, Ruth-Ann packets of coffee, and Nate—well, I had no idea.

"It's a big continent, but we'll find them," Nate said grimly, and I was pretty sure he did not mean the Norsemen.

"Well, at least we seem to be nowhere near a ghost zone right now," I said in an effort to lighten the mood. Jacob, in the other kayak, had launched into a story that seemed to involve the unlikely combination of quicksand and thin lake ice. (Not one of our researchers had ever come close to being sucked down into quicksand, if such a thing was possible. And the thin-ice incident had had a happy ending.) "Plus, it's such a nice spring morning," I added, taking in a lungful of wonderfully unpolluted air and the earthy scents of forest, lake, and soil that the rising sun had coaxed out.

Nate was having none of it. "There are natural dangers. We could run into a cougar or pack of wolves."

Well, if he was determined to be such a sourpuss about the whole thing, there was not much I could do.

"Here, Julia, take the paddle for a bit. I want to check something."

He handed me the paddle and consulted his compass and the map he had brought along, which he was using to mark our progress. We had started from what would one day shrink to modern Wally Lake on Nate's map, though it was hard to tell for sure, and portaged twice, the first time barely a few steps, and the other a good half a mile, and now we were rowing on what he thought might be Quam Lake blended into Halleque Lake. "This map is not very useful because nothing on it matches...I don't think we've reached Barsness Lake yet...Hmm." He took his compass out. "North is that way—"

Dr. B interrupted him. "You know, right, that the Vikings used only the sun and the stars and oral accounts to navigate? No maps, charts, or astronomical instruments. My point is that a *day's journey north from this stone* might just have meant that the sun rose roughly to their left and set to their right as they traveled."

"We have to start somewhere, and we might as well head toward compass north."

Now that we were actually here, the "triangle to the north" that he had drawn back in the lab seemed awfully big.

"We need a hill," I suggested.

"Other than the runestone one?" Dr. B said from in front of me in the kayak.

"A high one, so that we can spot the Norse camp. Andes Tower Hills, where the ski area is now, isn't that nearby?"

"We passed it a bit back," Nate said, still studying the map.

"Wouldn't it be something?" I had been trying to match Dr. B's rhythm with my paddle, but it was tricky and we kept drifting to one side. "To see the Norsemen, I mean. I wonder what it was like for them, so far from home. Did they sit in the evening around a campfire, retelling the Norse sagas and resting their tired muscles? Just think, if we spot them first and snap a photo, then we'll get the honor of returning with proof of pre-Columbian contact, not Quinn."

Nate held his arm out for the paddle. He straightened the kayak and said, "Are we here to find Quinn and Dr. Holm or to try to prove that the runestone is genuine?"

I never got the chance to answer him. There was a splash in the water behind us. Someone had tumbled out of the other kayak.

# 24

We'd put some distance between ourselves and the village, though not much, since the marshland curved in the wrong direction and we soon ran out of lake. The woods with their old-growth trees offered some cover and a place for Jacob to dry off. Unless we managed to light a fire, he would have to warm up as best he could. We pulled the kayaks to shore and onto a small beach that lead up to a clearing. The first order of business was the fire.

"Wait," Nate said to Ron, who had bent to gather firewood. "Let's check if it's even worth gathering the wood." Nate flicked his lighter and this time the flame emerged just fine. "Yay," I heard Jacob say between chattering teeth as Ron and Nate set about gathering firewood. I surveyed the situation and sent Jacob behind a tree to change into his spare clothes.

Once they had a decent-size stack of wood, Nate tried his lighter again and the dry, brittle branches soon crackled to life. Jacob inched himself as close as he could to the fire without actually setting himself aflame. Nate joined him and took off his boots, placing them next to the fire. Ruth-Ann wrung out Jacob's wet clothes and set them on a boulder to dry, then turned her attention to warming up water in an aluminum kettle for coffee and oatmeal. Jacob tried to protest that he didn't drink coffee, but she kindly shushed him. "Now's the time to start, then. You don't want to catch a cold. And before anyone tells me that you can't catch a cold just by *being* cold and wet—I disagree. Your body is more likely to catch something if it's busy trying to keep itself warm. The last thing we need is anyone getting sick out here."

There was no arguing with that.

Dr. B was humming as she helped Ruth-Ann ready the coffee and oatmeal packets. Time travel was the ultimate dream for harried academics. We had been in the fourteenth century sunset to sunrise, so not even half an hour had passed back in the lab, which meant that she still had plenty of time to prepare next week's lecture for her undergraduate class, *From Sir Isaac Newton to Caroline Herschel: Anecdotes in the Lives of Famous Scientists*.

Truth be told, if Quinn hadn't been involved in the present incident, I would have been enjoying my mini-vacation too. I hadn't taken one in a while. I had been meaning to visit my parents, but something at work always required my attention, not to mention the task of getting Sabina and Abigail settled.

As the fire crackled and the water warmed up, we took turns using impromptu bathroom facilities in the woods. Nate had instructed us to cover up anything we left behind, not only for History's sake, but to minimize our footprint in the wild, which amounted to the same thing. While the others chatted and went about their chores—Nate was fixing a small puncture on the outside of one of the kayaks with Ron's help—I sat down next to Dr. B to join her in warming my hands by the fire. She made room for me and said, "She's my friend, you know. Dagmar. We both jog."

"I didn't know you knew her." I should have realized. A university campus is a small place.

"Chief Kirkland wanted to know whether she had ever talked about the runestone."

I was glad Nate was pursuing all avenues of investigation, though I couldn't help but notice that he hadn't mentioned his conversation with Erika. This was officially his investigation, of course, and I was only unofficially involved. He was under no obligation to divulge all particulars of his various avenues of inquiry to me. Still. If Helen had been with us, she probably would have at this point reminded me about jealousy being "the green-eyed monster."

"So did she?" I asked, repeating Nate's question back to Erika.

She stirred the fire with a stick. "Dagmar and I did talk about our work, although most of the talking was done by me—she was interested in time travel and what it was like. People usually are, and it's particularly understandable in her case since she hoped to get on STEWie's roster. I suggested that she take a workshop or two, which she did. As to her own work, she did say she had her fingers crossed that she'd be offered a junior professorship at St. Sunniva."

I shook my head. "There's no funding for it. Her postdoc will expire at the end of the school year."

A look of been-there passed over the professor's face. "I have to say—if Quinn did kidnap her and she returns safely with us, I hope the school will feel badly enough about what happened that they'll find the money to offer her a professorship. Does that make me sound very pragmatic?" She gave a brief, self-conscious laugh. "It's just that in academia you have to jump at opportunities as they arise."

I rather figured that was true of all professions, but her career track was more uphill than most.

Erika gave a small shrug. "Like I told Chief Kirkland, Dagmar only mentioned the runestone once, in passing. She said that she felt her peers were too critical of it. According to her, aberrations were to be expected since the runes had been chiseled an ocean away from the 'standard' to which they were being compared, probably by a group of men who had varying backgrounds and life experiences."

I rummaged around in my backpack until I found the map from Dagmar's proposal, the one I had torn from the section titled *Strategy for Finding Vinland*. "I found this in her office."

Nate lost his interest in the kayaks and came over to look, Ron on his heels. The older man held a hand out to me. "May I, Julia?"

I handed him the map and he studied it for a moment.

"Ahh, yes," he said after a moment. "If I was the two of them and I had a . . . what did you call it?"

"A Slingshot," Dr. B suggested. "Slingshot 2.0, to be precise."

"If I had the Slingshot 2.0 at my disposal and wanted to find Vinland, I'd probably do just what she's proposing. Hide behind a bush at L'Anse aux Meadows and listen to their conversations and follow them when Vinland's mentioned."

Ruth-Ann left the kettle to do its thing and came over to join in the discussion. "Are we saying they may not even be coming here?"

"It might depend on who's in charge," Nate said. "Quinn or Dr. Holm."

"Let's hope we guessed right," Dr. B said.

I gave myself a mental kick for not mentioning the map before we climbed into STEWie's basket. "Too bad our STEWie basket didn't return home without us, like last time. At least then we'd know they were in the vicinity. If they pop up on Runestone Island now, we'll have no warning."

"They'll won't wait there," Dr. B said, "for the same reason we left—it's too exposed. There's nowhere for them to hide. These lovely woods—" She gestured around us with the small spoon she was using to stir warm water into her oatmeal—"offer plenty of opportunities for concealment."

They did. I still felt the eyes on us, as I had since we first inflated the kayaks on Runestone Island. I didn't want to say anything to the others yet; all I had to go on was a feeling.

"I guess your estranged husband is planning to film the skirmish with the Psinomani, Julia, or the Black Death flare-up, or whatever it was, for his reality show." Ruth-Ann tut-tutted as she passed out the small packets of instant coffee for us to stir into our mugs. "It seems disrespectful, to tell you the truth."

"I imagine it would be toned down and edited for the show." I said, more in an effort to defend our program than out of any loyalty to Quinn. STEWie researchers had come back with footage of many a disturbing and tragic event from the past. Sometimes, like with the time-traveling camera that had gone out on an ocean buoy to film the sinking of the Titanic (with an automatic timer set to send it back home), the footage was taken from far enough that it didn't have to be edited for the somewhat inappropriately named *History Alive* exhibition. In other instances, like with video grabbed from Civil War battlefields, the camera had gotten uncomfortably close. Sometimes it seemed to me that history was mostly made of tragic events.

Nate took Dagmar's map from Ron. "Most people aren't as squeamish as we think they are. Everyone slows down to look at car accidents. As for Quinn's reality show, the bloodiest episodes would probably get the highest ratings."

He was right. No one had complained yet about the gruesomeness of a single one of the *History Alive* exhibits.

"I imagine that the fact that it happened so long ago gives people an excuse not to feel bad about it," Ruth-Ann said. "After all, there's nothing we can do, is there?"

Dr. B sighed over her oatmeal. "True. You can't change History. We know because we tried. At least, Dr. Mooney and Dr. Rojas tried in the beginning, back when they were still figuring out the rules of time travel…STEWie wasn't even called that yet. They made an attempt to save the lost Mayan books. It wasn't long before they realized that the codices could only be rescued for future generations, not past ones—that is to say, they could not save the originals, only scan them before they made it onto the conquistadors' bonfires."

The manuscripts she was talking about were displayed in the *History Alive* exhibition on regular paper, not like they would have been made originally, on cloth pounded from tree bark and folded into a book. But we had learned that the Mayans weren't as obsessed with astronomy as we'd thought—the four codices that had survived into the present before STEWie came along just happened to focus on astronomy.

"Could Mr. Olsen and Dr. Holm be using their Slingshot 2.0 to jump around the continent in their quest to find the Norsemen?" asked Ron over Nate's shoulder.

Dr. B shook her head over her coffee mug. "I doubt it. That would quickly drain the battery, especially if they go against the arrow of time."

"Would Dr. Holm know that?" Nate asked.

"It's Time Travel 101," Dr. B replied. "I'm pretty sure the principle was covered in the workshops she took. No, they'll more likely hunker down to conserve their battery power—either in the woods here or, if the map Julia found is any indication, on Newfoundland. If they spot the Norsemen, they'll most likely follow them on foot."

"Could they have horses?" I asked. "Quinn and Dr. Holm, I mean. Don't ask me how or where they might have gotten them."

"No horses here," Ron said.

"Are we too far north?"

"No. Ask me more about it later."

I shook my head. "I don't know. It all sounds like a lot more work than Quinn likes to do."

Nate snorted. "More than going into bankruptcy because of his debts and losing everything?"

"Possibly. You don't know him like I do."

Almost like she was trying to change the subject, Ruth-Ann asked to hear some more about ghost zones. "Are they really as dangerous as they sound?"

Dr. Baumgartner chuckled. "When people ask me what I do, I give one of two answers. Both are true, incidentally. Sometimes I just say that I document the lives of seventeenth- and eighteenth-century scientists, which always earns me a yawn. Other times, I mention that I also work on compiling a database of ghost zones in those centuries so that we know not to fall into them on future runs, and they perk right up. I wouldn't worry too much about ghost zones," she reassured Ruth-Ann and Ron. "There's a more relevant question. We don't know much about what happens if there are two teams of time travelers side by side in the same time period who aren't cooperating with each other. Will we interfere with each other, causing each team to get time-stuck more frequently than usual? Or will History funnel us into the same path?"

"Jacob told us all about ghost zones," Ruth-Ann said. "He was demonstrating the thin-ice one when he fell out of the kayak and never had the chance to finish the story—Jacob?"

"Has he disappeared again?" I asked. "You'll find him some-where with his phone in hand."

I was right. Jacob wandered over; he had been by himself next to the kayaks. "Sorry, everyone, I was just typing in some thoughts. First impressions of the fourteenth century, that sort of thing."

"And what are your thoughts so far, young man?" Ruth-Ann asked kindly.

"Only a few, tweet-sized. The awesome night sky. The weirdness of there being no electrical wires in sight. The silence—"

I raised an eyebrow at him. "Silence? What about the chirping birds, the buzzing insects, and the hooting owls last night?"

"It's weird not hearing cars or planes."

"Give it time," Nate said. "It takes a few days of being in the wilderness to really tune in into nature. Speaking of which—"

He got to his feet.

Something had moved in the woods across the lake.

We all scrambled to our feet, but it was only a pair of white-tailed deer. The buck and doe stared at us for a long moment, then went on their way through the trees.

It seemed like a signal for us to leave. We finished off the coffee and oatmeal, rinsed the cups where a small stream entered the lake, and doused the fire with water, scattering the ashes around with a stick. We took a last look around to make sure we hadn't left anything behind and picked up the kayaks to portage them to the north.

It was a no-go, however.

We were time-stuck. Not like on Runestone Island, where Ron had been forbidden from approaching the stone but we had been free to leave.

Completely. On all sides.

# 25

"So we can't leave?" Ruth-Ann asked.

"It's just temporary," I explained. "We're stuck until History's paths rearrange themselves."

"There's got to be a way out," Nate said. He headed in the opposite direction of the one we'd wanted and was forced to come to a stop again. He started feeling his way around in the air, like a mime. "Anyone care to help me?"

While the others put down their backpacks and formed a company of mimes with Nate, I stayed where I was. I had that feeling again, of being watched. But we wouldn't be time-stuck if Quinn and Dr. Holm were near us, I reasoned. And it had to be against History's rules for the Psinomani to keep surveillance on us, though it was possible that we were being held in place to prevent an encounter with them. As far as nature-related possibilities went, the lake hummed with wildlife, with a pair of loons gliding along its calm surface, their black heads held high in the air almost as if they were turning their noses up at our presence. The buck and the doe we had seen on the far shore hadn't seemed particularly disturbed to see us, just curious. A squirrel had run up a tree as we lit the fire, but surely History wasn't keeping us in place because we were scaring or fascinating the local wildlife?

On the other hand, with History and its quirks, you never did know. I shook my head.

"What is it, Julia?" Dr. B asked from where she seemed to be checking her equipment, on a log by the water's edge. "Do you see something?"

"I just can't shake the feeling that we're being watched. Never mind."

The others returned in defeat. We seemed to be trapped in a room-size sphere centered on the extinguished fire, part of it grazing the water's edge where Dr. B had set up. "You might as well make yourselves comfortable," the professor said. "I figured I'd prepare the Slingshot in case we're stuck here awhile and want to adjust our position."

"I thought we were only bringing it along for emergencies," I said, settling down with my back against my backpack. "I'm not sure that being time-stuck—even if it turns out to be for hours—constitutes an emergency. Besides, when the Slingshot generates a new time travel basket, won't the one on Runestone Island return home without us? Is it wise to rely on the Slingshot alone?"

Dr. B shrugged above the device, which looked like a chunkier, junkyard version of a laptop. "It will be a good opportunity to get another data point. Xavier and Steven have been running experiments to test how far the new basket has to be from the old one for both to stay."

"What's the distance?" Nate asked. "Have we exceeded it? We're probably a good five, six miles from Runestone Island by now."

"It's not really a set distance—it's more a combination of place and circumstance. A few blocks in a city, farther in non-urban areas."

As our wait stretched on, Jacob, who was picking at the long-extinguished remnants of the fire with the toe of one hiking boot, said, "I think it's me."

"You what?" I asked.

"I think I'm the one who got us stuck here."

"How do you figure?" Dr. B asked her student.

"We lit the fire because I needed to dry off and now we're stuck."

"Could be," Nate said. "Maybe dousing the campfire with water and spreading the ash around wasn't enough. All right, let's completely cover it with dirt."

We did, Nate using his pocketknife to loosen the soil. The end result was that the ash and charcoal were no longer visible but the dirt above them looked disturbed. A good dose of rain would probably have completely erased all traces of our presence, but the morning clouds had dissipated to a clear, cloudless blue.

Still, Nate did his circle again, trying to push through. No luck. Then, as if something had just occurred to him, he headed purposefully over to the kayaks. Ron helped him carry them to the water, but the lake we had rowed in on didn't seem to want to accept them anymore. "Well, so much for that idea," Nate said.

"Jacob, are you typing again?" I asked. He was speedily keying in text with his thumbs.

"I'm jotting down what it feels like to have nothing holding you up. It's like History overruling gravity, you know? Besides, it's not like there's a lot to do here, Julia. No point in taking pictures for my blog—the lake is just a lake. It could belong in any century."

Apparently deciding that our predicament could at least be used as a learning experience, Dr. B said, "Jacob, put your phone aside for the moment. Can you explain to Ruth-Ann and Ron here why we can't jump in time without also moving in space?"

"Uh—all right, professor, I'll take a stab at it. The short answer is that space and time are one, of course. Spacetime. Some people write it with the dash, some without. Or is it called a hyphen? Anyway, I prefer to spell it as one word—why waste a character? Plus, the whole point is that space and time are one. Anyway, the reason we can't just stand in this spot and jump forward in time is that this spot itself will move and change as time passes. We have to keep up with it." He started ticking off the reasons on his fingers. "One, the Earth rotates. Two, we orbit the Sun. Three, the Sun orbits the center of the Milky Way Galaxy. Four, the galaxy itself moves in space. Five, the axis of the Earth wobbles, like a top—it's called precession. Six, the continents are drifting apart—"

Ruth-Ann put a hand on Jacob's shoulder to stop him. "I think we get the idea, dear. Sounds like a very complicated calculation."

"It is," Dr. B agreed. "It can't be done by hand. That's why I brought my laptop."

Nate squatted down by Dr. B. They were just about the same height. Erika had tied her long blonde hair back. She pushed her bangs out of her eyes, not because they were bothering her, but as an almost flirtatious gesture. Then I decided that the whole thing was in my mind.

"Can you do it, Dr. B?" Nate asked, as if remembering all the problems the Slingshot had given us the last time. Who could forget? "Nudge us forward in time safely? I'd rather get going than be stuck here indefinitely."

"Like I said, there's no reason to expect that we'll fall into a ghost zone."

"Can you give me the odds?"

"How can I give you the odds? I have no data on which to base any projections."

"Ballpark, then."

Dr. B seemed uncomfortable with the idea of ballpark figures. Many of the scientists at St. Sunniva University, whose job it was to be exact, tended to shy away from such broad approximations. I'd had plenty of experience with that. I stepped in and said, "What is your recommendation, Professor?"

"There's no reason for us *not* to jump."

"How long will the calculations take?" Nate asked.

Dr. B opened her backpack to retrieve her laptop. "It's not the fastest computer. A good hour or so."

"Well, time is the one thing we seem to have plenty of," Nate said, taking a seat. Jacob pulled out his suntan lotion and started applying it.

Dr. B unzipped the waterproof cover, removed the laptop, and set it down on the log next to the Slingshot, then hooked its cable to a pouch that she unfolded into three panels.

"What is that?" I asked. "Some special battery that the Department of Engineering cooked up?"

"Nope, just a portable solar recharger." She moved the panels so that they caught the maximum amount of sun. "You can get one at the Emporium."

"Will we be able to jump back immediately if we do drop into a ghost zone?" Nate asked.

Dr. B shook her head without looking up from the laptop, where she was busily entering commands. "This is the old Slingshot, remember? We can't go backward in time with it, only forward. Let me say it again—when you used the Slingshot before, the reason you fell into so many ghost zones was that Dr. Mooney had no way to calculate coordinates to guide the Slingshot. I do."

Nate nodded. "I'll leave you to it, then."

Remembering something Ron had said, I moved closer to where he was sitting on a log, his sketchpad on one knee. "You said there are no horses here, Ron? Where are they?"

He put down the pencil and tugged at the beads in his beard. "It's quite a story. A long time ago—more than a million years, if we could go back that far in time with your STEWie—"

"It's never been tried," Dr. B offered, briefly glancing back over her shoulder as she worked.

"If we did, we would have seen them, horses, dog-size ones, munching on leaves in the woods. This is where evolution bred them. Then, some ten thousand years ago, they went extinct. No one's quite sure why."

Jacob put away his phone and devoted his full attention to Ron's tale.

"Luckily for rodeos and chariots and racing tracks, some of the animals crossed the Bering Strait land bridge before they died off here, heading in the opposite direction the ancestors of the Psinomani took. Then the land bridge disappeared under rising ocean levels...Meanwhile, the horse thrived in Asia and Europe. But here in the Americas—today, at this very moment in time—there are no horses. None. Not one. Was it climate change? Being hunted to extinction by man? Drought? Disease? Like I said, no one knows."

It was daytime and our fire was out, but his story could not have been more effective if he had been telling it at night around a campfire.

He went on. "When the animal did return, it happened not over land, but over water."

For a second I had a vision of a herd of horses ambitiously swimming across the Atlantic or the Pacific, but Ron continued: "The ships of Columbus and other Europeans carried pigs, cattle...and horses. Nature did what it does best when a door is opened—she jumped at the chance. Some of the horses escaped and soon spread throughout the Great Plains. There weren't any big herds immediately, not of horses, and not of buffalo either. That happened later, when the balance between man and nature was lost after smallpox, which also came in on the ships, took its toll on the Indian population.

"Imagine a modern city left with few caretakers—vegetation and wildlife would soon overrun the place. Nature always wins. And so it will be in this case. The orchards and woods and animal populations that had been shaped by the hand of man—"

An image of the well-tended grove of black walnut trees back on Runestone Island flashed into my head.

"—would slowly lose the mark of civilization and the new-comers would assume that it had always been so. Without any check on their populations, animals multiplied. Great herds of horses and bison may have been what the Europeans saw, but that's not how it was before their arrival. The massive flocks of passenger pigeons reported by John James Audubon, the painter, were not the mark of a pristine continent untouched by the hand of man; they were a sign of unchecked animal population growth. Audubon described the flocks as darken-ing the skies for hours on end, obscuring the sun like a bird eclipse."

"I'm hoping to snap a photo of a passenger pigeon," Ruth-Ann said. "They are completely gone in our own time. Be on the lookout for a blue-gray head above a breast the hue of red wine," she added poetically.

The mid-day breeze stirred the budding leaves on the trees around us and I thought of the palisaded village again and of its small group of inhabitants. Listening to Ron and Ruth-Ann, and talking to Nate's grandmother the other day, had made it clear to me how little I knew of history. I felt ashamed that I knew so little about the past of my own country. I had heard of Vinland and Columbus but not about the horses, the passenger pigeons, or some of the things Dr. Payne had mentioned, such as that no one was sure how long ago the ancestral Indians had arrived or along which route.

Ruth-Ann took over the tale. "The Psinomani have the land in hand—they hunt deer and other small game, occasionally buffalo and bear, and they also fish, gather plants, farm wild rice, encourage the growth of trees they find useful. Wild rice, incidentally, isn't rice at all but a water grass harvested by two people in a canoe."

"Is anyone having trouble breathing?" Dr. B suddenly asked.

If we weren't before she said that, we certainly were as soon as she did.

Nate scrambled to his feet. He turned to check for the invisible wall again and didn't have to take a single step. The wall had *moved*. Closer.

"Dammit," Dr. B said. "We're not time-stuck. Someone is coming."

Unnoticed by us, History's walls had been inching in on us minute by short minute, putting pressure on us to leave.

I felt myself start to breathe heavily, as if I had been running, and willed myself to inhale and exhale normally. It was clear History wanted us gone, but how?

"Professor, is the Slingshot ready?" Nate asked in a calm voice.

"No, I need more time."

"Let's hope we have it. Wait—if we're not time-stuck, that means there has to be a way out, right? Time-travel's fourth rule: *There's always a way back*. We just need to find it."

I hoped he was right. I could definitely feel it now. The air had become thinner and it was a chore to breathe in and out, as if there was something pressing down on my chest.

"The water." Nate smacked his forehead. "I think we can go into the water and *swim* across instead of using the kayaks like we've been trying. We'll have to deflate the kayaks to take them with us—"

I suddenly felt a bit woozy and stepped into the water—it was cold but I let myself slip down into it and took a few tentative strokes. I immediately felt better.

"It's working," I called out.

"Julia—wait, come back—" I heard Dr. B's voice.

I made a U-turn in the water. I had forgotten my backpack.

"It's too dangerous," Dr. B spit out between shallow breaths. "Don't you see? What if we all get into the water and swim out and then suddenly we aren't *allowed* to swim any more?"

"Oh," I said. "I didn't think of that."

The feeling of something pressing down on my chest was back. Next to me, Jacob was also fighting for breath. Dr. B was on her knees by the computer, as if willing it to work faster.

"Everyone, get into a huddle," I heard her command. She sounded faint, as if either she or I were disappearing. "Holding hands is best—stand the kayaks on their ends so that they fit into the basket—"

# 26

"Hey, where are we?" Jacob asked. "This looks completely different."

"It shouldn't be." Dr. B glanced around wildly. "I sent us just a few minutes ahead. I think—yes, there must have been a minor adjustment by History. The destination we wanted wasn't available so we arrived as close as History would permit."

Nate pulled out his compass and map to orient himself. "We were over there..." he said, pointing behind him. "And that's where we want to go, north." He pointed ahead.

"STEWie's basket?" I asked.

Dr. B checked the instrument in her hand. "Still where we left it."

"Good," Nate said.

Shivering in my wet clothes, I noticed that Jacob had his cell phone out again.

"Jacob, this is no time to be jotting down thoughts for future blog posts and tweets. We're finally free to get going. I'm just going to go change behind that tree—" If there was one motif for the week, it was water.

"Wait, Julia. I have an app for binoculars. I thought I saw—yes, look, the place where we were...there are some Indians there now—sorry, Mrs. Tuttle, is it rude to say Indians? I meant the Dakota—the Psinomani."

"Here." I took the phone from him, careful not to get it wet, and looked through it. Several Dakota men and boys were passing through from the woods into the more sparsely vegetated prairie to the west. Had we remained at our previous location, they would have run smack into us. I couldn't help but notice that they were carrying spears. They were blocking our way to STEWie's basket but luckily the other direction was where we wanted to go, farther north and deeper into the woods.

"Look, we should have anticipated this," I heard Dr. B explain as I toweled off and changed into my backup clothing behind the tree. "The best we can expect to do is tiptoe through the woods. If anyone had any visions of mingling with the Dakota or the Norsemen, put them aside immediately. Our clothes are strange. Everything we carry—and the way we carry ourselves—stands out. The very imprints left by the soles of our hiking boots do not belong here. The same will be true for Quinn and Dr. Holm, but at least that works in our favor. They'll be as limited as we are. If they do come, I expect that we will converge on the same spot sooner or later."

Ruth-Ann sounded a little disappointed. "I had expected more of a front row seat than one way up in the balcony."

"Time travel is like that," Dr. B went on. "First-time STEWie users find that it never lives up to their expectations. It's always— *smaller*, I guess. They forget that time travelers, like the locals, have only one pair of eyes. They can only see one slice of the battle or take a quick peek into the window of, say, Galileo's villa. Answering questions is never easy. It takes multiple runs, wise choices, and a lot of luck."

"And funding," I called out from behind the tree.

Ruth-Ann and Ron chuckled at that. I had worried that they might slow us down, but they'd struck a good pace, both paddling and when the kayaks needed to be carried.

"What now?" Ruth-Ann asked when I emerged dry, with the small towel wrapped around my hair. At least it had started to warm up as the sun rose higher in the sky.

"We keep heading north," Nate said. "Into the woods."

After a bit of experimentation, though, we realized that History didn't seem to want to let us go deeper into the woods. We were free to head the other way, into the open fields of the prairie with their dry, yellow growth spreading toward the western horizon. Where the Psinomani men were going.

"I guess we have to take a detour," Nate said. "Hopefully we'll be able to swing back into the woods sooner rather than later. Do you need any help, Dr. B?"

The professor slung the Slingshot across one shoulder, on top of her backpack. "All ready."

"Can we stay a bit longer?" Ruth-Ann had been snapping pictures of the Psinomani men as they grew smaller in the distance, hacking at the knee-high grass as they walked.

"We're not here to sightsee," Nate said as the rest of us divided up the kayaks and started walking.

"Aren't you curious about our ancestors, yours and mine?" Ruth-Ann asked, putting the camera away and hurrying to catch up with us.

"I am curious," he said, turning around. For some reason he was looking at me and not Ruth-Ann, "but now isn't the time. We have a job to do."

He picked up his pace as he guided our little group forward. I hoped he wouldn't walk smack into one of History's invisible walls.

Soon it became clear that we were being led on an arc through the gently rolling prairie. "One thing is for sure,"

Dr. B commented. "Our path seems to be tied to the coming and goings of the village."

"Maybe we just need to put some real distance between us and the villagers and that will break this time-stickiness that we've been experiencing," Jacob suggested.

"That could very well be the case," Dr. B said. "It's certainly happened often enough on other STEWie runs. You leave the circle of influence of a person or settlement and suddenly it's like the gates of History have opened and you can go wherever you want."

I thought it would be wise to eat something to fend of the chill, so when we stopped to allow Ruth-Ann to snap some photos—Jacob had spotted a flock of the red-breasted passenger pigeons—I reached for a snack from my backpack.

"If we carried one or two back with us," Jacob suggested, studying the flock of passenger pigeons gliding gracefully above our heads, with their long tails and broad wings, "they would no longer be extinct."

Ruth-Ann caught her breath. "Can we?"

Dr. B sighed. "No. It's a slippery slope. The photos and video will have to do. Maybe some future generation will be wiser than we are and they'll figure out how to bring all the extinct animals back without destroying the fragile harmony of our modern-day ecosystem, but we're far from ready."

Munching on a cookie, I reflected again on how privileged I was to see the Psinomani village, the passenger pigeons, and all the other fourteenth-century surprises that awaited us. And I owed it all to Quinn. Not that I was happy about the situation, but if it hadn't been for him, I would have been at my desk attending to everyday work matters. I had to admit to myself that I understood his motivations . . . at least partially. I just wished he had gone about things in a different way.

As we resumed walking, following the pigeons, I reached for another cookie. Nate, who had somewhat impatiently waited for the pigeon photo shoot to end, said from behind me, "You brought cookies, Julia? Haven't you heard that it's better to shop on the perimeter of the grocery store than in the middle? You know, where the fresh fruit and fish and milk are."

Was he teasing me? That was very unlike him. Perhaps the sun was getting to him.

"I could hardly have brought fresh fish and milk with me. Besides, cookies are comfort food in my family. We don't all have grandmothers who are gourmet cooks, you know." In my family, pre-sliced white bread and peanut butter and jelly had counted as a treat for dinner. My parents had always been busy with work; chores like grocery shopping and cleaning were done on the weekends, if at all.

"You buy fancier stuff for fundraisers and other school occasions, I've noticed," he said, falling into a stride next to me. "Goat cheese and grapes, bagels and lox, and whatnot."

"Not to mention champagne. But the school pays for it, you know that. In the grocery store the stuff that's in the middle of the store is cheaper and requires little actual cooking."

"You wouldn't put the cheapest, subpar gasoline into your car, why put subpar food into your body—"

I increased my pace so I could eat my cookies in peace.

∞

"Those clouds are starting to concern me," Ruth-Ann, who was carrying the paddles, said. I had one end of a kayak and Jacob had the other. Nate and Ron were carrying the second kayak, while Dr. B led the group, occasionally signaling us to adjust our route when she felt herself being slowed down by History's constraints.

I glanced back. "Hmm, I hope it doesn't rain." Some grayish clouds, which had been hugging the ground to the east, deep in the prairieland, had started to rise skyward in our direction.

"Nothing our rain jackets can't handle—" Nate said with a shrug, then stopped. Jacob bumped his end of the kayak into the small of Nate's back.

"Oops, sorry, Chief Kirkland."

Nate shaded his eyes with his hand and, with a frown, scanned the horizon.

Ruth-Ann said, "Rain clouds don't billow up like that. It's almost like—"

She didn't finish her thought. In the minute or two we had been standing there, the clouds had broadened and were rising steadily in the previously blue sky. It struck me that they were spreading entirely too fast in the breezeless afternoon and were an odd shade of gray—smoky, charcoal-tinted, ashy.

Nate swore. "Those aren't rain clouds—it's smoke from a wildfire."

As we all stood frozen to the spot, he added, "Though the smoke plumes are so uniform I could almost swear that someone started the fire intentionally..."

Ruth-Ann gasped. "Yes...the villagers might be hunting and want to drive bison or other game into the lake, or are clearing the land to discourage the growth of trees and underbrush so that fresh grass will grow for grazing—"

I wanted to hear more about it, but not at the moment. A pair of white-tailed deer—I couldn't tell if they were the ones we had seen before—thundered past us and over the rise ahead. There was no mistaking the stench of burned grass and shrubs that followed them.

We had fallen into a ghost zone after all.

"Follow the animals," Nate commanded. "Run!"

# 27

Like I said, Nate had experience with wildfires from his years in the Boundary Waters wilderness, by the border with Canada. Wanda the cocker spaniel was a constant reminder of that time, a string tied around his finger that said *Don't trust too easily again.* Or not. He had probably chosen to keep the dog because he felt sorry for her after her owner went to jail.

Which was completely irrelevant at the moment, except for the experience with wildfires part, which was hugely relevant.

"This is what ghost zones are like, huh?" said Jacob, panting as we hurried along. Under the circumstances, I was glad to see that he seemed calm. It was a sign that he might be successful in leading his own research team a few years down the road. If we made it back.

We crested a rise, which gave an unnerving view of the burning prairie behind us. A jagged line of red-orange gobbled at the prairie grass with an eerie crackling that drifted in and out on the breeze. The nearing edge of the fire had not caught up with us yet, but its heat was creating a wind that drove the smoke and heat in our direction, making it hard to breathe.

We hurried downhill into a bowl-shaped depression. It had to be the only valley in the entire state without a lake. Nate swore again and turned to Dr. B. "Can we use the Slingshot?"

"You mean jump blindly, without running the necessary calculations? Not a good idea. We could end up someplace worse."

"Worse than this?" Nate jerked his thumb in the direction of the fire.

In the depression, the air was not yet thick with smoke, but it soon would be. I could *taste* the fire, a gritty mouthful of ash and heat that made it hard to speak. I managed to get a few words out anyway. "Xavier had no problem using it to whisk us out of a ghost zone—"

"—and into another. I'm not Xavier Mooney. I won't just hit a button and send us into the unknown. We could end up in the middle of the ocean, or some place even less survivable, like, I don't know, outer space or something. I'd rather face a known danger."

The others reluctantly nodded their agreement.

"Can we outrun the fire?" Ron asked.

"We can't. It's too late." Nate already had a blanket out and was pouring our drinking water on it. Ruth-Ann pulled a blanket out of her own bag and did the same with Ron's help.

Moving as quickly as we could, we found a rocky spot clear of vegetation and wedged our bodies into it. We covered ourselves with the wet blankets, hauled the kayaks over us, and hoped for the best.

# 28

"Well, now you've been through a ghost zone," I said to the Tuttles, who looked a little wild-eyed. I suspected that the rest of us looked a bit wild-eyed too. Ghost zones were not the kind of thing you could get used to. There was no sense of exhilaration like you might get from, say, skydiving or climbing Mt. Everest (neither of which I had ever done), only a feeling of being blind-sided and the realization that it might happen again at any time, without warning.

Coughing and with watery eyes, we staggered away from the charred area with its blackened remnants of vegetation, heading back into the woods without regard for direction, our only goal to get as far away as possible. The fire had mostly run its course, tapering off by design or because it had run out of fuel, leaving behind gently falling ash and six coughing time travelers.

Ron was limping, having twisted his ankle during our run into the valley, and was holding on to Ruth-Ann's arm for support as he hobbled along. I hoped they didn't regret coming with us. I wanted to ask Nate if he was all right—I knew the fire might have brought back some painful memories, however stoic he tried to be—but I didn't want to ask him about it in front of the others. Next to me, Jacob was clutching his backpack, and up ahead, Dr. B was swatting ash off her clothes.

The kayaks were gone, melted into an unrecognizable black mass that we had left behind. It meant that we would be on foot from this point on, and unless we wanted to chance using the Slingshot again, were going to have a hard time getting back to STEWie's basket on Runestone Island.

Well, at least my hair had dried quickly.

I had completely lost my sense of orientation, but thought that we'd doubled back a bit, into what would one day become the Andes Tower ski hill area. Soon we reached a small lake. In silent agreement, we dropped our backpacks onto the ground, happy to catch our breath and wash the soot off our faces in the cool water.

"It sent us right into a ghost zone," Jacob said as he splashed water on his face. "The Slingshot."

"I'm not sure it did, actually," Dr. B said. "I think we actually walked into that one. We chose to go into the prairie, but there were other directions open to us. Just not the one we wanted."

I lowered myself onto the uneven ground, feeling the coolness of the spongy moss on my hands, and asked the question that needed to be asked. "Do we keep trying to find Quinn and Dr. Holm even if it means risking falling into another ghost zone? Perhaps the wildfire was a sign that we should turn back."

"I know you don't think Dr. Holm needs rescuing, Julia," Nate said. He was still on his feet, rubbing his jawline with one hand as if trying to decide which course of action would be best.

"I don't. Do you?"

"I'd like to make sure, that's all."

"Besides, we could have guessed wrong…they might not even be coming here. What if they are camping out in Duluth or Hudson Bay or Newfoundland? Even if they *are* here, we still might miss them."

"I've been thinking about that," Nate said. "I think we might be here too early in the year. Judging from the vegetation, it must have been a long winter. I think we should jump ahead a few weeks."

"Ron's ankle might require medical attention," I pointed out.

Ron had found a seat on a boulder and was loosening the laces of his hiking boots. He gingerly felt his left ankle as Ruth-Ann looked on with a furrowed brow. "It's an old snowshoeing injury. I'll be fine I just need to rest the ankle a bit." He reached up to wipe a bit of soot off Ruth-Ann's cheek. "Ruth-Ann, what do you think?"

She handed him her water bottle. "That I'm in no hurry to go back. I don't think you are either."

"You know my opinion," Dr. B said. "There's no reason to think that we're going to keep falling into ghost zones."

"Jacob, you get a vote, too," I said to him. The ginger-haired graduate student was sitting on a tree root with his arms wrapped around his knees, poking at the moss with a reed.

"Hmm, what, Julia?"

"You get a vote, too. Stay and keep looking for Quinn and Dr. Holm, or go home?"

The danger of what we had just been though must have finally sunk in. Instead of answering my question, he said with something of a dazed look, "Time travel isn't at all like I imagined...I've been thinking about Sunniva." I thought he meant the university, but he went on. "As a thesis topic, I mean. But that would mean going to the tenth century, and who knows *what* I'd encounter that far back?"

I realized that he was talking about the school's namesake, the woman whose name meant "sun gift." Sunniva, the patron saint of Western Norway, had an unusual story—the tenth-century Irish princess had fled aboard a ship to escape an unwanted marriage to a pagan king. She had ended up hiding in a cave off the coast of Norway, where she died after a rockfall blocked the entrance, causing her and her followers to starve. When the cave was opened decades later, her body was found intact, as if she had simply fallen asleep. Or so the legend went. Dr. Edberg of the European History department had not had much luck on his investigative runs to the region and so had moved on to other things. It *was* a good idea for a thesis topic. "I wonder what everyone is doing," Jacob added pensively.

I sat down on the tree root next to him. "Everyone home at St. Sunniva? Here, have some water."

"No, everyone in the whole world. I miss being connected."

I guessed he was talking about his online buddies. "You can catch up on Twitter news when you get back. Are you saying you'd rather go home, then?"

"Hmm? What? No. We can't give up now, can we?" He dropped the reed onto the forest floor and brushed soot off his jeans. "I'm ready."

I turned back to the others. "Sounds like we're pushing on."

Nate nodded to me and sat down with a penknife to fashion a walking stick for Ron. "Same location but three weeks from now, please, Dr. B."

# 29

A safe jump of three weeks and a meal of granola bars and fresh water gave us renewed energy. The steady pace through the woods kept us too busy for conversation. The air was warmer and the forest now denser, with only intermittent shafts of light filtering in through the canopy, illuminating bountiful wildflowers and ferns. Birds chirped and dragonflies flitted among old oak and elm trees like miniature helicopters. A squirrel toddled by. I wondered if we might run into a moose or a caribou this far south—or, more unnervingly, a bear or a wolf. I had a sudden vision of us getting lost in the seemingly endless forest and slowly starving to death over the course of several weeks as we unsuccessfully tried to hunt down deer and other large game with nothing but a pointy stick...which was when I remembered that Nate had brought a gun. Of course we weren't going to get lost—Dr. B had left a beacon on Runestone Island—but I was suddenly happy that we had a means of self-defense. Hopefully it would work if we really needed it.

"Nice woods," said Jacob, who seemed to have completely perked up.

We struggled through for a good two hours, pushing low-hanging branches out of the way, stepping over fallen and decomposing logs and thriving ferns, all the while swatting mosquitoes out of our faces. All of us were scratched up and bug bitten. I had never realized how difficult it was to walk through the woods without an established path to follow. North, south, west, east, no matter what the direction, there were just…more trees. If we had not possessed a compass, it would have been hard to know which direction we were heading in, not that we had much choice in the matter—even with the adjustment in time, History's hand was still leading us where it wanted. It took all my energy to focus on staying on my feet without tripping or twisting an ankle to match Ron's injured one. It probably helped him that we were making such slow progress, but as the afternoon wore on, his face took on an increasingly pale hue. I caught Ruth-Ann casting a concerned look in his direction several times, as if she was wondering if we'd made the right decision in continuing our quest.

"Dammit, I wish we hadn't lost the kayaks," Nate said as we wound our way around the marshy shores of another sprawling lake. Like all of us, he no doubt realized that the kayaks would have made things a whole lot easier for Ron.

Dr. B, as if reading my mind, said, "Maybe we should think about setting up camp here, Chief Kirkland. It's as good a spot as any. Sheltered, with access to water." Almost imperceptibly, she nodded in Ron's direction.

The end of our second day in the fourteenth century found us much worse off than the first—cold, without our kayaks, and in low spirits. Like the previous night, Nate's lighter and the Tuttle's matches wouldn't produce a flame and the stove stayed cold, but our various electronic devices, with their tiny lights, worked just fine. By the glow of Jacob's cell phone and a setting half-moon, Ron told us of Vinland and the Norse sagas as we munched on dry food and rested our tired legs.

"The Vikings would not have had firearms," he said, "like Columbus did. They only had spears, axes, bows and arrows, perhaps a sword if they could afford it. They came here not as invaders but looking to settle a land, as they had with Iceland around 870 AD," he explained. "After that they pushed farther west, to Greenland, led by Erik the Red. He was a hot-blooded outlaw who had been exiled for committing murder—more than once—back home in Iceland. He chose to sail west, to the land that had been spotted by ships blown off course. The sagas tell his story and that of his offspring, three sons, Leif, Thorvald, and Thorstein, and one daughter, Freydis. As for his Greenland—" Ron paused for a drink of water from his bottle. "The name is all wrong, you know, an example of an early PR machine at work. Erik the Red was trying to woo colonists over from Iceland. Most of Greenland is covered with ice throughout the year—the only parts that are green are the edges of the fjords. Erik the Red and his colonists built two settlements, one at the southern tip and the other a bit farther north on Greenland's west coast. The problem was that they used up the trees quickly and found it a struggle to survive on their farming lifestyle—cattle and sheep didn't adapt easily to Greenland's harsh climate.

"But a forested land had been sighted even farther to the west, again by ships that had been blown off course. The oldest son, Leif, set sail with a crew of thirty-five. They first made landfall probably somewhere on the coast of Labrador. After two more days at sea, the sagas say, they came across a place that suited them just fine—a fertile, warmer land where wild grapes grew, a place the Norse called Vinland the Good. They decided to winter there and build their houses. But people were already living there. *Skraelings*, the Norse called them in a not very complimentary fashion. Wretches who screech. The sagas talk of skirmishes with the locals and the colonists soon went back to Greenland, though they occasionally returned for lumber."

"They would have been Peoples of the Dawnland," Ruth-Ann said quietly, "those who lived where the sun first rises. Speakers of Algonquian."

"The sagas tell of five voyages made to Vinland by Greenlanders. But here's the thing about L'Anse aux Meadows. Helge and Anne Stine Ingstad found the remnants of eight houses, four boat sheds, an iron smithy, and other workshops...but no wild grapes, which all of the stories mention. It must have just been a stepping-stone to Vinland, like your Dr. Holm guessed, with Vinland itself being farther south down the coast, where wild grapes would have been sure to grow.

"As for our Norsemen, of whom we haven't seen a trace— well, they could be traders looking to set up a new route to the west to match their established one to the east. Another theory is that that they might be Knights Templar. Fascinating but far-fetched. I have a different take."

"Ron," said Ruth-Ann, with a fond look at her husband, "thinks he might know what happened to the Greenlanders."

"All these theories assume that the runestone carvers came to North America directly from Scandinavia, sailing across the North Atlantic. Here's the thing. The two Greenland colonies struggled in the unforgiving climate and in the end disappeared, the more northern one by 1362—does that date sound familiar?—and the other one a bit later. No one knows what happened, where they went. I think at least some of them gave up on treeless Greenland, where it was difficult to support their way of life, and followed Leif Erikson's footsteps and the lure of Vinland."

"The date fits with the runestone," I said. "But why would they call themselves Norwegians and Gotlanders on the stone?"

"I don't think they would have thought of themselves as Greenlanders as such. They had strong ties to Norway and depended on it for goods, bishops, and the latest social mores." Ron frowned. "It's more problematic that the runestone talks of fishing. Greenlanders didn't fish."

"What do you mean they didn't fish?" Nate asked. "They must have."

"Nope. They made cheese from cow's, sheep's, and goat's milk and hunted caribou and seals. The seals were the poor man's meat, caribou the farm owner's. But maybe things changed when they came here." He paused. "As for what happened—will happen—to our Norsemen from Greenland..."

"Never mind the verb tense," Dr. B said. "There's no good solution. We tend to use the present tense to minimize confusion."

"Okay, then. Here's how I picture it. Vinland is on the eastern seaboard. Our runestone carvers set out early in the spring, perhaps with a local guide to take them along the St. Lawrence River trade route, or they wing it. The main center of the Psinomani culture was—is—the large inland lake halfway between where we are now and Duluth. In the twenty-first century we call it, somewhat redundantly, Mille Lacs Lake.

"It could be that the Norsemen spend some time with the Psinomani there and trade iron for some furs and a canoe or two. They depart to do a bit of exploring on their own and set up camp. One morning, a smaller group splinters off to go fishing at dawn, only to return in the afternoon to find that disaster had struck the camp. Maybe there was a misunderstanding with the Psinomani, or the theory about the Black Death is the correct one. Either way, there's nothing they can do. They wait until morning, perhaps fearing that the same thing might happen to them."

"Could it have been a fire like the one we just lived through?" Nate asked.

Ron shook his head. "Would they have used the description 'red from blood' on the stone if that had been the case? I don't think so. In any case, at dawn they bury their dead, gather their things and leave, moving fast to get away from the place of death. Clearly they feel safe once they reach Runestone Island. They camp there the two or three days necessary to carve their tale into the stone. Perhaps that means the Black Death was responsible after all, since they didn't think the danger would catch up to them."

I brought up a point about the runestone that had been bothering me for days. "The runes look so—fresh. I had a hard time believing they were a hundred years old, let alone almost a thousand."

Ron, his ankle elevated on his backpack, didn't seem too disturbed by my comment. "Collateral damage from the stone having been cleaned. After it was dug up, mud was scraped from most of the runes with a nail. Only a few were left undisturbed, on the side of the stone."

"In reading your book," I said, looking from Ron to Ruth-Ann and back, "I couldn't tell which way the two of you come down on the issue, for or against."

"We take turns," Ruth-Ann said. "There are times when Ron is quite convinced the runestone is genuine and I'm not, and times when it's the other way around. We have yet to agree on it."

"And today?" I asked.

Ron hung his head. "I came out here feeling certain that we'd find them, especially when I saw the stone just lying there waiting. Now I'm not so sure. Like I said, we haven't seen a single trace of them. We came across the Psinomani, but there have been no signs of the Norsemen..."

Jacob piped up. "Time travel kind of messes with your head, doesn't it? Yesterday the moon was full and then we jumped ahead and now it's a first quarter moon."

"It's more than that," Ron said. "I guess I thought they'd be here because we were coming to look for them. Silly, I know."

Ruth-Ann rubbed her husband's shoulder fondly. "I wasn't convinced at all as we climbed into the Time Machine basket. But... there's a legend."

This must be the Dakota legend that Nate's grandmother had mentioned.

"Tell us about it, please, Ms. Tuttle," Jacob said, passing his cell phone with its light to her. Ruth-Ann took over as the campfire-story teller.

"The account was given by the Good Earth Woman— Makawastewin was her Dakota name, Susan Windgrow her English name. She lived on Prairie Island, on the Mississippi near the Wisconsin border. Her story tells of events that happened long ago, before her own lifetime. Good Earth Woman was born in the 'month of yellow corn,'" Ruth-Ann quoted. "November, that is. She said that her ancestors—and mine— lived in a northern land where the winters were long and game and other resources were scarce. Our forefathers and foremothers journeyed south and west, until they found a home by a large lake where the climate was more temperate and the game more plentiful. It might have been Lake Superior."

She went on. "Picture the Good Earth Woman, ninety years old, stooped in her coat and flowered dress as she sat in a chair, her hair tied back with a scarf. She told her story in 1935 to anthropologist Ruth Landes in the Dakota tongue, with her twenty-eight-year-old grandson sitting by her side to translate. One spring long ago, she said, our people sighted a sailboat on the large lake. The boat had a mast with carved snakes and a figurehead at the prow—a horse-like creature with horns, a scaly body, and wings. Thirty-eight sailors with horned headpieces manned the oars."

"To me it's always sounded like she's describing a longship," Ron said, "what with the oars and the carved figurehead. But Greenlanders would not have built such an elaborate thing, nor would they have had horned headpieces."

"Thirty-eight sailors. It doesn't match, either," I heard Nate mutter. "The stone says twenty-two Norwegians and eight Gotlanders, which is thirty."

"It's runestone math," Ron said. "Were there thirty Norsemen total who left Vinland—*Eight Gotlanders and twenty two Norwegians on a journey from Vinland*—or does that count only include those who went inland? Or only those who survived to carve the stone?" He shook his head.

"I wish it would all line up," Jacob complained. "Is this normal for history?"

"More or less," said Dr. B.

"You can make any story fit if you try hard enough," Nate said. "Didn't you say that there were no horses here that far back, Ron? If we're assuming it all happened in the fourteenth century, how would they have known that the boat figurehead was supposed to be a horse?" He seemed to be channeling Dr. Payne for some reason. It had been a long day and it probably wasn't easy to be responsible for the safety of six people—eight, if you counted Dr. Holm and Quinn.

I shushed him. "You can't have it both ways. You said an eyewitness report where every detail lined up was more suspicious than one where every detail didn't mesh. It was a boat with strangers on it. Go on, Ruth-Ann, please."

"A story is like a birthday card passed around the office— everyone adds a bit of themselves to it. Anyways, a Native American story is meant to be an interpretation of events, rather than a factual briefing—you know that, Chief Kirkland. But I'll let you judge for yourselves. Here is what the Good Earth Woman said next. The strangers gave gifts of iron knives and axes and were taught in return how to canoe and portage. They stayed for three seasons—the summer, fall, and winter—then left the next spring, saying they would return one day. They never did. In time, our ancestors moved westward from the large lake under pressure from their neighbors, the Ojibwe and the Winnebago tribes. Then the French fur traders entered the picture in the seventeenth century and everything changed—"

Jacob's cell phone suddenly winked out, leaving us in the dark. I knew that the battery hadn't died; he had just switched to a backup one.

"Hey, what's that noise?" he whispered, looking around nervously. "That's not normal for the woods, is it?"

Was this it? Were we about to clash with those unseen eyes?

# 30

Drums. A rhythmic beat, accompanied by rising and falling voices, had broken through the soft background noises of the night. The beat washed over the shadowy tree trunks around us like a wave over seashore, disguising the direction of its source and making the hairs on my arms stand on end more than the chill of the evening had. Had History led us to this spot only to corner us? The darkness of the old woods was absolute except for the moon peeking though a web of dark leaves. We had found shelter under a canopy of intertwined branches, suddenly menacing and eerily limb-like. Next to me, Jacob's eyes were wide, two beacons of fear in the darkness.

Nate had jumped to his feet and was listening intently, trying to decide where the sound—and possibly the danger—was coming from.

"It's all right," Ruth-Ann whispered. Her head was cocked as she listened.

Dr. B pushed herself to her feet and said, her voice equally low, "Shall we see if we can take a look?"

"Can we? Will we be able to do it without being seen?" Ruth-Ann whispered back. I couldn't see her expression, but she had turned in Nate's direction as if daring him to even suggest that our mission was too important to bother with what he had called *sightseeing*.

Nate's body still projected tense energy, but he nodded. We formed a line—each person putting a hand on the shoulder of the person in front of them—and crept through the woods single file. Twigs snapped and leaves crunched under our hiking boots no matter how softly we put one foot in front of the other as we felt our way along a path that seemed to get narrower and narrower—but not because of any tangible constraints—before coming to an abrupt stop at the edge of the woods. We managed to inch forward a bit more into a clearing until our noses were pressed against a head-height wooden fence that curved left and right in the darkness.

We had come almost full circle in a wide, zigzagging arc back to the village. I opened my mouth to comment on this, but no words came out, not even the whisper I had been planning. Not surprisingly, even the faintest sound would have given away our presence. We were closer than we would have been able to get had we belonged to the present, History's hand guiding us into the village's blindspot. We were so close that I could have flung the granola bar in my pocket and bounced it off the back off the bark house just on the other side of the fence.

I'd had an uneasy feeling ever since I had seen the village half empty. Maybe it was still a lingering fear from Pompeii, where we had known the town would be destroyed without being able to do anything about it.

The village was no longer empty. Peeking through the thin gaps between the wooden stakes of the palisade, we saw that a celebration of some kind was underway by the light of the flickering fires. The prairie fire technique had resulted in a good haul—the scent of the stew simmering in the clay pots wafted invitingly toward us. There were hand drums and dancing, and, to one side, a clutch where a tense game with carved-bone dice was being played. Voices rose and fell, the dancers' thumping feet kicking up dust from the dry soil, their necklaces jiggling along as the drums beat on. Some of the village kids were dancing in their own circle off to one side. The younger ones had what Ruth-Ann would later explain were maple-sugar cones, like lollipops; she figured that much of the village must have been away on a maple-tapping expedition.

We could not go in, I knew—a social, cultural, and historical gap of over six hundred years separated us more than the solid wooden fence did. Still, to hungry and weary travelers from afar, it was all very inviting, even if not in any realizable sense. I wondered what the villagers would have made of us, with our strange clothes and lack of fourteenth-century life skills, if we had burst out of the woods. Would we have been met as friends, as foes, as supernatural beings of the good kind...or the evil kind because we had approached so effortlessly and so stealthily?

I saw Ron dab at his eyes. Next to him Ruth-Ann was aiming her camera in the direction of the celebrating villagers. She let out a small grunt of frustration. The camera's button did not seem willing to respond to her touch. Dr. B silently offered Ruth-Ann her own camera, the lab one, which I knew had a night setting and a quiet mechanism. I was already planning to get a copy of the pictures to Nate's grandmother when we got back.

Nate was watching the village festivities with his back to the rest of us, his arms crossed. Dr. B signaled to me that she was ready to head back, and next to her Ruth-Ann started putting her camera away. Weary from the wildfire and all the walking we had done, I, too, was ready to call it a night and tumble into my sleeping bag.

I was pretty sure History would lead us right back to our site, but didn't want to take any chances getting separated. I put a hand on Nate's shoulder to alert him that the others had begun backing away, their hiking shoes noiseless under the curtain of the beating drums.

He grabbed my hand and held it for a moment, then pulled me to him.

In the darkness of the woods, with the fourteenth-century moon and stars as the only witnesses, to the sound of the celebration of life going on in the village a stone's throw away from us, we kissed. It was all very romantic and, for an all-too-brief moment, I forgot about my tired feet and Quinn and the Norsemen, and just let myself go.

# 31

"We're on the right track. Look."

Something on the forest floor had captured Nate's attention.

It was a single footprint, made by a hiking boot of modern design, with the indentations from the curves and the brand name from the shoe sole still discernible in the dirt. Only two people on the whole continent (other than the six of us) could have a modern shoe like that.

"Looks like they headed that way," Nate said. "Deeper into the woods."

It was mid-day, and a slow and steady hike to the north had yielded the prize.

"How long ago?" Jacob asked.

Nate eyed the young graduate student. "How long ago what?"

"How long ago did they walk by? Can you tell?"

"You mean because I'm part Indian? Or because I'm in law enforcement? Either way, I'm no Sherlock Holmes."

"You mean you can't tell us if it's going to rain today?" I said jokingly. It had been steadily clouding up as we pushed our way northward. The shafts of sunlight that had brightened the forest floor were slowly shrinking and disappearing. Instead of answering, Nate shoved a low-hanging branch out of the way and held it up for me to go under. He was back to his business-like self and hadn't said much all day.

Soon we came upon a second clue, this one hardly bigger than a postage stamp—the tiniest bit of green packaging. I recognized where it had come from instantly. Thin Mints, Quinn's favorite Girl Scout cookies. He had been their best customer on our street, keeping our small pantry stocked with the cookies at all times. The piece had fallen into a bed of starflowers that someone had walked on, crushing the white, delicate blossoms into a sad mess.

Nate wordlessly placed the green piece of cardboard into his pocket and we pushed on.

"Hey, look over there," Jacob said at one point, and we all shuffled to a stop. A few yards ahead, a well-trodden path opened up. There was no way anyone would choose to keep battling the thick of the forest when there was a perfectly good path available. Clearly Quinn and Dr. Holm had taken it, but in which direction?

"I'll see if I can spot their footprints," Nate said.

"And I'll see if there's a History barrier on one side or the other," Erika said.

Nate went to the left and Dr. B to the right. Nate's head was angled toward the ground as he carefully scanned the pine needles and last season's leaves on the forest floor; Erika held her arms up in front of her in anticipation of an invisible wall. As the rest of us watched, they came back and passed each other in opposite directions. We heard Erika say, "Ooof," and Nate call over his shoulder, "Watch out for the wall."

I was half-hoping we would be stuck in both directions so that we could get a bit of rest. The increasing humidity was making me sweat and my legs were sore. Ron had bound his ankle inside the hiking boot with a wrap from Dr. B's emergency medical kit, but even with a walking stick to lean on, a look of pain snuck onto his face every time he took a step.

Nate and Dr. B came back.

"There's a wall blocking the path," Dr. B said, rubbing her arm, which must have slammed up against the barrier.

"Well, there aren't any tracks or anything the other way," Nate said, "but there don't seem to be any walls either."

Without looking at Ron, Ruth-Ann said, "Chief Kirkland, do you mind if we rest a bit before continuing on? I need a break."

"Me too," said Jacob. "I'm starving."

"Yes, all right." Nate put down his backpack. "Everyone, have some water and something to eat. Meanwhile I'm going to walk up that hill to see what's ahead."

I eagerly set down my backpack as well, feeling twenty pounds lighter immediately. "I'll join you," I called out after him.

I don't know what made me say it. Some kind of sixth sense, perhaps. Or maybe I just wanted to steal a moment alone with him.

As we followed the narrow, single-file path in the uphill direction open to us, I watched Nate bend his head to navigate his way under a tree branch. "Did you have to get your campus security uniform specially made?"

"Hmm, what, Julia?" he asked as if his mind was on other matters.

"Your campus security uniform. Being so tall and all, I mean."

"They make them in all sizes...I was just thinking about Sabina, actually."

"What about her?"

"I've been assuming that it would be best for her to make a clean break with the past, but I'm not so sure anymore. Seeing how excited Jacob is about being here, and the fact that she tried to run away…And then there's this runestone thing, which is like a cold case. Those are old unsolved crimes."

The word came out before I could stop it. "Yes."

"Yes, what?"

"STEWie would be a great for solving cold cases. If it's ever used for that, I'd love to help. I'm good at combing through documents and photos and all that stuff. And Sabina—I think she'd jump at the chance to time travel back home."

"I think she might need to find out what happened to her father and grandmother. I know it's unlikely they made it through the eruption—and I suspect she knows that too—but it might give her closure."

A rumble of thunder pre-empted my answer. Nate threw a look up at the sky. "We might think about setting up shelter early. I don't like the look of those clouds."

I didn't either. The fluffy white clouds that had greeted us upon waking that morning had been driven away by fast-approaching thunderheads. The leaves of the trees were starting to stir in the approaching storm.

"How safe are we from lightning?" I asked, eyeing the clouds through a gap in the canopy.

"Well, we should probably try not to stand under the tallest tree in the area."

I was about to point out that most of the trees around us seemed pretty tall to me, but before I could, he said, "Ron's leg seems to be really bothering him."

"More than he's letting on, I think."

"The prudent thing to do might be to split up."

"You mean let the others head back to Runestone Island?"

"Well, yes—if you want to stay. The others can take their time heading back so that Ron doesn't overexert himself."

"Ruth-Ann might want to stay as well," I said over the rumble of thunder in the distance. "It's not like Ron's injury is life-threatening."

"No, true enough. You're right, I shouldn't have assumed that."

"After all, how many chances does a person get to go into the fourteenth century?"

He glanced in my direction with a smile. "I get it, Julia—all I meant was that the two of them seem inseparable."

"They do, don't they? I suppose you're right."

"Either way, Dr. B can leave us the Slingshot after she programs it with the coordinates for home. And if we have trouble getting back, they know where to find us...where to..."

He had stopped short and I had walked straight into him. "Oof, sorry—"

"Shhh. Look."

We had reached the top of the hill. There was a circular clearing on the other side, bordered all around by the woods. The strengthening wind had sent brown leaves into a dance around the boulders strewn on the sparse grass. The view out of the forest had opened up and I noticed that there was an ominous green tint to the sky, but at the moment I was more interested in what was going on in front of us.

I hadn't known what to expect. From the beginning, I'd had my doubts about Dr. Holm. The evidence, and what I knew about Quinn, seemed to indicate that she had gotten onto STEWie's platform willingly. I had suspected that Quinn might have charmed her into taking him into the fourteenth century to shoot footage for his *History's Dirty Secrets* show. I had even considered the possibility that that *she* had charmed *him* into doing it, perhaps because she needed someone to carry her tent and backpack.

But I had not expected this.

# 32

The repetitive clink of chisel on stone drifted to where Nate and I were crouching behind a white pine. Quinn was on his knees by the chair-size stone, a hammer in his right hand, the chisel in his left. He had pinned a piece of paper to the ground with a stick to prevent it from flying off in the wind. Occasionally he would pause to reference the paper, then return to the chiseling.

"You can stop now, Quinn," I called out without considering whether it was a good idea to do so.

Quinn gave a startled oath and dropped his tools. Mine must have been the last voice he'd expected to hear in the fourteenth-century woodland. He jumped to his feet as Nate and I emerged from behind the tree. You'd think he would have at least had the decency to look chagrined as he greeted us. "Jules, you startled me. And who do we have here, the chief of campus security? What are you two doing here in the woods? No, don't say it, I know—you're looking for me. Do you realize what this means?" He blew on his hand—I hoped the chisel had given him a good scrape—and dabbed it on his Hawaiian shirt.

"What might that be?" Nate asked.

"That I acquired all my blisters for nothing." He said this as if he had gotten a broken bone by saving a drowning puppy. His shirt was looking a little worse for wear; there was a tear on one parrot-and-palm-tree-covered shoulder and a fine white dust all over from the chiseling.

"Well, it was worth a try." Quinn gave a no-worries shrug. "How have you been, Chief? Haven't seen you since that Walleyes cookout."

The Walleyes was the town fishing club. Quinn had belonged to it briefly. He hadn't brought back many fish, but it had afforded him an opportunity to fill the weekend hours with an activity that was of no interest to me. Nate was a member, too. Which was all beside the point. The point was that I couldn't believe my ears. Worth a try? *Worth a try?* He had thrown the whole Time Travel Engineering department into disarray, disrupted people's roster spots, wasted the security office's time, not to mention put Sabina at risk of exposure. Before I could do what I really wanted to do (yell at him), Nate asked in an even tone, "Where is Dr. Holm?"

I realized that I had completely forgotten about her.

Quinn acted as if he hadn't heard. "You're looking a little charred, Jules, were you lighting a fire or something?"

"Where is Dr. Holm?" Nate repeated his question more forcefully. His hand crept onto the weapon on his hip.

"Isn't my company enough for you, Chief? Dagmar went to gather raspberries. We're running a bit low on food—one of our backpacks was stolen by a bear. I can tell that you've been through some adventures, too," he said with another glance at our clothes. "Like I said, Dagmar went off to gather berries before the storm hits, and I offered to take over the chiseling for a bit." He said it as if it had been a gentlemanly, chivalrous thing to do. "We only did it because we got tired of looking for the Vikings, you know. Did you happen to see them while you were looking for us?"

"Not a footprint," I said.

"Darn. Dagmar and I looked, believe me, we looked until I was sick of eating granola bars and walking and the mosquitoes and I lost track of how many jumps we'd made and the battery in our Slingshot-thingie was drained."

I thought I heard the rustle of a squirrel or another small animal behind me, just inside the forest line, but saw nothing.

Quinn was still reminiscing. "I pitched my idea to Dagmar over wine during our first dinner together. We were going to jump around a bit, find the Vikings, prove Farfar's runestone is real, and everybody would be delighted about it. But no one's shown up. So…" He trailed off, then added, "She's going to be disappointed that our, uh, *project* didn't pan out. All that hard work for nothing." He dabbed his hand on his shirt some more. "I should have brought work gloves. Setting up the stone was an undertaking—we had to chip off a bit of it to get a smooth surface. And then the chiseling…I already have, let's see, one…two…*three* blisters."

I stared at Quinn open-mouthed. He seemed to be treating the whole thing as a prank rather than what it was, a serious criminal matter. He also seemed to be saying in no uncertain terms that Dr. Holm had brought *him*, not the other way around. I glanced at Nate. He and Quinn were facing each other across the new runestone, with Nate looking ready to punch Quinn, if only such actions were permitted to a law enforcement officer. He still had his hand on the holster but hadn't pulled out his weapon. Which was unfortunate because he didn't have time to react to what happened next.

Someone stuck a gun into the small of my back.

"No one move," a woman's high-pitched voice said in a parody of a bad thriller. She had crept silently out of the woods.

My knowledge about guns amounted to what I'd learned from TV melodramas, but the one in the small of my back felt bigger and sturdier than the one Nate pulled out in slow motion and pointed at Dagmar over my shoulder. I hoped for the best scenario—that neither gun would work—but if one of them *did* work, that it would be Nate's.

"I knew it," I said, without daring to turn to look at Dagmar. She was shorter than me, so Nate had to be aiming at the top of her head. "I knew that Quinn didn't drag you here against your will."

Quinn, for his part, suddenly got very chatty again. "Dagmar, there you are. The chisel slipped and I managed to scratch both the stone and myself. Excuse me while I spray some antiseptic on it. My hand, not the stone, of course, ha ha." He headed for the lone backpack sitting on the ground by the stone and started to rummage, carrying on a one-sided conversation all the while. "Did you find any berries? Oh, here's the first aid kit. By the way, have you met Jules? And the man pointing the weapon at you is Chief Kirkland from the campus security office."

"She and I have met," I said.

Quinn spritzed antiseptic on his hand. "So Chief Kirkland, how did you find us?"

Nate didn't seemed inclined to answer, so I did. I thought it would be better not to mention the others. "You've been leaving behind footprints and cookie packaging. Before that—well, Dr. Holm sent me a text message asking for help and Nate thought she might be in trouble. I had my doubts. We found a disturbed computer station in the TTE lab, like she had been dragged into STEWie's basket against her will."

"You're on a first name basis with our security chief here, Jules? A text message and a disturbed computer? Excuse me for a moment while I apply a bandage...I thought I heard a crash while I waited in the Time Machine basket for her to program in our destination. Dagmar said it was nothing out of the ordinary, just one of the mirrors jumping its track. Then we got to Woodstock. Now *that* was something. Nobody even gave us a second look. My shirt must have done the trick."

I was happy to see that mosquito bites covered Quinn's arms beneath his short-sleeved shirt. His beige khakis, their knees brown from squatting in the dirt, completed the look. Quinn threw a look down at his pants. "Should have brought a black pair and a garden kneeler. Too bad neither of us has a green thumb, eh, Jules?"

I didn't dignify that with an answer.

"It's over, Dr. Holm," Nate said as a rumble of rolling thunder filled the sudden silence between us. Nate's hands were steady as he pointed the gun above my shoulder. I noticed that there were calluses on his fingers from the first night's attempt to make a fire by rubbing sticks together. The barrel in the small of my back had started to shake slightly, as if Dr. Holm's hands were getting tired. Must have been all that chiseling.

"If I let you go back, my career is over," Dr. Holm pointed out, and I felt the barrel jam into my back with renewed force. Nate might have made the wrong move by using the honorific before her name.

"As things stand," Nate said evenly, "your worries should be bigger than whether or not your career is over. What you should be concerned about is prison time. The length of it. Put the gun down."

"Was your plan to slap all the blame on Quinn?" I asked over my shoulder. "Were you going to return alone with some sob story about being kidnapped? Let me guess. You were going to say that you stumbled across this new runestone but then he pointed the gun at you. While you tried to wrestle it away, it went off, leaving you to come back the hero—and with firm knowledge of the location of a Norse artifact? By the way, the message asking for help, why did you send it to me and not the police?"

"Who texts the police? I thought it was a nice touch. You were so obsessed with the whole thing anyway... Why was that?"

I just stood silent. I certainly wasn't going to mention Sabina.

Having finished with his bandage, which was ridiculously large for the size of his rather minor wound, Quinn sprang lightly to his feet. "No one would have bought that story. People know me better than that. Jules, you didn't believe for a minute that I—"

"Maybe for a minute," I allowed. "By the way, where are the divorce papers?"

Quinn smacked himself on the forehead with his uninjured hand. "I forgot to mail them off."

"Isn't this a nice family reunion?" Dagmar said. "And don't kid yourself, Quinn. You were using me as much as I was using you. Episode one of *History's Dirty Secrets*—stumbling on a genuine Viking artifact in the middle of a fourteenth-century woodland."

Quinn gave Dr. Holm a frank look. "Dagmar, dear, I thought this was a joint venture on our part—that we'd come back hand in hand, hero and heroine, co-discoverers of the true story of the runestone. In fact, I was going to ask you to be my partner and co-host for the reality show."

The gun against my back slipped a bit. "Did you really have backing for the show?"

"I had a plan. For the show, for me, for us. You would have been happy."

This was getting sickening.

"Happy?" She gave a back-of-the-throat snort. "Happy? I'm on my third post-doc. I thought this was the one, that I would finally get a junior professorship. A find like this runestone would have had universities fighting for the chance to hire me."

That would likely have been true. Quinn's chance visit to her office had given her a way out of the academic sinkhole she was in. She must have quickly hatched a plan that Quinn was more than willing to go along with. But looking for the Norsemen had turned out to be the equivalent of finding a needle in the haystack of History, just like Dr. Payne had said it would be. So Dagmar had turned to Plan B, to carve a stone. After Quinn had finished helping her chisel it and the "discovery" was filmed, she wouldn't have needed him anymore. I highly doubted that she would have let the one witness to her crime live to tell the tale.

The barrel of the hunting handgun was still firmly lodged against my back. The thunder was getting nearer and louder, so there was always a chance that lightning might strike Dagmar. I could hope.

I wondered idly if the lightning would travel down the metal barrel of the gun and into me.

"I'd like to avoid a shoot-out, Dr. Holm," Nate said as the first drops of rain started to fall. After a moment's deliberation, he added, "Here, I'll put my weapon down first."

He laid it down on the ground. I hoped the gamble would pay off.

Dagmar jabbed me in the back. "Go stand over there, by Chief Kirkland."

I did. Dr. Holm's gun was now pointed at both of us.

Quinn sauntered over toward her.

"Dagmar, darling, I'm afraid I have to side with Chief Kirkland on this one. I've had enough blood for one day. I might need stitches, what do you think, Chief Kirkland?"

He unwrapped the bandage to reveal a tiny scrape, shoving it under Nate's nose, undoubtedly in an effort to defuse the situation. It didn't work. At that moment we heard our friends' approaching voices over the sound of the storm. They would be over the hilltop in seconds. I felt my hand slide into my pocket for something, anything to defend myself with.

I saw Dagmar's eyes open wide and her finger tense as she pressed the trigger.

# 33

There was no shot. The only thing that actually happened was that the granola bar I threw at Dagmar bounced off her body and fell to the ground.

She pulled the trigger again, a look of confusion on her face.

"When you have more time travel experience under your belt," said Dr. B, emerging from the tree line, "you'll find that modern devices often do not work as you'd expect while you're in the field. History is a force to be reckoned with." Ruth-Ann and Jacob were on her heels, burdened not only with their own gear but also with the backpacks Nate and I had left behind. Ron leaned on his walking stick a few steps behind them. "The retort of a gun this close to the village is just not possible, I'm afraid. You should have brought a knife instead."

"Don't give her any ideas," I said.

Dagmar's face had gone bright red, making her look like an unusually angry pixie.

"Let's leave the discussions for later," Nate said, flinching as Dagmar shouted in frustration. He bent down to pick up his weapon and return it to its holster.

The others caught sight of the stone, on which Dagmar and Quinn's combined efforts had yielded a scant two lines of text. I heard Ruth-Ann emit a gasp of surprise at the blatant attempt at deception. Jacob was already snapping photos of the stone.

Dr. B dropped her backpack and shook her head, "Of all the things to do in the past..." She didn't bother finishing the sentence.

Nate reached around to retrieve something from his belt. Handcuffs. He had brought handcuffs.

"Well, now that we're all here," said Quinn, "I suppose we should head back, Dagmar—Dagmar, where are you going?"

Dagmar had picked something up from where our things were gathered and was trotting away from us, the gun still in one hand. A brief flash of lightning split the sky to the southwest of us and she stopped in her tracks as if an idea had struck her the instant the lightning struck the ground.

She turned, lifted the gun, and fired as the thunder broke over the forest. I threw myself on the ground and Nate ducked, but she wasn't aiming at us. The shot went clean through the Slingshot 1.0, which was sitting on the ground next to where Dr. B had set her backpack, leaving behind a penny-size hole in the device.

"The stone doesn't matter anyway," Dagmar spat out as the wind and rain whipped her hair around her face. "It was just a rung in a ladder—I want to find Vinland."

"Vinland?" Quinn said as if this was the first he was hearing of her plan. "How on earth would we do that?"

"By following the Norsemen back, you...you *dolt*."

"Dr. Holm," Nate began.

"But Dagmar, darling, we never saw any Norsemen. Not a one," Quinn interjected, still in a cheery tone. "I suppose bringing back photos of the new stone would have resulted in more runs in the Time Machine for you. Well, none of it is likely to happen now, is it? By the way, Jules, you never did tell me how you found us?"

Before Dr. B had a chance to explain about History funneling us into the same spot, Dagmar took off.

"We'll catch up with her," Quinn said. "It's not like she can really go anywhere..." His eyes were focused on the rapidly retreating back of the linguistics postdoc.

"Sorry, Jules," he said and took off after Dr. Holm.

"STEWie's basket," Dr. Baumgartner said with a gasp, the punctured Slingshot 1.0 at her feet. "She took the Callback. If they get to Runestone Island first, we'll be stranded here."

A few steps more and Dagmar was in the trees, Quinn on her heels.

"Did I mention she's a runner?" I said to Nate as lightning split the sky above us again.

# 34

We raced after them through the green, humid forest, branches scratching at our faces, rain soaking our bodies, our backpacks bouncing hard against our backs. "Leave me behind," Ron had called out between heavy breaths, but Nate had just offered him a supporting shoulder. At one point we lost sight of Dagmar and Quinn, but then we saw them ahead of us, slowed down by a thick patch of forest. All the while, the storm drew closer. The sky had darkened as if someone had thrown a cloak over the whole area, trapping us in with the storm and blocking the sunshine out. I knew that if I was back home under conditions like these, my cell phone would be beeping with tornado alerts and I would have been keeping an ear out for the sirens. Minnesota got a handful of twisters a year, nowhere near as many as the states to the south, but I knew what a sky *that* dark foretold.

"Should we try to make it back to the village to warn them?" Jacob asked. "Maybe History will let us do it—"

"*Warn* them?" Nate said, in a rare snippy moment. "I have no doubt they know the significance of those clouds just as we do. We need to find a ditch."

This was the source of the uneasiness I'd felt since our arrival; there *was* a disaster bearing down on the village, one the carefully erected defensive palisade would be useless against.

The wind was whipping the rain into our faces with such force that the trees around us were mere shadows, engulfed by the storm's fury. We had completely lost sight of Dagmar and Quinn, and it was all we could do to keep on our feet. Hail had started to fall, the descent of the rock-hard pellets slowed down by the forest canopy, but not enough.

Peering into the rain, Jacob said, "I could have sworn I saw...hold on..." and hurried off into the trees.

Nate turned to go after him. "We have to find a low spot and stay together—"

I grabbed his arm. "Wait."

Lightning split the sky and for the briefest of moments we had a downhill view through the trees.

"I see it, Julia, there's a funnel cloud—" he said, his eyes dark.

"No, *there*. Look."

We had all fallen into the same boiling cauldron of History, our group of six, the villagers, Dagmar and Quinn—and our elusive Norsemen, phantom-like in the blinding rain. They were here, finally...and they were right in the path of the twister.

# 35

As the storm raged around their camp and their brown woolen cloaks billowed in the wind, the figures, tiny from where we were, worked quickly to weigh down with rocks their fur-lined sleeping sacks and other possessions. They didn't know enough about this land to read its signs—the bruising hail, the rolling lightning, the ghostly daytime dark that had enveloped the forest. The dangers they were used to were harsh seas and cold, not this. The site they had chosen for their camp was by two Psinomani burial mounds, the landmarks mentioned on the runestone.

I knew a smattering of Norwegian, one of the words being danger (*fare!*) and I opened my mouth to call out the warning, forgetting about History, more worried about whether they could hear me over the thunder and wind whipping the tree branches.

"Julia, why are you standing there with your mouth open?" Nate shouted into the wind. "Let's get moving."

Quinn tapped me on the shoulder. I had no idea how or when he had joined us; there was no sign of Dagmar. "Jules, I'm as thunderstruck as you are—bad word choice, ha—but we need to get into a ditch. Now is not the time for photos."

Somehow I had the lab camera in my hand.

"In here." Jacob's head popped out from what looked to be a narrow opening in a rocky overhang. "Come on," he beckoned frantically, adding something I didn't understand. "He waited until he was sure we had seen him. Hurry…"

The last I saw of the Norsemen was the ten of them on their feet as the black funnel cloud closed in, tearing out trees in its path and blurring the line between land and sky. And that was the photo I managed to snap just as Nate and Quinn pulled me toward the narrow opening.

Hail.

Wind.

No time—

The small shelter.

Inside, a pair of eyes stared at us from the shadows.

# 36

A young boy sat with his back against the dirt wall, his knees pulled up to his chin, his jet-black hair tied back and hanging long against his slender body, which was clad in breechcloth and moccasins. I absorbed all of this in an instant as we tumbled in with our heads down, soaked from the rain and dragging our backpacks. We barely fit into the tent-size space, and both Dr. B and Nate had to bend their heads. I hoped the walls would hold. Someone had made a below-ground shelter by deepening the rocky overhang and closing it on all sides with copious amounts of rock and dirt.

We might have been a strange group for the boy to behold, but he was no doubt happy to have company in the storm. We all huddled on the earthen floor and gave our attention to what was happening outside—fierce, golf ball–size hail pelted the ground, wind-driven branches and twigs flew by, and the man-made and natural walls sheltering us shook violently, although that last one might have just been an illusion. I thought I could faintly hear the shouts of the men outside, although that too might have been my imagination, for they were surely too far away. And then I heard a sound that did not belong here, *could not* belong here, one that was all too real. If I hadn't known better, I would have thought it was an approaching freight train. But I knew what it really was.

We crawled back from the opening, jamming our bodies next to the boy, against the rock wall.

I wondered how Dagmar was faring.

Then, as quickly as it had started, it was all over. The train passed and the hail slowed down and then stopped completely, leaving behind gently falling rain. Soon the thunder seemed more distant, too. We looked at each other to make sure everyone was all right, and then turned toward the boy.

He was maybe Sabina's age, twelve or thirteen, and he didn't seem alarmed by our presence, either because the storm was more worrisome than we were or because he had thought it over and come to the conclusion that we were neither enemies nor evil spirits. He had partly risen when we first tumbled into the alcove, and he had stayed in that half-crouched position, dividing his attention between the storm outside and his visitors. Once the storm abated, his shoulders finally relaxed. His eyes moved from our colorful jackets to Quinn's Hawaiian shirt, which was soaked from the rain. He reached out to touch the compass hanging on Nate's belt; it had become cracked during the chaos of the storm.

When we filed out of the shelter, devastating destruction awaited us—a great swath of the forest was gone. It was like the deadly train I thought I'd heard *had* rumbled through the area. Trees lay on their sides, roots and all, as if they'd been tossed around by a giant's hand, while their neighbors stood untouched. The hail had left behind a carpet of white, and the air was markedly cooler. Downhill, where the tornado track continued, trees had been uprooted all the way to the Norsemen's camp and beyond. There was an eerie silence in that direction. I had to remind myself that there was nothing we could have done.

It didn't help.

Cupping their hands, Nate and Quinn were calling out Dagmar's name, but at a kind of half-yell, muted by History's constraints. There was no sign of her.

"He made sure that I saw him and the shelter," Jacob said again of the boy. As if to lend proof to the adage that life goes on, he and the boy squatted down and began playing some version of marbles with the golf-ball sized chunks of hail. Dr. B, looking a bit stunned, told the Tuttles in her professorial voice, as if she were giving a lecture or a workshop on the subject, "With time travel, social interaction with children is usually easier. Young people, with their limited life experience, are used to seeing unexpected things. And if they see something *really* odd like the six of us with our bright jackets and strange hair styles, their brains will deal with it by categorizing it as a day dream or a wonderful secret to be kept."

"The boy—I think he might be on a vision quest," Ruth-Ann said, studying the child's dark head. "That's a rite of passage that marks the transition to adulthood. He probably hasn't eaten or slept in a couple of days."

"Are we to be his vision, then?" I asked.

"Maybe, maybe not. The tornado made more of a statement than we did, I'd say."

"I sort of wish we could bring him back with us, like you did with Sabina," Jacob said as the boy rolled a chunk of hail and expertly struck another. "Oops, should I not have said that?" he asked with a nervous glance at the Tuttles. Dr. B already knew; it would have been hard to keep the secret from any the TTE professors.

"Not that he'd want to leave his village and family, of course," Jacob added. "Just for a visit or something. Hopefully his village is okay."

"Who's Sabina?" Ron asked. "And where did you bring her back from?"

"It's a bit of a long story. Ask me later," I said, echoing his favorite phrase back at him.

Jacob and the boy had exchanged a few phrases as they played, with Jacob in English and the boy in ancestral Dakota. Somehow they were managing to understand each other well enough. Ruth-Ann added quietly, "Do you think I can chance a photo?"

Dr. B gave a small shrug. "Never hurts to try."

But the camera would not work for her. "No matter," Ruth-Ann said and took a tentative step forward. For a second I thought she might reach out and touch the top of the boy's head, but she held off. The boy looked up and said something. Ruth-Ann blinked tears out of her eyes as he returned his attention to the game of hail marbles.

Quinn took a break from calling Dagmar's name and turned in our direction. "Jules, aren't you going to introduce me?"

"Quinn, this is Dr. Erika Baumgartner of the Time Travel Engineering department," I explained. "And over there, with the Jedi sweatshirt, is her graduate student, Jacob. And they're Ruth-Ann and Ron Tuttle, our guides to the fourteenth century. Everyone, this is Quinn. He's a—"

"A man of many interests," Quinn cut in, smoothly finishing the sentence for me. I was going to say that he was a wannabe reality TV star. Instead I asked, "Ruth-Ann, what did the boy say to you?"

"He said hello...and called me *thunwin*, auntie."

Nate was still shouting Dagmar's name hoarsely. Dr. B said, "I'll check in that direction," and went to help.

I turned to Quinn. "Why didn't you bring her with you?"

"I tried, Jules. She lost all interest in getting back to STEWie's basket or taking shelter. You can guess why."

Ruth-Ann's brow was crinkled in concern, "Did she go down to try to warn them?"

"She should have known that was impossible," I said.

Nate and Dr. B came back.

"Let's split up to look for her," Nate said. "She may be lying somewhere injured—or worse. Ron and Jacob, you stay here and the rest of us will search."

# 37

The boy took off, pausing here and there to examine downed trees and swinging Nate's compass on its chain as he walked. I had a feeling—reinforced by my knowledge of History's rules—that it would become a hidden treasure, not to be shared with others.

"Wait," I said as we watched the boy's lean figure disappear into the woods. "Did we get his name?"

"Tokala," said Jacob.

"Tokala?" Ruth-Ann repeated, letting the name linger on her tongue. "Fox."

I don't know how I knew, perhaps because he had shown so little surprise upon seeing us, but I was certain that it was Tokala's eyes that had been watching us all along. I guessed that he had first seen us the moonlit evening we arrived on Runestone Island, and perhaps had been part of the group of hunters that crossed paths with us on their way to set the fire. He must have spent much of his vision quest following us as we stumbled through the woods after our jump of three weeks.

Like the rest of us, he had made it to the other side of a ghost zone. I crossed my fingers that his village was okay. Our path home would take us some distance from it and making a side trip just to look seemed like the time travel equivalent of rubbernecking.

We couldn't avoid seeing what had happened to the other travelers from afar.

The Norsemen's teammates, returning as the sun edged toward the horizon in the dugout canoes they had been given as detailed in the Good Earth Woman's ancestral story, would find their comrades' bodies in their camp by the two mounds. They would not know what to make of the uprooted trees and the intense destruction the storm had inflicted on the land. That was the thing about a tornado—it leveled its touchdown site but left neighboring areas undisturbed. The men who had gone fishing might have spent the day in the sun only to return to carnage and destruction. I had a feeling that the Norsemen and the villagers would cross paths this very day and that the villagers would take them to the island with the black walnut trees and leave them there to make their memorial. *Ave Maria Save Us from Evil.*

Dagmar had been so close to realizing her goal. But she couldn't have known that, so she and Quinn had set about carving the stone. I was still convinced that she would have engineered an accident for him before returning home.

"I'd say it's lucky for you that we happened to come along," I said to him as we walked.

Quinn turned an outraged stare on me. "Lucky? Lucky, you say, Julia? Lucky would have been running into the Vikings as soon as we stepped into the fourteenth century. With that kind of footage, Dagmar and I would have become instant stars. That's how it was in my head: I would be the team leader. Dagmar would be my consultant. And we'd be assisted by two cameramen whose faces would never be seen on the screen. Together we would solve mysteries in history—who shot JFK, did we really land on the Moon, what happened at Roswell, and so on. I mean, who wouldn't watch that? It was a good idea, wasn't it?

But we spent days and days looking for the Vikings, so many I lost track. Three times we went back home for supplies and to do laundry until we couldn't do that anymore because we ran out of battery power—"

Dr. B shook her head at this. "That may be what Dagmar thought, but if the Slingshot 2.0 stopped working, it was probably because our basket was already here for the last of your jumps. Did you jump to Runestone Island?"

"Yes."

"Where from?" Nate demanded. "Did you go back to Dr. Holm's apartment or your hotel or what?"

"Neither. We were using a cabin as our base."

"Whose cabin?"

"Dagmar's family's cabin. It has a deck overlooking the St. Croix River. We popped in and out at will."

"Sorry," Jacob said. "It was all my fault. I didn't want to say anything, but I gave her the code to the lab."

Nate eyed him. "You gave Dr. Holm the code? Why?"

A pink flush spread across Jacob's freckled face. "She said she had mislaid it, and she was older than me and a postdoc—"

"No one thinks any of this was your fault, Jacob," I said with a look at Quinn.

"Hey, don't blame me either," Quinn said. "I thought we were just here to look for the Norsemen—I didn't know about any of this Vinland business. But we didn't find them, and then Dagmar suggested we carve the stone ourselves, and I thought— well, where's the harm in that?"

"And the hunting handgun?" Nate asked.

"She asked me to bring one along in case we got attacked by a bear or something. We did have a close call—like I said, one made off with a backpack in the middle of the night. Frankly, I'm a little unnerved that she was thinking of using it on me."

"I believe you," I said.

"Hmm. I'll take your word for it, Julia," Nate said, grunting under the weight of what he was carrying.

"I told you the runestone is real, Jules," Quinn added. He was helping Nate, and there was a strained look on his face. "My grandfather may have been many things, but he was not a liar."

"I never said he was," I pointed out as we continued on with our grim task. About halfway between our shelter and the camp of the Norsemen, we'd come upon Dagmar's broken body lodged under a tree trunk flung violently by the storm. There would be no race to STEWie's basket.

It seemed wrong to leave her. It took all of us to move the heavy tree trunk with its summer-green branches, after which we wrapped her in one of the bivy sacks. We took turns carrying her body in pairs as we slowly wound our way out of the woodland in the direction of Runestone Island and home.

# PART FOUR:
# HOME

# 38

"Is that it?" D. Payne asked.

The stone was real. Against all odds, a party of Norse explorers had reached the middle of what would centuries later become the United States of America. We had seen them. They had not been the tall, fierce warriors with horned helmets and spears that I had foolishly imagined the first time Quinn had brought up the topic, but bare-headed, frightened men far from home. Why they had come, whether their comrades had made it back to their ship, and where Vinland was—these were questions that Dr. Payne would have to tackle.

It was a job he had taken on with the swiftest change of heart I'd ever seen. He had asked for extraordinary evidence. It was the lousiest photo imaginable as far as quality went, most of it blurry with rain and my shaking hand, but it was enough. He slid the photo under the lit lamp on his desk. His computer seemed out of place in his office, which—with all its dark wood and filled-to-the-brim bookcases—could have been an old-fashioned gentleman's study in the days when they still had them. Dr. Payne was only missing a monocle as he bent over the photo. He cleared his throat. "Hmm, intriguing...Well, yes, that certainly changes things somewhat...A STEWie run to investigate further would not be amiss."

When I left, he was already drafting a STEWie run proposal to document the Psinomani villagers' culture and to follow the Norsemen back to Vinland in an unconscious echo of Dagmar Holm's plan. He hadn't asked about her final moments. I managed to feel bad for her as I passed by the locked door to her office. She would have so wanted to be part of Dr Payne's team.

I doubted she would have ever been happy, building a career around the stone she had carved, knowing it was fake. Quinn had said they were carving something simple, along the lines of *Vinlanders on a journey inland*, and the date. All of the scientists and academics I knew had a deep-rooted drive for the truth. In the end, that was what it was about, really, as firm as the concrete foundations of the buildings that circled Sunniva Lake. Though they might scorn that description, the researchers under my care had an almost sacred respect for truth. Still, they were human. Like athletes who used performance-enhancing drugs, a person might forget what it was all about, the lure of the medal—the Olympic or the Nobel kind—proving irresistible.

But she did get to breathe the fourteenth-century air, walk the woodlands, eat berries, and hear the drum beat of Psinomani dancers. And, in the end, she found her beloved Norsemen. I wondered what kind of life she would have managed to have if by some chance she had survived the tornado and stayed behind while the rest of us made it to STEWie's basket. She would have been constrained both by History's rules and her own unfamiliarity with fourteenth-century life. Would she have been able to find a home with the Dakota, or perhaps in Vinland itself? Either way it would have been a very small life. She would have been unable to reveal any knowledge from the future, either the big things (that the white explorers would come back one day and bring a disease with them) or the mundane ones that corn would be sold in crinkly bags to be popped in the microwave for two minutes and eaten in front of screens with moving pictures.

Dr. Payne would focus on the broad strokes of what we had seen; I knew that he wouldn't return with the answers I really wanted—whether Tokala's village had been spared that day, or if he had grown up to be a hunter, a village leader, a dreamer. But one thing was certain. The investigation to discern whether our Norsemen were indeed the lost Greenlanders would be an easily funded one—this was big news.

I walked over to the RV in the parking lot to say good-bye to Ruth-Ann and Ron, having called Abigail and Sabina to let them know we were back. Nate had gone straight from the TTE lab to his office to take care of what needed to be done in reporting Dagmar's death after the ambulance had taken her body away. Ruth-Ann and Ron had decided not to stick around. I understood why. Time travel. As Jacob had said, it messed with your head.

I found the Tuttles deep in conversation with Quinn by the steps of their RV. Officer Van Underberg gave me a wave as he drove out of the parking lot at the posted campus speed limit, having dropped the three of them off. Quinn had his suitcase.

"Are you really interior decorators?" I heard Quinn say as I approached them. "That seems fated—I have a fixer-upper I'm working on in Phoenix. Two, actually—well, three—and they could all use an expert hand. I don't suppose you'd be interested in driving me down and taking a look?"

Ruth-Ann and Ron glanced at each other. Ron's ankle was wrapped up, but he looked like himself again as he leaned on a crutch, his beard freshly combed above a bright yellow St. Sunniva University T-shirt, which he must have picked up at the hospital. "We have been talking it over," Ruth-Ann said. "It would be nice to have a change of scenery for a bit, get some thinking done on how to organize our experiences into a book, wouldn't it, Ron?"

"Hmm. There *are* some very interesting petroglyphs in the Phoenix area," Ron said.

Ruth-Ann added, "And we could use the money."

"Quinn doesn't have any money," I said as I walked toward them. "He *owes* money."

"Jules, there you are. I'm surprised you would worry about money at a time like this. Like Ruth-Ann here pointed out, after what we've just been through in the fourteenth century—the bear, the tornado, the *guns*—we all need some time to unwind. Except for me. The media is going to be clamoring for the Norsemen story and we need a spokesperson. I might not get my reality show, but I've already booked three TV interviews as soon as I get to Phoenix. Ron, you'll have to fill me in on the Vinland connection…"

"It's not exactly the best publicity for the school," I said. *Or for Sabina*, I wanted to add but didn't.

"Jules, any publicity is good publicity, haven't you figured out that yet?"

"You were faking a runestone, Quinn. That's not exactly the headline you want."

He waved the charge away. "That was all Dagmar. I believed in the Kensington Runestone, and I was proven correct. As for the rest of it…" He didn't finish the thought, suddenly looking crestfallen. I knew he was thinking of Dagmar. "Maybe the two of us should have been more patient."

I wasn't sure I believed him that the whole thing was Dagmar's idea, but he was right. Like Dagmar herself had said to me in the Coffey Library the first time we met, good things come to those who wait. Of course, had she waited for a proper STEWie run, the Norsemen might have remained a legend, and Dr. Payne's jaw would never have dropped when he saw the photo

I had brought back home. In a sense, she had accomplished just what she'd set out to do.

I told the Tuttles they had a standing invitation to drop by the TTE lab or my office any time. Ruth-Ann hopped into the driver's seat while Ron readied the RV, Quinn having secured a spot on their couch for the drive down to Arizona. I hoped he would find a way to pay them for their time, especially if they did help him with the luxury house flips he had left unattended in Phoenix.

He handed me a pair of keys from the RV steps. "Would you mind returning my rental car?"

"Fine. Where is it parked?"

"Dagmar's cabin on the St. Croix. It needs gas."

"Of course it does. Remember your promise," I reminded him.

He flashed a grin at me as he dragged his suitcase up the steps of the RV. "What promise would that be? The divorce papers?" He pulled an envelope from his pocket and grinned at me. "Last chance to change your mind, Jules...I could rip them up."

I knew he didn't mean it. "It wouldn't work, Quinn. I'm not sure it ever did."

"No, it didn't really, did it."

"Anyway, I meant the promise about Sabina," I said, checking that all the papers were in the envelope and signed properly.

"Ah, that one. Will do. Can I tell the Tuttles?"

I had meant to fill them in on the story but never got the chance. I nodded. "But only the Tuttles."

∞

"Don't say it," I said to Helen, who was waiting for me at the edge of the parking lot.

"Don't say what?"

"That we haven't seen the last of him."

"Julia, as long as we keep Sabina's story secret, Quinn will always be able to hold it over us."

"I want to give her as much time as possible. Besides, it's Abigail's call. She's her guardian. I'm just their landlord."

"You know that you're much more than that. Abigail has followed your lead in this matter. You know, I don't know why you say you're not motherly," she added.

"Because I don't know anything about the day-to-day stuff. Keeping kids fed and clothed and clean and all that."

"Hmm. Speaking of young people, how did Jacob do?" she asked as we neared the Hypatia House.

Jacob, I explained, had emerged from the experience a little wiser about time travel, but only a little. I related a text message exchange he and I had on my way back from Dr. Payne's office, which had gone something like this:

*Julia, I wanna do run to Norway to find Sunniva, who do I talk to?*
*STEWie roster full until end of year. Where will you get funding?*
*Can u help?*
*Library research first, then proposal writing, then seek grants.*
*Oh.*
*Plus Dean Braga needs to give approval - IF you have funding.*

I felt bad about squashing his youthful enthusiasm, but he needed to learn about the reality of life as a time travel researcher, really any researcher. As Dr. Holm had found out, money was key. No matter how exciting your idea, it simply wasn't doable until you had secured lab time and funding. Even if you were a theoretical physicist or a philosopher and made do with a pencil and paper, you still needed food to eat, a desk and chair to sit in, and the pencil and paper (and laptop) to write up your thoughts and publish them.

"To be young again," Helen said. I thought she would supply a quote from Shakespeare, but she went on, smiling, "Jacob has a crush on St. Sunniva, our Sabina has a crush on him, and no doubt someone at Sabina's high school has a crush on her. Well, making Sunniva the focus of his PhD is not a bad idea. Like anything else, it will take a lot of hard work and some luck."

We walked in silence for a moment.

"So Chief Kirkland decided there was nothing he could charge Quinn with? Illegal use of school resources?" she suggested as we stopped in the courtyard of the Hypatia House. "Wasting everyone's time?"

"Quinn claims Dagmar told him that she had secured last-minute permission from Dr. Payne for a STEWie run. She hadn't, of course, but he had no way of knowing that. At least, we can't prove otherwise. And it's not illegal to purchase a hunting handgun—Quinn says it was Dagmar's idea anyway. Nate considered a charge of attempted fraud because of the fake stone, but even he admitted that that would be a long shot."

My cell phone rang just as I got to my office. It was Nate. "I have a couple of things to attend to here and a shower to grab, but would seven-thirty work for you?"

"Seven-thirty? For what?"

"Remember, shrimp curry at my place?"

I had forgotten it was still Friday. The whole thing was odd, as it usually was with time travel. We had spent two nights and days in the fourteenth century, but only a couple of hours had passed for Helen and everyone else on campus.

"Shrimp curry it is," I said. Thinking that it would be nice to talk about something lighthearted for a change, I said, "But only on one condition. No time travel talk."

∞

As I was trying to decide whether to wear a strappy dress, which would expose my mosquito-bitten arms and require nicer shoes, or a more casual combination of jeans and shirt, Sabina popped into my room.

"Good," I said. "Let me run something by you. Dessert or not? I think I should bring dessert—Nate probably doesn't serve dessert to his guests. Or if he does, it's probably fruit salad or something." Maybe we could meet halfway, I thought. That is to say, I could learn to like healthy dishes as long as I didn't have to cook them myself. And perhaps he'd be open to occasionally introducing—what had he called it?—subpar food into his body. Though when you put it that way, it didn't sound appetizing at all.

Sabina hadn't come over to talk about food. Getting right to the point, she said, "Reveal secret, Julia."

I moved the two outfits, which I had been studying in my robe, off the bed, transferring them to a chair. "Here, have a seat. The prudent thing would be to give yourself more time to get used to things before—well, before becoming a celebrity and fielding offers to go on TV news shows and write an autobiography—that's a book about your life—and have a movie made about you. All that stuff."

"Yes, that sound no fun. Except for movie."

We had shown her a few classics like *Some Like It Hot*, which she enjoyed very much, and also the romantic comedy *Around the World in Eight Days* starring heart-throb and St. Sunniva alum Ewan Coffey, on whom Abigail had a bit of a crush.

Sabina asked about *Tee-Vee* news shows.

I decided the jeans and a shirt were the way to go since my feet were way too sore for heels. "I suppose it's time we let you watch more television. I'll talk to Abigail about it. Just— well, ignore most of what you see, especially the commercials." At Sabina's raised eyebrows, I added, "They're like what your father had on the wall above his shop to let people know how good his garum was, only the information is acted out and, uh, exaggerated." I sat down next to her on the bed. "Look, Abigail and I just want you to be more comfortable in our culture before we reveal your background to the world."

"Wait to get my teeth white, yes? All right. We wait. But not long. I want to get reveal over with."

# 39

An uneventful week had passed and things were just starting to get back to normal when my cell phone beeped in the middle of the night. I didn't hear it at first, but the second beep woke me out of the nightmare that was making me toss and turn. I had been dreaming of Dagmar running toward the tornado and her Norsemen and never reaching them. I shook off the dream and reached for my cell phone.

The text was from Jacob.

*Celer trending on Twitter*

Graduate students keep odd hours. I texted him back that it was the middle of the night—3:00 a.m. to be exact—and what did he mean Celer was trending?

*Tons of tweets about how you rescued a dog from Pompeii & he's living at your house*

He followed that with *Except they're spelling it Keller.*

I sat up in bed, turned on the light, and texted back *Are they saying anything about Sabina?*

*No, just Celer*

Quinn. It was his way of keeping the upper hand, reminding me that he still knew our secret, making sure he didn't get retroactively charged with anything. I couldn't decide if I was furious at Quinn for revealing the truth about the dog or grateful that he hadn't said anything about Sabina.

In the morning, very early even by my standards, I called Nate. I reached him on his way out the door. He had been busy the past week—I had never realized how much work needed to be done when a death occurred in circumstances as unusual as this one. I hadn't seen him since our shrimp dinner, when we had talked long into the night and finally fallen asleep, exhausted for more than one reason.

His Jeep screeched into my driveway not fifteen minutes later. He dropped off Wanda the spaniel and drove off with Celer. After a quick consultation with Abigail, we had come up with a temporary solution. Cavalier King Charles Spaniels, as everyone who had access to the Internet knew, traced their lineage to only six dogs (with delightful names, I found out, researching the matter over breakfast: Ann's Son, Aristide of Ttiweh, Carlo of Ttiweh, Duce of Braemore, Kobba of Kuranda, and—perhaps my favorite—Wizbang Timothy). Wanda could not, therefore, with rock-solid genetic certainty, have been brought back from 79 AD. I resolved to tell anyone who asked that the rumor was a prank pulled by students who had too much free time on their hands. I'd even offer, if necessary, to send one of Wanda's chestnut hairs to anyone who wanted to do a DNA analysis.

Nate had driven Celer to his grandmother's house. I pictured the mellow, gray-coated mutt curling up by her fireplace as she cooked him delicious dog meals. I had a suspicion they would get along very well. Sabina was still asleep, but I was sure she'd understand the need for the dog switch. Like I said, it was just a temporary measure anyway, until things died down.

It didn't work out that way.

After a somewhat harried day trying to keep up with Wanda, I was having a calming cup of tea, having confirmed that *Keller* was no longer trending on Twitter. Sabina, who had been somewhat quiet all day, was next door catching up on homework—I could hear the TV and was a bit surprised she had it on so loud. Abigail was picking up some pizza for them on her way back from campus.

As for my side of the house—Nate was coming over and I had picked up a bottle of wine for us and some of Ingrid's Swedish meatballs, which were sitting in the oven to stay warm. I was mulling over whether to light some candles for the dinner table, when my phone rang.

I thought it might be Nate calling to say he was running late.

It was Professor Mooney.

"Julia, we have a problem."

I put down the tea. What was it now—another blackmailer like Quinn, a wannabe murderer like Dean Braga's predecessor, what?

"Sabina—she's gone."

"What? Where?"

"Back in time."

## THE END

# ACKNOWLEDGMENTS

This is the second book in my time-travel series and I want to repeat something I said in the first: *Like Julia Olsen, I am not a historian.* Julia's journey into the nineteenth and fourteenth century was one for me as well. Put more plainly, I'm uncomfortably aware that despite my best efforts, historical oversights are sure to have snuck in. I can only hope they will be looked on kindly by the reader.

The central question, whether the Kensington Runestone is a phantom or a real data point on History's timeline, is one whose answer will have to wait for more weighty evidence on one side or the other. I followed the writer's prerogative in choosing the more interesting story, and took the liberty of adding a small eyewitness to the discovery event.

Books like this one owe a debt to other books: Alice Beck Kehoe's *The Kensington Runestone: Approaching a Research Question Holistically* explores the runestone evidence from all sides; the Olof Ohman letter and affidavit can be found in Theodore C. Blegen's *The Kensington Rune Stone: New Light on an Old Riddle* and other sources; Annette Kolodny's *In Search of First Contact: The Vikings of Vinland, the Peoples of the Dawnland, and the Anglo-American Anxiety of Discovery* is a good in-depth read about the Norse sagas; the Good Earth Woman's story related by Ruth-Ann Tuttle is given in Ruth Landes's 1968 book *The Mystic Lake Sioux: Sociology of the*

*Mdewakantonwan Santee*; and Jared Diamond's *Collapse: How Societies Choose to Fail or Succeed* includes a section on the Greenlanders and the mystery of their disappearance. Newton Horace Winchell was the state geologist at the time; I relied on his 1910 report to the Minnesota Historical Society as the starting point for Dagmar Holm's translation of the stone's text. Newton Horace Winchell was the state geologist at the time; I relied on his 1910 report to the Minnesota Historical Society as the starting point for Dagmar Holm's translation of the stone's text. The poster she shows Julia is based on the reading of the stone's text from John D. Bengtson's article, *The Kensington Rune Stone: A Study Guide*, available at http://jdbengt.net.

As always, grateful thanks go out to my editor, Alex Carr, my agent, Jill Marsal, and the book's trusty team at 47North. John Baron, Jill Marsal, and Richard Ellis Preston, Jr. all read a pre-publication version of the manuscript and provided much appreciated feedback. Angela Polidoro is the most dedicated developmental editor an author could hope to have and the book benefited greatly from her input, as well as that of copyeditor Richard Camp. MPS Ltd. did the lovely runestone illustrations and The Book Designers are overdue thanks for the covers of both the first book and this second one.

The power of the electronic age is that an author can ping people with questions that arise during the creation of a manuscript, and my thanks go out to everyone who responded to requests I sent out regarding pronunciation, copyright, and other issues.

A shoutout also goes to all 47North authors, about as lively and supportive bunch as you could hope to meet.

Finally, as always, my deepest thanks go to my family—the Maslakovic and Baron clans, and, most of all, to my son, Dennis, and my husband, John.

# ABOUT THE AUTHOR

 Neve Maslakovic is the author of the Incident series, as well as a stand-alone novel, *Regarding Ducks and Universes.* Before turning her hand to writing fiction, Neve earned her PhD in electrical engineering at Stanford University's STAR (Space, Telecommunications, and Radioscience) Laboratory. Born in Belgrade, Yugoslavia (now Serbia), Neve currently lives with her husband and son near Minneapolis/ St. Paul, where she admits to enjoying the winters. Find out more on www.nevemaslakovic.com or follow Neve on Twitter, @NeveMaslakovic.